THE HORROR, THE HORROR, WHERE DID IT ALL BEGIN?

Here is your chance to relive the spine-chilling tales that began the careers of some of today's masters of the horrific. So turn on your brightest lights to drive all the ghosts away, and settle down with such eerie and terrifying tales as:

"Lilies"—The old lady came by every Saturday to bring them some of the flowers she and her son had picked in the country. And this Saturday would prove no exception . . . or would it?

"The Church in High Street"—He'd come to the town of Temphill at his friends's request. But now his friend was nowhere to be found and discovering his friend's fate might prove his own undoing. . . .

"Optional Music for Voice and Piano"—It began when he was ten, a nightmarish experience that left him with a gift for music. But was his incredible voice a blessing or a curse?

HORRIBLE BEGINNINGS

HORRIBLE
BEGINNINGS

**Edited by
Steven H. Silver
and Martin H. Greenberg**

DAW BOOKS, INC.
DONALD A. WOLLHEIM, FOUNDER
375 Hudson Street, New York, NY 10014

**ELIZABETH R. WOLLHEIM
SHEILA E. GILBERT
PUBLISHERS**
www.dawbooks.com

First Printing, March 2003
1 2 3 4 5 6 7 8 9

ACKNOWLEDGMENTS

Introduction © 2003 by Steven H. Silver.

Introduction to "Lilies," copyright © 2003 by Stefan R. Dziemianowicz.

"Lilies" by Robert Bloch. Copyright © 1934 by Robert Bloch. First published in *Marvel Tales,* Winter 1934. Reprinted by permission of the agent for the Author's Estate, Ralph M. Vicinanza, Ltd.

Introduction to "The Graveyard Rats," copyright © 2003 by Frederik Pohl.

"The Graveyard Rats" by Henry Kuttner. Copyright © 1936 by Popular Publications, Inc. First published in *Weird Tales,* March 1936. Reprinted by permission of the agent for the author's Estate, Don Congdon Associates, Inc.

"The Church in High Street": Introduction copyright © 2003 by Ramsey Campbell.

"The Church in High Street" by Ramsey Campbell. Copyright © 1962 by Ramsey Campbell. First published in *Dark Mind, Dark Heart.* Reprinted by permission of the author.

Introduction to "Eustace," copyright © 2003 by Tanith Lee.

"Eustace" by Tanith Lee. Copyright © 1968 by Tanith Lee. First published in *The Ninth Pan Book of Horror Stories.* Reprinted by permission of the author.

"First Gear," copyright © 2003 by Edward Bryant.

"They Only Come In Dreams" by Edward Bryant. Copyright © 1970 by Edward Bryant. First published in *Adam Magazine,* January 1970. Reprinted by permission of the author.

Introduction to "The Cleaning Machine" copyright © 2003 by F. Paul Wilson.

"The Cleaning Machine" by F. Paul Wilson. Copyright © 1971

1986 by Gary A. Braunbeck. First published in *Twilight Zone's Night Cry*, Fall 1986. Reprinted by permission of the author.

Introduction to "Colt .24," copyright © 2003 by Rick Hautala.

"Colt .24" by Rick Hautala. Copyright © 1987 by Rick Hautala. First published in *Isaac Asimov's Magical Worlds of Fantasy #8: Devils*. Reprinted by permission of the author,

Introduction to "Prince of Flowers," copyright © 2003 by Elizabeth Hand.

"Prince of Flowers" by Elizabeth Hand. Copyright © 1988 by Elizabeth Hand. First published in *The Twilight Zone Magazine*, February 1988. Reprinted by permission of the author.

"From a Distance," copyright © 2003 by Kathe Koja.

"Distances" by Kathe Koja. Copyright © 1988 by Kathe Koja. First published in *Isaac Asimov's Science Fiction Magazine*, Mid-December 1988. Reprinted by permission of the author.

Introduction to "The Wind Breathes Cold" copyright © 2003 by P.N. Elrod

"The Wind Breathes Cold" by P.N. Elrod. Copyright © 1992 by P.N. Elrod. Copyright © 1992 by P.N. Elrod. First published in *Dracula: Prince of Darkness*. Reprinted by permission of the author.

Introduction to "Deep Sleep," copyright © 2003 by Matthew Costello.

"Deep Sleep" by Matt Costello. Copyright © 1992 by Matthew Costello. First published in *Dracula: Prince of Darkness*. Reprinted by permission of the author.

To Elaine for her support
and Robin and Melanie for their inspiration.

CONTENTS

xi

CONTENTS

CONTENTS

INTRODUCTION

Everyone has their own first horror. It could be falling from a high place or the fear of abandonment. As we grow older, the things that fill us with dread become more sophisticated, although there are certain primal fears that remain with us no matter how much logic tells us that we shouldn't worry about them.

Last week, I was working in my den when my three-year-old daughter wandered in, well past her bedtime. She meekly informed me that there were monsters in her room. I started to explain that the monsters weren't real, but I realized that while the monsters may not have been real, her fears were. We went into her room, looked around and determined that in this case the "monsters" were pieces of lint on her blanket. I tucked her in, picked off the lint, and gave stern orders to her stuffed animals to protect her from any further monster incursions.

Even as my daughter is afraid of the monsters in her room, she is obviously thrilled by the terror they incite. Even as I try to allay her fears, she openly *tries* to hold on to the idea that she can have nightmares each night. It is this sort of fascination with horror that leads so many authors to encapsulate the feelings in their writing and to make their readers eagerly reach for the next volume by Tanith Lee, Ramsey Campbell, or any of a multitude of authors.

The authors included here have the special ability of taking the fears and horrors they feel and stretching them to encompass the fears of their readers. However, while it may be easy to dream up a horror story that will terrify people, it is another thing to present that horror in such a manner that people will choose to share it.

Before these authors had gathered their fans, they published their first stories practically anonymously. Readers decided to read the stories not because they recognized a favorite author's name, but because the title of the story looked interesting or because they trusted the editor who bought that first story.

This collection presents the debut stories of several authors. These stories may not represent the best these authors have to offer (after all, they are their first stories), but as Ed Bryant says in his introduction to "They Come Only in Dreams," he's "not at all ashamed of [the story]."

All of these authors have gone on to achieve continued success in the horror field. That success can be traced directly back to these stories, the first selected by editors as good enough to see the light of publication as well as a paycheck. They represent not horror, but the glimmer of success for authors who had been trying to break into their chosen field at the end of a stream of rejection letters.

Many of these stories have not been reprinted until now. This collection gives readers a chance to reintroduce themselves to this collection of horror authors as they introduced themselves to the world at large. In some cases, these stories will convince readers to search out an author's later works. In other cases, it might inspire a budding author who sees in these stories the hope that he (or she), too, can become a published author.

Open this book, either at random, or to a favorite author, or to an author as yet undiscovered. Sit in front of the fire while the wind howls outside the locked door. Immerse yourself in these horrific visions and hope that the sound you hear is only the creak of the wind or your imagination.

INTRODUCTION TO

"LILIES"

by Stefan Dziemianowicz

It is tempting to introduce "Lilies" as the first published fiction of the man who would later write the modern horror classic *Psycho,* but that would be to commit the grievous error of treating critical hindsight as foresight. The truth is, "Lilies" is a story written by a sixteen-year-old in his first flush of infatuation with a weird muse.

In 1934, Robert Bloch was a precocious Milwaukee high-school student still somewhat in shock that he had begun corresponding with H. P. Lovecraft only a year before. Lovecraft's groundbreaking stories appeared regularly in *Weird Tales,* the pulp fiction magazine Bloch had been reading religiously since stumbling upon it a Chicago railway station in 1927, and Bloch was one of many readers who regarded Lovecraft as the best reason to toss away a precious quarter each month during the height of the Great Depression on a magazine of pure escapist fiction. In the naivete that distinguishes a newly minted fan,

Bloch had written to Lovecraft asking where he might track down out-of-print stories by the author whose stories the worshipful *Weird Tales* readership constantly evoked. Lovecraft, in his generosity, offered to send Bloch tear sheets of his work. In a very short time, Bloch reciprocated by sending his own stories—all unpublished—to Lovecraft for critique.

Lovecraft told Bloch what he could do with them—and fortunately, that amounted to steering his protégé toward magazines in which Lovecraft himself had been published. Through Lovecraft, Bloch made the acquaintance of *Marvel Tales,* a semiprofessional magazine of fantasy and science fiction edited and published by William L. Crawford. It was a match meant to be, for at the same time Bloch aspired to publish fiction professionally, Crawford aspired to publish a professional fiction magazine. One of the first generation of science fiction fans, Crawford owned a printing press and was convinced that he could put out a magazine that would rival any of the pulp magazines available at the newsstands. Crawford persuaded topflight science fiction writers and the cream of the *Weird Tales* roster—including not only Lovecraft, but Robert E. Howard and Frank Belknap Long—to provide stories for *Marvel*. He filled the gaps between their contributions with submissions from as yet unheralded scribes like Robert Bloch.

"Lilies" appeared in the third issue of *Marvel Tales,* dated Winter 1934. It was Bloch's first work of fiction to see print, although it was not intended to be. In a headnote to the story, Crawford explained that "Lilles" was "presented in lieu of Mr. Bloch's scheduled yarn—'The Madness of Lucian Gray'—as a result of a mix-up in manuscripts." It didn't matter to Bloch that a different story debuted, or that "Lucian Gray" seemed so embarrassed by the confusion that he never showed his face in print. The story appeared smack in the middle of the magazine, and rubbed shoulders with tales by seasoned veterans such as Lloyd A. Eshbach, David H. Keller, and P. Schuyler Miller.

And how did Bloch's effort stack up against the competition? Not too shabbily, considering that there were no expectations for it aside from Bloch's own. "Lilies" is a simple weird tale with a sentimental streak that shows a Robert Bloch who had yet to fall completely under the spell of Lovecraft's eldritch horrors or become master of the mordant pun-manship that distinguished his mature writing. Although Bloch chose not to include it in any of the short fiction collections published in his lifetime, its premise clearly appealed to him, and he revisited it obliquely in his better-known *Weird Tales* story "Floral Tribute," published in 1949.

Marvel did not feature a letters column, so it's hard to gauge the reception of "Lilies," but Crawford thought well enough of it to buy yet another Bloch story, "The Black Lotus." This story, which appeared in *Marvel*'s companion publication *Unusual Stories* in mid-1935, might have been Bloch's second published work of fiction but for a bolt of professional savvy that struck the fledgling writer before "Lilies" had even seen print. "While Crawford had nothing to lose, it turned out I had little to gain," Bloch writes of the *Marvel Tales* experience in his autobiography, *Once Around the Bloch.* "The so-called magazines bore little or no resemblance to anything found on the newsstands or even produced from under the overcoats of pornography peddlers, where their wares were concealed in that puritanical period. Showing copies of these crudely printed periodicals around would scarcely serve to establish my credentials as a 'published' writer."

So Bloch moved on to greener graveyards, and began submitting his fiction to *Weird Tales,* the magazine that any weird fiction writer who earned his spurs in fan publications ultimately aspired to. It proved the most important move of his career. Crawford's magazines never achieved professional status and disappeared by the end of 1935 (though Crawford himself was a publishing presence in fantasy and science fiction for another half century). But in July of 1934, Bloch cracked the pro market with his first *Weird Tales* sale, "The Secret in the Tomb."

And thereby hangs a truly weird tale, for this proved *not* to be Bloch's first professionally published story. Spurred by his success, Bloch sent more submissions to the magazine, and *Weird Tales* editor Farnsworth Wright decided Bloch's second sale, "The Feast in the Abbey," was a stronger story with which to introduce the new writer. Published in the January 1935 issue of *Weird Tales,* it proved one of the most popular selections for that issue in reader voting and catapulted Bloch instantly to the professional stratosphere.

No one has noted the eerie parallels in the circumstances surrounding Bloch's *Marvel Tales* and *Weird Tales* debuts, but the juggled ordering that saw "The Feast in the Abbey" in print before "The Secret in the Tomb"—like "Lilies" before "The Madness of Lucian Gray"—is the kind of strange coincidence one finds only in a Robert Bloch story.

LILIES

by Robert Bloch

THE Colorado Apartments is a substantial building, its red-brick walls rising to a four-story eminence that sets it definitely apart from the squalid sordidness of the surrounding neighborhood. Its tenants are likewise removed from the general wretched run of tenement scum that dwells in the ramshackle pest-holes adjoining the dignified brick edifice.

Most of these tenants have been in the building since its construction twenty-three years ago; they are solid, middle-aged and infinitely respectable—the men white collar clerks or accountants, the women plump, comfortable and childless, filling lonely hours with parential ministration to pet canaries. There are widowers, too—gray old men, and widows—gray old women; a very solid, conservative group of tenants indeed. They are a clannish group, the women exchanging gossip and recipes across the back porch of a morning; the men greeting each other from behind their evening papers on the front porch. They would visit one another perhaps, were it not for the unseen barrier of an apartment, the alien sense of espionage that is implied in the phrase, "across the hall." Apartment dwellers love privacy. Still, they do exchange foods—a cut of pie or pudding or perhaps a cool drink in the spring or summer.

There was, for example, Mrs. Hahn and her flowers.

Mrs. Hahn was an elderly widow who dwelt directly below our third floor apartment in Number 13. She was German, a motherly soul much given to puttering around in her kitchen. She never left her house save on a Saturday afternoon when her married son called for her in his car and they spent the rest of the afternoon in the country. Invariably on Saturday evening she would laboriously mount the stairs to our apartment and present my mother with an armful of wildflowers gathered in the country by "me and my son Willie."

Her pathetic pleasure in this humble task and her reward in our thanks she enjoyed with wistful pride. She was grateful for this, her one weekly rite, the one chance she still had to be giving and doing in a world that had passed her by.

This weekly incident was repeated regularly for nearly a year. Every Saturday the old woman and her flowers came in the midnight dust—the floral tributes varying with the season; violets, sweet peas, marigolds, gladioli, nasturtiums, poppies, roses.

Finally there came a Saturday late in October when the expected visitor did not materialize. Night deepened, and still no familiar ring upon our doorbell. We had not seen the old woman all week, and my mother was greatly relieved when at eight o'clock the bell finally rang and she opened the door to find the bent, familiar figure of the old woman standing outside in the darkness of the shadowed hall.

"Good evening." The usual greeting, cheerful yet hesitant.

"Why, good evening, Mrs. Hahn. Been out in the country again this week?"

"Well, no, not exactly. Anyway, my son Willie come and bring me these flowers—what a thoughtful boy he is, my son! And I thought if you might like a few——"

She proffered the bouquet. My mother thanked her; she turned and slowly descended the stairs once more. We heard the door of her apartment close softly, and closed our own.

My mother snapped on the light. Then she gasped— for the flowers in her arms were white calla lilies. She held them, staring oddly at the waxen blooms; was still holding them, in fact, when she looked through the window. A big car pulled up—black it was and shiny, with a closed back, and very long—and two men stepped out. One of them was Willie Hahn, and he was crying. Mother stepped over to the window. Hahn and the stranger were coming up the steps. They were in the hall now, on the way upstairs, and I heard a flash of their conversation.

"Yes, I brought some flowers—lilies, of course. Left them here about an hour ago on the—"

Mother looked out of the window at the funeral car. Then she glanced down at the flowers again, and for the first time noticed the tag around the stems.

"In memory of my dear mother, Mrs. Ludwig Hahn."

Downstairs they were moving the coffin, and nobody noticed that the flowers on her breast were gone.

INTRODUCTION TO

" THE GRAVEYARD
RATS "

by Frederik Pohl

Henry Kuttner was an engaging young man—tragically, he never lived to become an old one—with a great sense of humor. The other thing he had in considerable degree was writing talent; Tony Boucher called him "one of SF's most literate and intelligent storytellers," and so he was. Alone or with his wife, Catherine (whose solo works appeared under the byline of C. L. Moore), Kuttner wrote a score of successful novels and any number of shorter pieces in the brief couple of decades that comprised his writing career. A minor fraction of the novels are mysteries. Most are science fiction, and more often than not Kuttner's science-fiction stories are tinged with a delicious strain of humor. . . .

In this they are quite unlike his first venture into print, "The Graveyard Rats." There is nothing comical about "The Graveyard Rats." It isn't science fiction, it isn't fantasy, it isn't a mystery novel. What it is is horror, of the purest kind. It is meant to make your blood curdle and to disturb your sleep with nightmares, and, by gosh, it does what it sets out to do.

At least, it certainly did that for me when I first read it in the March 1936 issue of the famous old fantasy magazine, *Weird Tales*. I was sixteen at the time, an avid science fiction and fantasy fan and by no means yet a professional writer. I was, however, fairly regularly published in most of the sf and fantasy magazines of the day, though only in their letter columns. As soon as I had finished that issue I sat down to write a fan letter. It was not in my usual style, however. Seduced by the perfect iambs of the story's byline and title—"Hank Kuttner's yarn, 'The Graveyard Rats' "—I wrote it in doggerel verse.

However, even at sixteen I was not without a reasonable amount of prudence. I took the precaution of keeping my own name off it, and so when it was published it appeared under a pseudonym, my true identity never revealed until this moment.

I mention this early indiscretion only in order to be able to boast that I was one of the very first to recognize the talent of this fine and sorely missed writer. I was by no means the last, however. Kuttner's work was of a very high order, and before long everyone knew it.

THE GRAVEYARD
RATS

by Henry Kuttner

OLD Masson, the caretaker of one of Salem's old-est and most neglected cemeteries, had a feud with the rats. Generations ago they had come up from the wharves and settled in the graveyard, a colony of abnormally large rats, and when Masson had taken charge after the inexplicable disappearance of the former caretaker, he decided that they must go. At first he set traps for them and put poisoned food by their burrows, and later he tried to shoot them, but it did no good. The rats stayed, multiplying and overrunning the graveyard with their ravenous hordes.

They were large, even for the *mus decumanus,* which sometimes measures fifteen inches in length, exclusive of the naked pink and gray tail. Masson had caught glimpses of some as large as good-sized cats, and when, once or twice, the gravediggers had uncovered their burrows, the malodorous tunnels were large enough to enable a man to crawl into them on his hands and knees. The ships that had come generations ago from distant ports to the rotting Salem wharves had brought strange cargoes.

Masson wondered sometimes at the extraordinary size of these burrows. He recalled certain vaguely disturbing legends he had heard since coming to ancient, witch-haunted Salem—tales of a moribund, inhuman life that was said to exist in forgotten burrows in the earth. The old days, when Cotton Mather had hunted down the evil cults that worshiped Hecate and the dark Magna Mater in frightful orgies, had passed; but dark gabled houses still leaned perilously toward each other over narrow cobbled streets, and blasphemous secrets and mysteries were said to be hidden in subterranean cellars and caverns, where forgotten pagan rites were still celebrated in defiance of law and sanity. Wagging their gray heads wisely, the elders declared that there were worse things than rats and maggots crawling in the unhallowed earth of the ancient Salem cemeteries.

And then, too, there was this curious dread of the rats. Masson disliked and respected the ferocious little rodents, for he knew the danger that lurked in their flashing, needle-sharp fangs; but he could not understand the inexplicable horror which the oldsters held for deserted, rat-infested houses. He had heard vague rumors of ghoulish beings that dwelt far underground, and that had the power of commanding the rats, marshaling them like horrible armies. The rats, the old men whispered, were messengers between this world and the grim and ancient caverns far below Salem. Bodies had been stolen from graves for nocturnal subterranean feasts, they said. The myth of the Pied Piper is a fable that hides a blasphemous horror, and the black pits of Avernus have brought forth hell-spawned monstrosities that never venture into the light of day.

Masson paid little attention to these tales. He did not fraternize with his neighbors, and, in fact, did all he could to hide the existence of the rats from intruders. Investigation, he realized, would undoubtedly mean the opening of many graves. And while some of the gnawed, empty coffins could be attributed to the activities of the rats, Masson might find it difficult to explain the mutilated bodies that lay in some of the coffins.

The purest gold is used in filling teeth, and this gold is not removed when a man is buried. Clothing, of course, is another matter; for usually the undertaker provides a plain broadcloth suit that is cheap and easily recognizable. But gold is another matter; and sometimes, too, there were medical students and less reputable doctors who were in need of cadavers, and not overscrupulous as to where these were obtained.

So far Masson had successfully managed to discourage investigation. He had fiercely denied the existence of the rats, even though they sometimes robbed him of his prey. Masson did not care what happened to the bodies after he had performed his gruesome thefts, but the rats inevitably dragged away the whole cadaver through the hole they gnawed in the coffin.

The size of these burrows occasionally worried Masson. Then, too, there was the curious circumstance of the coffins always being gnawed open at the end, never at the side or top. It was almost as though the rats were working under the direction of some impossibly intelligent leader.

Now he stood in an open grave and threw a last

sprinkling of wet earth on the heap beside the pit. It was raining, a slow, cold drizzle that for weeks had been descending from soggy black clouds. The graveyard was a slough of yellow, sucking mud, from which the rain-washed tombstones stood up in irregular battalions. The rats had retreated to their burrows, and Masson had not seen one for days. But his gaunt, unshaven face was set in frowning lines; the coffin on which he was standing was a wooden one.

The body had been buried several days earlier, but Masson had not dared to disinter it before. A relative of the dead man had been coming to the grave at intervals, even in the drenching rain. But he would hardly come at this late hour, no matter how much grief he might be suffering, Masson thought, grinning wryly. He straightened and laid the shovel aside.

From the hill on which the ancient graveyard lay he could see the lights of Salem flickering dimly through the downpour. He drew a flashlight from his pocket. He would need light now. Taking up the spade, he bent and examined the fastenings of the coffin. Abruptly he stiffened. Beneath his feet he sensed an unquiet stirring and scratching, as though something was moving within the coffin. For a moment a pang of superstitious fear shot through Masson, and then rage replaced it as he realized the significance of the sound. The rats had forestalled him again!

In a paroxysm of anger Masson wrenched at the fastenings of the coffin. He got the sharp edge of the shovel under the lid and pried it up until he could finish the job with his hands. Then he sent the flashlight's cold beam darting down into the coffin.

Rain spattered against the white satin lining; the coffin was empty. Masson saw a flicker of movement at the head of the case, and darted the light in that direction.

The end of the sarcophagus had been gnawed through, and a gaping hole led into darkness. A black shoe, limp and dragging, was disappearing as Masson watched, and abruptly he realized that the rats had forestalled him by only a few minutes. He fell on his hands and knees and made a hasty clutch at the shoe, and the flashlight incontinently fell into the coffin and went out. The shoe was tugged from his grasp, he heard a sharp, excited squealing, and then he had the flashlight again and was darting its light into the burrow.

It was a large one. It had to be, or the corpse could not have been dragged along it. Masson wondered at the size of the rats that could carry away a man's body, but the thought of the loaded revolver in his pocket fortified him. Probably if the corpse had been an ordinary one Masson would have left the rats with their spoils rather than venture into the narrow burrow, but he remembered an especially fine set of cuff links he had observed, as well as a stickpin that was undoubtedly a genuine pearl. With scarcely a pause he clipped the flashlight to his belt and crept into the burrow.

It was a tight fit, but he managed to squeeze himself

along. Ahead of him in the flashlight's glow he could see the shoes dragging along the wet earth of the bottom of the tunnel. He crept along the burrow as rapidly as he could, occasionally barely able to squeeze his lean body between the narrow walls.

The air was overpowering with its musty stench of carrion. If he could not reach the corpse in a minute, Masson decided, he would turn back. Belated fears were beginning to crawl, maggotlike, within his mind, but greed urged him on. He crawled forward, several times passing the mouths of adjoining tunnels. The walls of the burrow were damp and slimy, and twice lumps of dirt dropped behind him. The second time he paused and screwed his head around to look back. He could see nothing, of course, until he had unhooked the flashlight from his belt and reversed it.

Several clods lay on the ground behind him, and the danger of his position suddenly became real and terrifying. With thoughts of a cave-in making his pulse race, he decided to abandon the pursuit, even though he had now almost overtaken the corpse and the invisible things that pulled it. But he had overlooked one thing: the burrow was too narrow to allow him to turn.

Panic touched him briefly, but he remembered a side tunnel he had just passed, and backed awkwardly along the tunnel until he came to it. He thrust his legs into it, backing until he found himself able to turn. Then he hurriedly began to retrace his way, although his knees were bruised and painful.

Agonizing pain shot through his leg. He felt sharp teeth sink into his flesh, and kicked out frantically.

There was a shrill squealing and the scurry of many feet. Flashing the light behind him, Masson caught his breath in a sob of fear as he saw a dozen great rats watching him intently, their slitted eyes glittering in the light. They were great misshapen things, as large as cats, and behind them he caught a glimpse of a dark shape that stirred and moved swiftly aside into the shadow; and he shuddered at the unbelievable size of the thing.

The light had held them for a moment, but they were edging closer, their teeth dull orange in the pale light. Masson tugged at his pistol, managed to extricate it from his pocket, and aimed carefully. It was an awkward position, and he tried to press his feet into the soggy sides of the burrow so that he should not inadvertently send a bullet into one of them.

The rolling thunder of the shot deafened him, for a time, and the clouds of smoke set him coughing. When he could hear again and the smoke had cleared, he saw that the rats were gone. He put the pistol back and began to creep swiftly along the tunnel, and then with a scurry and a rush they were upon him again.

They swarmed over his legs, biting and squealing insanely, and Masson shrieked horribly as he snatched for his gun. He fired without aiming, and only luck saved him from blowing a foot off. This time the rats did not retreat so far, but Masson was crawling as swiftly as he could along the burrow, ready to fire again at the first sound of another attack.

There was a patter of feet and he sent the light stabbing back of him. A great gray rat paused and watched him. Its long ragged whiskers twitched, and its scabrous, naked tail was moving slowly from side to side. Masson shouted and the rat retreated.

He crawled on, pausing briefly, the black gap of a side tunnel at his elbow, as he made out a shapeless huddle on the damp clay a few yards ahead. For a second he thought it was a mass of earth that had been dislodged from the roof, and then he recognized it as a human body.

It was a brown and shriveled mummy, and with a dreadful unbelieving shock Masson realized that it was moving.

It was crawling toward him, and in the pale glow of the flashlight the man saw a frightful gargoyle face thrust into his own. It was the passionless, death's-head skull of a long-dead corpse, instinct with hellish life; and the glazed eyes swollen and bulbous betrayed the thing's blindness. It made a faint groaning sound as it crawled toward Masson, stretching its ragged and granulated lips in a grin of dreadful hunger. And Masson was frozen with abysmal fear and loathing.

Just before the Horror touched him, Masson flung himself frantically into the burrow at his side. He heard a scrambling noise at his heels, and the thing groaned dully as it came after him. Masson, glancing over his shoulder, screamed and propelled himself desperately through the narrow burrow. He crawled along awkwardly, sharp stones cutting his hands and knees. Dirt showered into his eyes, but he dared not pause even for a moment. He scrambled on, gasping, cursing, and praying hysterically.

Squealing triumphantly, the rats came at him, horrible hunger in their eyes. Masson almost succumbed to their vicious teeth before he succeeded in beating them off. The passage was narrowing, and in a frenzy of terror he kicked and screamed and fired until the hammer clicked on an empty shell. But he had driven them off.

He found himself crawling under a great stone, embedded in the roof, that dug cruelly into his back. It moved a little as his weight struck it, and an idea flashed into Masson's fright-crazed mind. If he could bring down the stone so that it blocked the tunnel! The earth was wet and soggy from the rains, and he hunched himself half upright and dug away at the dirt around the stone. The rats were coming closer. He saw their eyes glowing in the reflection of the flashlight's beam. Still he clawed frantically at the earth. The stone was giving. He tugged at it and it rocked in its foundation.

A rat was approaching—the monster he had already glimpsed. Gray and leprous and hideous it crept forward with its orange teeth bared, and in its wake came the blind dead thing, groaning as it crawled. Masson gave a last frantic tug at the stone. He felt it slide downward, and then he went scrambling along the tunnel.

Behind him the stone crashed down, and he heard a sudden frightful shriek of agony. Clouds showered upon his legs. A heavy weight fell on his feet and he dragged them free with difficulty. The entire tunnel was collapsing!

Gasping with fear, Masson threw himself forward as the soggy earth collapsed at his heels. The tunnel narrowed until he could barely use his hands and legs to propel himself; he wriggled forward like an eel and suddenly felt satin tearing beneath his clawing fingers, and then his head crashed against some thing that barred his path. He moved his legs, discovering that they were not pinned under the collapsed earth. he was lying flat on his stomach, and when he tried to raise himself he found that the roof was only a few inches from his back. Panic shot through him.

When the blind horror had blocked his path, he had flung himself into a side tunnel, a tunnel that had no outlet. He was in a coffin, an empty coffin into which he had crept through the hole the rats had gnawed in its end!

He tried to turn on his back and found that he could not. The lid of the coffin pinned him down inexorably. Then he braced himself and strained at the coffin lid. It was immovable, and even if he could escape from the sarcophagus, how could he claw his way up through five feet of hard-packed earth?

He found himself gasping. It was dreadfully fetid, unbearably hot. In a paroxysm of terror he ripped and clawed at the satin until it was shredded. He made a futile attempt to dig with his feet at the earth from the collapsed burrow that blocked his retreat. If he were only able to reverse his position he might be able to claw his way through to air . . . air . . .

White-hot agony lanced through his breast, throbbed in his eyeballs. His head seemed to be swelling, growing larger and larger; and suddenly he heard the exultant squealing of the rats. He began to scream insanely but could not drown them out. For a moment he thrashed about hysterically within his narrow prison, and then he was quiet, gasping for air. His eyelids closed, his blackened tongue protruded, and he sank down into the blackness of death with the mad squealing of the rats dinning in his ears.

INTRODUCTION TO

"THE CHURCH IN HIGH STREET"

by Ramsey Campbell

"There are myriad unspeakable terrors in the cosmos in which our universe is but an atom; and the two gates of agony, life and death, gape to pour forth infinities of abominations. And the other gates which spew forth their broods are, thank God, little known to most of us. Few can have seen the spawn of ultimate corruption, or known that center of insane chaos where Azathoth, the blind idiot god, bubbles mindlessly; I myself have never seen these things—but God knows that what I saw in those cataclysmic moments in the church at Kingsport transcends the ultimate earthly knowledge."

So began "The Tomb-Herd," the initial draft of my first professionally published tale. Aficionados of Lovecraft's work will recognize it as imitating "Life and Death," a synopsis from his commonplace book of a story or prose poem that he may have written and seen into print. Some folk less familiar with Lovecraft will take my opening paragraph as reading like him. When I was fifteen I thought it did, but in fact it merely parodies his prose at its most excessive, which his writing seldom was. Here are a few more choice passages from "The Tomb-Herd":

"The house which I knew as my friend's, set well back from the road, overgrown with ivy that twisted in myriad grotesque shapes, was locked and shuttered. No sign of life was discernible inside it, and outside the garden was filled with a brooding quiet, while my shadow on the fungus-overgrown lawn appeared eldritch and distorted, like that of some ghoul-born being from nether pits.

"Upon inquiring of this anomaly from the strangely reticent neighbors, I learned that my friend had visited the deserted church in the center of Kingsport after dark, and that this must have called the vengeance of those from outside upon him."

I suspect most of us would be strangely reticent if a stranger came knocking at our door to ask why his shadow resembled that of a ghoul-born being, but let's go on:

"In that stomach-wrenching moment of horrible knowledge, realization of the abnormal ghastlinesses after which my friend had been searching and which, perhaps, he had stirred out of aeon-long sleep in the Kingsport church, I closed the book. But I soon opened it again . . ."

Best of all:

"(Now followed the section which horrified me

41

more than anything else. My friend must have been preparing the telegram by writing it on the page while outside unspeakable shamblers made their way toward him—as became hideously evident as the writing progressed.)

"To Richard Dexter. Come at once to Kingsport. You are needed urgently by me here for protection from agencies which may kill me—or worse—if you do not come immediately. Will explain as soon as you reach me . . . But what is this thing that flops unspeakably down the passage toward this room? It cannot be that abomination which I met in the nitrous vaults below Asquith Place . . . IA! YOG-SOTHOTH! CTHULHU FHTAGN!"

This was one of several tales I sent to August Derleth at Arkham House. You may be as astonished as I am in retrospect that he found anything in them to encourage. He told me to abandon my attempts to set my work in America and in general advised me in no uncertain terms how to improve the stories, not least by studying the work of M. R. James to learn the restraint I'd overlooked in Lovecraft. I suspect he would have been gentler if he'd realized I was only fifteen years old, but on the other hand, if you can't take that kind of forthright editorial response you aren't likely to survive as a writer.

I was still in the process of adopting his suggestions when he asked me to send him a story for an anthology he was editing (then called *Dark of Mind, Dark of Heart*). Delighted beyond words, I sent him the rewritten "Tomb-Herd," which he accepted under certain conditions: that the title should be changed to "The Church in the High Street," (though he later dropped the latter article, along with the prepositions from the title of his book) and that he should be able to edit the story as he saw fit. They story as published, there and here, therefore contains several passages that are Derleth's paraphrases of what I wrote; indeed, it's more of a collaboration than those tales of his to which he added Lovecraft's name. As I think he realized, it was the most direct way to show me how to improve my writing. It saw print in such company as Robert Bloch, John Metcalfe, William Hope Hodgson, and M. P. Shiel. Quite a thrill for a fledgling horror writer, never mind a sixteen-year-old, and it set me on my dark solitary road. I spent two years trying to be Lovecraft before devoting the rest of my life to the task of being myself.

THE CHURCH IN HIGH STREET

by Ramsey Campbell

". . . the Herd that stand watch at the secret portal each tomb is known to have, and that thrive on that which groweth out of the inhabitants thereof . . ."
—ABDUL ALHAZRED: *Necronomicon*

If I had not been a victim of circumstances, I would never have gone to ancient Temphill. But I had very little money in those days, and when I recalled the invitation of a friend who lived in Temphill to become his secretary, I began to hope that this post—open some months before—might still be available. I knew that my friend would not easily find someone to stay with him long; not many would relish a stay in such a place of ill repute as Temphill.

Thinking thus, I gathered into a trunk what few belongings I had, loaded it into a small sports car which I had borrowed from another friend gone on a sea voyage, and drove out of London at an hour too early for the clamorous traffic of the city to have risen, away from the cell-like room where I had stayed in a tottering, blackened backstreet house.

I had heard much from my friend, Albert Young, about Temphill and the customs of that decaying Cotswold town where he had lived for months during his research into incredibly superstitious beliefs for a chapter in his forthcoming book on witchcraft and witchcraft lore. Not being superstitious myself, I was curious at the way in which apparently sane people seemed to avoid entering Temphill whenever possible—as reported by Young—not so much because they disliked the route, as because they were disturbed by the strange tales which constantly filtered out of the region.

Perhaps because I had been dwelling upon these tales, the country seemed to grow disquieting as I neared my destination. Instead of the gently undulating Cotswold hills, with villages and half-timbered thatched houses, the area was one of grim, brooding plains, sparsely habited, where the only vegetation was a gray diseased grass and an infrequent bloated oak. A few places filled me with a strong unease—the path the road took beside a sluggish stream, for instance, where the reflection of the passing vehicle was oddly distorted by the green, scum-covered water; the diversion which forced me to take a route straight through the middle of a marsh, where trees closed overhead so that the ooze all around me could barely be seen; and the densely wooded hillside which rose almost vertically above the road at one point, with trees reaching toward the road like myriad gnarled hands, all wearing the aspect of a primeval forest.

Young had written often of certain things he had learned from reading in various antique volumes; he wrote of "a forgotten cycle of superstitious lore which would have been better unknown"; he mentioned strange and alien names, and toward the last of his letters—which had ceased to come some weeks before—he had hinted of actual worship of trans-spatial beings still practiced in such towns as Camside, Brichester, Severnford, Goatswood and Temphill. In his very last letter he had written of a temple of "Yog-Sothoth" which existed conterminously with an actual church in Temphill where monstrous rituals had been performed. This eldritch temple had been, it was thought, the origin of the town's name—a corruption of the original "Temple Hill"—which had been built around the hill-set church, where "gates," if opened by now long forgotten alien incantations, would gape to let elder demons pass from other spheres. There was a particularly hideous legend, he wrote, concerning the errand on which these demons came, but he forebore to recount this, at least until he had visited the alien temple's earthly location.

On my entrance into the first of Temphill's archaic streets, I began to feel qualms about my impulsive action. If Young had meanwhile found a secretary, I would find it difficult, in my indigence, to return to London. I had hardly enough funds to find lodging here, and the hotel repelled me the moment I saw it in passing—with its leaning porch, the peeling bricks of the walls, and the decayed old men who stood in front of the porch and seemed to stare mindlessly at something beyond me as I drove by. The other sections of the town were not reassuring, either, particularly the steps which rose between green ruins of brick walls to the black steeple of a church among pallid gravestones.

The worst part of Temphill, however, seemed to be the south end. On Wood Street, which entered the town on the northwest side, and on Manor Street, where the forested hillside on the left of the first street ended, the houses were square stone buildings in fairly good repair; but around the blackened hotel at the center of Temphill, the buildings were often greatly dilapidated, and the roof of one three-story building—the lower floor of which was used as a shop, with a sign—*Poole's General Store*—in the mud-spattered windows—had completely collapsed. Across the bridge beyond the central Market Square lay Cloth Street, and beyond the tall, uninhabited buildings of Wool Place at the end of it could be found South Street, where Young lived in a three-story house which he had bought cheaply and been able to renovate.

The state of the buildings across the skeletal river bridge was even more disturbing than that of those on the north side. Bridge Lane's gray warehouses soon gave way to gabled dwellings, often with broken windows and patchily unpainted fronts, but still inhabited. Here scattered unkempt children stared resignedly from dusty front steps or played in pools of orange mud on a patch of waste ground, while the older tenants sat in twilit rooms, and the atmosphere of the place depressed me as might a shade-inhabited city ruin.

I entered into South Street between two gabled

three-story houses. Number 11, Young's house, was at the far end of the street. The sight of it, however, filled me with foreboding—for it was shuttered, and the door stood open, laced with cobwebs. I drove the car up the driveway at the side and got out. I crossed the gray, fungus-overgrown lawn and went up the steps. The door swung inward at my touch, opening upon a dimly-lit hall. My knocks and calls brought no answer, and I stood for a few moments undecided, hesitant to enter. There was a total absence of footprints anywhere on the dusty floor of the hall. Remembering that Young had written about conversations he had had with the owner of Number 8, across the road, I decided to apply to him for information about my friend.

I crossed the street to Number 8 and knocked on the door. It was opened almost immediately, though in such silence as to startle me. The owner of Number 8 was a tall man with white hair and luminously dark eyes. He wore a frayed tweed suit. But his most startling attribute was a singular air of antiquity, giving him the impression of having been left behind by some past age. He looked very much like my friend's description of the pedantic John Clothier, a man possessed of an extraordinary amount of ancient knowledge.

When I introduced myself and told him that I was looking for Albert Young, he paled and was briefly hesitant before inviting me to enter his house, muttering that he knew where Albert Young had gone, but that I probably wouldn't believe him. He led me down a dark hall into a large room lit only by an oil lamp in one corner. There he motioned me to a chair beside the fireplace. He got out his pipe, lit it, and sat down opposite me, beginning to talk with an abrupt rush.

"I took an oath to say nothing about this to anyone," he said. "That's why I could only warn Young to leave and keep away from—that place. He wouldn't listen—and you won't find him now. Don't look so— it's the truth! I'll have to tell you more than I told him, or you'll try to find him and find—*something else*. God knows what will happen to me now—once you've joined *Them,* you must never speak of their place to any outsider. But I can't see another go the way Young went. I should let you go there—according to the oath—but *They'll* take me sooner or later, anyway. You get away before it's too late. Do you know the church in High Street?"

It took me some seconds to regain my composure enough to reply. "If you mean the one near the central square—yes, I know it."

"It isn't used—as a church, now," Clothier went on. "But there were certain rites practiced there long ago. They left their mark. Perhaps Young wrote you about the legend of the temple existing in the same place as the church, but in another dimension? Yes, I see by your expression that he did. But do you know that rites can still be used at the proper season to open the gates and let through *those from the other side*? It's true. I've stood in that church myself and watched the gates open in the center of empty air to show

49

visions that made me shriek in horror. I've taken part in acts of worship that would drive the uninitiated insane. You see, Mr. Dodd, the majority of the people in Temphill still visit the church on the right nights."

More than half convinced that Clothier's mind was affected, I asked impatiently, "What does all this have to do with Young's whereabouts?"

"It has everything to do with it," Clothier continued. "I warned him not to go to the church, but he went one night in the same year when the Yule rite had been consummated, and *They* must have been watching when he got there. He was held in Temphill after that. *They* have a way of turning space back to a point—I can't explain it. He couldn't get away. He waited in that house for days before *They* came. I heard his screams—and saw the color of the sky over the roof. *They* took him. That's why you'll never find him. And that's why you'd better leave town altogether while there's still time."

"Did you look for him at the house?" I asked, incredulous.

"I wouldn't go into that house for any reason whatever," confessed Clothier. "Nor would anyone else. The house has become theirs now. *They* have taken him *Outside*—and who knows what hideous things may still lurk there?"

He got up to indicate that he had no more to say. I got to my feet, too, glad to escape the dimly-lit room and the house itself. Clothier ushered me to the door, and stood briefly at the threshold glancing fearfully up and down the street, as if he expected some dreadful visitation. Then he vanished inside his house without waiting to see where I went.

I crossed to Number 11. As I entered the curiously-shadowed hall, I remembered my friend's account of his life here. It was in the lower part of the house that Young had been wont to peruse certain archaic and terrible volumes, to set down his notes concerning his discoveries, and to pursue sundry other researches. I found the room which had been his study without trouble; the desk covered with sheets of notepaper—the bookcases filled with leather- and skin-bound volumes—the incongruous desk lamp—all these bespoke the room's onetime use.

I brushed the thick dust from the desk and the chair beside it, and turned on the light. The glow was reassuring. I sat down and took up my friend's papers. The stack which first fell under my eye bore the heading *Corroborative Evidence,* and the very first page was typical of the lot, as I soon discovered. It consisted of what seemed to be unrelated notes referring to the Mayan culture of Central America. The notes, unfortunately, seemed to be random and meaningless. "Rain gods (water elementals?) Trunk-proboscis (ref. Old Ones). Kukulkan (Cthulhu?)" —Such was their general tenor. Nevertheless, I persisted, and presently a hideously suggestive pattern became evident.

It began to appear that Young had been attempting to unify and correlate various cycles of legend with one central cycle, which was, if recurrent references were to be believed, far older than the human race. Whence Young's information had been gathered if not from the antique volumes set around the walls of the room, I did not venture to guess. I pored for hours over Young's synopsis of the monstrous and alien myth-cycle—the legends of how Cthulhu came from an indescribable milieu beyond the furthest bounds of this universe—of the polar civilizations and abominably unhuman races from black Yuggoth on the rim— of hideous Leng and its monastery-prisoned high priest who had to cover what should be its face—and of a multitude of blasphemies only rumored to exist, save in certain forgotten places of the world. I read what Azathoth had resembled *before* that monstrous nuclear chaos had been bereft of mind and will—of many-featured Nyarlathotep—of shapes which the crawling chaos could assume, shapes which men have never before dared to relate—of how one might glimpse a dhole, and what one would see.

I was shocked to think that such hideous beliefs could be thought true in any corner of a sane world. Yet Young's treatment of his material hinted that he, too, was not entirely skeptical concerning them. I pushed aside a bulky stack of papers. In so doing, I dislodged the desk blotter, revealing a thin sheaf of notes headed *On the legend of the High Street Church*. Recalling Clothier's warning, I drew it forth.

Two photographs were stapled to the first page. One was captioned *Section of tesselated Roman pavement, Goatswood,* the other *Reproduction engraving p. 594 "Necronomicon."* The former represented a group of what seemed to be acolytes or hooded priests depositing a body before a squatting monster; the latter a representation of that creature in somewhat greater detail. The being itself was so hysterically alien as to be indescribable; it was a glistening, pallid oval, with no facial features whatsoever, except for a vertical, slitlike mouth, surrounded by a horny ridge. There were no visible members, but there was that which suggested that the creature could shape any organ at will. The creature was certainly only a product of some morbid artist's diseased mind—but the pictures were nevertheless oddly disturbing.

The second page set forth in Young's all too familiar script a local legend to the effect that Romans who had laid the Goatswood pavement had, in fact, practiced decadent worship of some kind, and hinting that certain rites lingered in the customs of the more primitive present-day inhabitants of the area. There followed a paragraph translated from the *Necronomicon*. "The tomb-herd confer no benefits upon their worshipers. Their powers are few, for they can but disarrange space in small regions and make tangible that which cometh forth from the dead in other dimensions. They have power wherever the chants of Yog-Sothoth have been cried out at their seasons, and can draw to them those who will open their gates in the charnel-houses. They have no substance in this dimension, but enter earthly tenants to feed through them while they await the time when the stars become fixed and the gate of infinite sides opens to free That Which Claws at the Barrier." To this Young had appended some cryptic notes of his own— "Cf. legends in Hungary, among aborigines Australia. —Clothier on High Church, Dec. 17," which impelled me to turn to Young's diary, pushed aside in my eagerness to examine Young's papers.

I turned the pages, glancing at entries which seemed to be unrelated to the subject I sought, until I came to the entry for December 17. "More about the High Street Church legend from Clothier. He spoke of past days when it was a meeting-place for worshipers of morbid, alien gods. Subterranean tunnels supposedly burrowed down to onyx temples, etc. Rumors that all who crawled down those tunnels to worship were not human. References to passages to other spheres." So much, no more. This was scarcely illuminating. I pressed on through the diary.

Under date of December 23, I found a further reference: "Christmas brought more legends to Clothier's memory today. He said something about a curious Yule rite practiced in the High Street Church—something to do with evoked beings in the buried necropolis beneath the church. Said it still happened on the eve of Christmas, but he had never actually seen it."

Next evening, according to Young's account, he had gone to the church. "A crowd had gathered on the steps leading off the street. They carried no light, but the scene was illuminated by floating globular objects which gave off a phosphorescence and floated away at my approach. I could not identify them. The crowd presently, realizing I had not come to join them, threatened me and came for me. I fled. I was followed, but I could not be sure *what* followed me."

There was not another pertinent entry for several

days. Then, under date of January 13, Young wrote: "Clothier has finally confessed that he has been drawn into certain Temphill rites. He warned me to leave Temphill, said I must not visit the church in High Street after dark or I might awaken *them,* after which I might be *visited*—and not by people! His mind appears to be in the balance."

For nine months thereafter, no pertinent entry had been made. Then, on September 30, Young had written of his intention to visit the church in High Street that night, following which, on October 1, certain jottings, evidently written in great haste. "What abnormalities—what cosmic perversions! Almost too monstrous for sanity! I cannot yet believe what I saw when I went down those onyx steps to the vaults— that herd of horrors! . . . I tried to leave Temphill, but all streets turn back to the church. Is my mind, too, going?" Then, the following day, a desperate scrawl— "I cannot seem to leave Temphill. All roads return to No. 11 today—the power of those from *outside.* Perhaps Dodd can help." And then, finally, the frantic beginnings of a telegram set down under my name and address and evidently intended to be sent. *Come Temphill immediately. Need your help* . . . There the writing ended in a line of ink running to the edge of the page, as if the writer had allowed his pen to be dragged off the paper.

Thereafter nothing more. Nothing save that Young was gone, vanished, and the only suggestion in his notes seemed to point to the church in High Street. Could he have gone there, found some concealed room, been trapped in it? I might yet then be the instrument of freeing him. Impulsively, I left the room and the house, went out to my car, and started away.

Turning right, I drove up South Street toward Wool Place. There were no other cars on the roads, and I did not notice the usual pavement loafers; curiously, too, the houses I passed were unlit, and the overgrown patch in the center, guarded by its flaking railing and blanched in the light of the moon over the white gables, seemed desolate and disquieting. The decaying quarter of Cloth Street was even less inviting. Once or twice I seemed to see forms starting out of doorways I passed, but they were unclear, like the figments of a distorted imagination. Over all, the feeling of desolation was morbidly strong, particularly in the region of those dark alleys undulating between unlit, boarded houses. In High Street at last, the moon hung over the steeple of the hill-set church like some lunar diadem, and as I moved the car into a depression at the bottom of the steps the orb sank behind the black spire as if the church were dragging the satellite out of the sky.

As I climbed the steps, I saw that the walls around me had iron rails set into them and were made of rough stone, so pitted that beaded spiders' webs glistened in the fissures, while the steps were covered with a slimy green moss which made climbing unpleasant. Denuded trees overhung the passage. The church itself was lit by the gibbous moon which swung high in the gulfs of space, and the tottering gravestones, overgrown with repulsively decaying vegetation, cast curious shadows over the fungus-strewn grass. Strangely, though the church was so manifestly unused, an air of habitation clung to it, and I entered it almost with the expectation of finding someone—caretaker or worshiper—beyond the door.

I had brought a flashlight with me to help me in my search of the nighted church, but a certain glow—a kind of iridescence—lay within its walls, as of moonlight reflected from the mullioned windows. I went down the central aisle, flashing my light into one row of pews after the other, but there was no evidence in the mounded dust that anyone had ever been there. Piles of yellowed hymnals squatted against a pillar like grotesque huddled shapes of crouching beings, long forsaken—here and there the pews were broken with age—and the air in that enclosed place was thick with a kind of charnel musk.

I came at last toward the altar and saw that the first pew on the left before the altar was tilted abnormally in my direction. I had noted earlier that several of the pews were angled with disuse, but now I saw that the floor beneath the first pew was also angled upward, revealing an unlit abyss below. I pushed the pew back all the way—for the second pew had been set at a suitably greater distance—thus exposing the black depths below the rectangular aperture. The flickering yellow glow from my flashlight disclosed a flight of steps, twisting down between dripping walls.

I hesitated at the edge of the abyss, flashing an uneasy glance around the darkened church. Then I began the descent, walking as quietly as possible. The only sound in the core-seeking passage was the dripping of water in the lightless area beyond the beam of my flashlight. Droplets of water gleamed at me from the walls as I spiraled downward, and crawling black things scuttled into crevices as though the light could destroy them. As my quest led me further into the earth, I noticed that the steps were no longer of stone, but of earth itself, out of which grew repulsively bloated, dappled fungi, and saw that the roof of the tunnel was disquietingly supported only by the flimsiest of arches.

How long I slithered under those uncertain arches I could not tell, but at last one of them became a gray tunnel over strangely-colored steps, uneroded by time, the edges of which were still sharp, though the flight was discolored with mud from the passage of feet from above. My flashlight showed that the curve of the descending steps had now become less pronounced, as if its terminus was near, and as I saw this I grew conscious of a mounting wave of uncertainty and disquiet. I paused once more and listened.

There was no sound from beneath, no sound from above. Pushing back the tension I felt, I hastened forward, slipped on a step, and rolled down the last few stairs to come up against a grotesque statue, life-size, leering blindly at me in the glow of my flashlight. It was but one of six in a row, opposite which was an identical, equally repulsive sextet, so wrought by the skill of some unknown sculptor as to seem terrifyingly real. I tore my gaze away, picked myself up, and flashed my light into the darkness before me.

Would that a merciful oblivion could wipe away forever what I saw there!—the rows of gray stone slabs reaching limitlessly away into darkness in claustrophobic aisles, on each of them shrouded corpses staring sightlessly at the ebon roof above. And nearby were archways marking the beginning of black winding staircases leading *downward* into inconceivable depths; the sight of them filled me with an inexplicable chill superimposed upon my horror at the charnel vision before me. I shuddered away from the thought of searching among the slabs for Young's remains—if he were there, and I felt intuitively that he lay somewhere among them. I tried to nerve myself to move forward, and was just timidly moving to enter the aisle at the entrance of which I stood, when a sudden sound paralyzed me.

It was a whistling rising slowly out of the darkness before me, augmented presently by explosive sounds which seemed to increase in volume, as were the source of it approaching. As I stared affrightedly at the point whence the sound seemed to rise, there came a prolonged explosion and the sudden glowing of a pale, sourceless green light, beginning as a circular illumination, hardly larger than a hand. Even as I strained my eyes at it, it vanished. In a few seconds, however, it reappeared, three times its previous diameter—and for one dreadful moment I glimpsed through it a hellish, alien landscape, as if were I looking through a window opening upon another, utterly foreign dimension! It blinked out even as I fell back—then returned with even greater brilliance—and I found myself gazing against my will upon a scene being seared indelibly on my memory.

It was a strange landscape dominated by a trembling star hanging in a sky across which drifted elliptical clouds. The star, which was the source of the green glowing, shed its light upon a landscape where great, black triangular rocks were scattered among vast metal buildings, globular in shape. Most of these seemed to be in ruins, for whole segmentary plates were torn from the lower walls, revealing twisted, peeling girders which had been partially melted by some unimaginable force. Ice glittered greenly in crevices of the girders, and great flakes of vermilion-tinted snow settled toward the ground or slanted through the cracks in the walls, drifting out of the depths of that black sky.

For but a few moments the scene held—then abruptly it sprang to life as horrible white, gelatinous shapes flopped across the landscape toward the forefront of the scene. I counted thirteen of them, and watched them—cold with terror—as they came forward to the edge of the opening—and *across it,* to flop hideously into the vault where I stood!

I backed toward the steps, and as in a dream saw those frightful shapes move upon the statues nearby, and watched the outlines of those statues blur and begin to move. Then, swiftly, one of those dreadful beings rolled and flopped toward me. I felt something cold as ice touch my ankle. I screamed—and a merciful unconsciousness carried me into my own night. . . .

*   *   *

When I woke at last I found myself on the stones between two slabs some distance from the place on the steps where I had fallen—a horrible, bitter, furry taste in my mouth, my face hot with fever. How long I had lain unconscious I could not tell. My light lay where it had fallen, still glowing with enough illumination to permit a dim view of my surroundings. The green light was gone—the nightmarish opening had vanished. Had I but fainted at the nauseating odors, at the terrible suggestiveness of this charnel crypt? But the sight of a singularly frightening fungus in scattered patches on my clothing and on the floor—a fungus I had not seen before, dropped from what source I could not tell and about which I did not want to speculate—filled me with such awful dread that I started up, seized my light, and fled, plunging for the dark archway beyond the steps down which I had come into this eldritch pit.

I ran feverishly upward, frequently colliding with the wall and tripping on the steps and on obstacles which seemed to materialize out of the shadows. Somehow I reached the church. I fled down the central aisle, pushed open the creaking door, and raced down the shadowed steps to the car. I tugged frantically at the door before I remembered that I had locked the car. Then I tore at my pockets—in vain! The key ring carrying all my keys was gone—lost in that hellish crypt I had so miraculously escaped. The car was useless to me—nothing would have induced me to return, to enter again the haunted church in High Street.

I abandoned it. I ran out into the street, bound for

Wood Street, and, beyond it, the next town—open country—any place but accursed Temphill. Down High Street, into Market Square, where the wan moonlight shared with one high lamp standard the only illumination, across the Square into Manor Street. In the distance lay the forests about Wood Street, beyond a curve, at the end of which Temphill would be left behind me. I raced down the nightmarish streets, heedless of the mists that began to rise and obscure the wooded country slopes that were my goal, the blurring of the landscape beyond the looming houses.

I ran blindly, wildly—but the hills of the open country came no nearer—and suddenly, horribly, I recognized the unlit intersections and dilapidated gables of Cloth Street—which should have been far behind me, on the other side of the river—and in a moment I found myself again in High Street, and there before me were the worn steps of that repellent church, with the car still before them! I tottered, clung to a roadside tree for a moment, my mind in chaos. Then I turned and started out again, sobbing with terror and dread, racing with pounding heart back to Market Square, back across the river, aware of a horrible vibration, a shocking, muted whistling sound I had come to know only too well, aware of fearful pursuit . . .

I failed to see the approaching car and had time only to throw myself backward so that the full force of its striking me was avoided. Even so, I was flung to the pavement and into blackness.

* * *

I woke in the hospital at Camside. A doctor returning to Camside through Temphill had been driving the car that struck me. He had taken me, unconscious and with a contusion and a broken arm, taken me from that accursed city. He listened to my story, as much as I dared tell, and went to Temphill for my car. It could not be found. And he could find no one who had seen me or the car. Nor could he find books, papers, or diary at No. 11 South Street where Albert Young had lived. And of Clothier there was no trace—the owner of the adjacent house said he had been gone for a long time.

Perhaps they were right in telling me I had suffered a progressive hallucination. Perhaps it was an illusion, too, that I heard the doctors whispering when I was coming out of anaesthesia—whispering of the frantic way in which I had burst into the path of the car—and worse, of the strange fungus that clung to my clothes, even to my face at my lips, as if it grew there!

Perhaps. But can they explain how now, months afterward, though the very thought of Temphill fills me with loathing and dread, I feel myself irresistibly drawn to it, as if that accursed, haunted town were the mecca toward which I must make my way? I have begged them to confine me—to prison me—anything—and they only smile and try to soothe me and assure me that everything will "work itself out"—the glib, self-reassuring words that do not deceive me, the words that have a hollow sound against the magnet of Temphill and the ghostly whistling echoes that invade not only my dreams but my waking hours!

I will do what I must. Better death than that un-speakable horror . . .

Filed with the report of P.C. Villars on the disappear-ance of Richard Dodd, 9 Gayton Terrace, W.7. Manu-script in Dodd's script, found in his room after his disappearance.

INTRODUCTION TO
"EUSTACE"
by Tanith Lee

Since this story is less than a hundred words long, these remarks on it will take up more space than *it* will. . . .

I was about nineteen when I wrote *Eustace,* and though it wasn't published until I was approaching twenty-one (in 1968), I had actually been asked for it by the editor, whom I had briefly met via my mother's employers. He said he would include a piece by me, providing it was *very* short (i.e. less than a page). Sometimes stipulations like these are impossible, but this time it wasn't. I got the idea, I now think, almost instantly. Either that, or I had already written it—thirty-four years on, it rather eludes me.

Obviously, in my then desperately unpublished state, I thought this crumb might be an actual start. (My naïveté has often been very helpful to me!) It wasn't a start, of course. Several more years elapsed before anything else was published, and even more until Donald Wollheim of DAW let me loose on a proper, full-time writing career, in 1975.

However, I think "Eustace" is pretty good. It still amuses me. And, if one thinks around the edges of it, the ramifications of this tiny fragment remain extremely uncomfortable.

EUSTACE

by Tanith Lee

I LOVE Eustace although he is forty years my senior, is totally deaf, and has no teeth. I don't mind that he is completely bald, except between his toes, that he walks with a stoop, and sometimes falls over in the street. When he feels it necessary to emit a short sharp hissing sound, gnaw the sofa, or sleep in the garden, I accept everything as quite normal. Because I love him.

I love Eustace because he is the only man who has not minded about my having three legs.

FIRST GEAR

by Edward Bryant

I'll admit to having at least the normal writer's ego—
that ego being a commodity that varies enormously
from one scribbler to the next. Egos in the arts community are entities that inspire thousands, probably
millions of mythic accounts. The typical writerly ego
can be charted on a spectrum ranging from the sort
of self-regard that could rip holes in the hulls and sink
a dozen *Titanic*s to levels of self-esteem so negligible,
they generate a dark event horizon that *almost* pre-
vents manuscripts from ever going out farther than
ten meters from the author's writing area. Almost.

Me, I'm somewhere in the middle. And having as-
serted that, I'll also admit that my first professionally published story is probably never going to end up in an
anthology of unaccountably overlooked American fictions
of the twentieth century. Mind you, I'm not ashamed of
it; but I do know the difference between a marginally
competent tale and a work of surpassing genius.

"They Come Only in Dreams" is among the latter.

Just kidding. I wanted to see if you were awake.

Allow me to recap a bit of history and give you a context for the story's appearance. In 1969 I completed a second summer stay at Robin Scott Wilson's Clarion SF Writers Conference (back then, there was no stigma attached to attending multiple times). I'd attended the very first Clarion in 1968 and had been delighted (putting it mildly) to be the first Clarion writer to make a professional sale. But that story didn't appear in print until 1972. I spent the year between Clarions working full-time in a stirrup buckle factory and cranking out a whole variety of science fiction and fantasy stories, few of which clicked on any level with editors. I was having a hard time getting started in my writing career. The transmission kept grinding and slipping, right there at first gear.

Then, early in the autumn of 1969, I accepted Harlan Ellison's kind invitation to come to L.A. and stay as a working guest in his home. I'm not sure Harlan really knew what he was in for, since I arrived and then lingered for much of the next four years! Harlan got some company and some dubiously useful help around the house; I benefited from an absolutely invaluable mentoring.

Soon after my arrival, Harlan listened to my tales of rejection-slip hell and suggested I might take the same route as so many other writers in Southern California—try writing for the fertile wealth of men's magazines published in and around L.A. These weren't the biggies, such as *Playboy, Gallery,* or *Penthouse.* Nor were they at the bottom of the heap, a la *Swingle* (which admittedly I eventually sold to). These were mid-level men's mags such as *Adam* and *Knight* and *Adam Bedside Reader*. True, their essential stock in trade was photo spreads of partially and totally unclad women, but stories and nonfiction articles were needed to fill in the space between the studies of nude female pulchritude. Pornography, a natural concern for a small-town boy like me, wasn't a concern. The editors Harlan introduced me to just wanted some decent writing. The articles should be hip, the stories could be titillating. These magazines were a voracious market (this was pre Internet porn sites, recall). I found out that a wide variety of known professional writers practiced in this arena, particularly recruited from science fiction. Harlan, Norman Spinrad, Theodore Sturgeon, and a host more sold here. The issue of *Adam* in which "They Come Only in Dreams" appeared also featured new work from Sturgeon, Alex Apostolides, and Theodore Mathieson.

I dragged out rejected manuscripts from the previous year, spiffed them up, and also learned to pitch nonfiction pieces. When Merrill Miller at *Adam* offered to take "Dreams," he offered $200. Not bad breaking-in pay, particularly in terms of 1969 dollars. More sales followed. Merrill and Jared Rutter and their colleagues helped keep me afloat while I continued attempting to batter down editorial doors at science fiction magazines such as *Galaxy* and *Fantasy & Science Fiction*.

It was major thrill-time when late in 1969, the January 1970 issue of *Adam* appeared at newsstands, the cover adorned with the photo of a cute Greek film starlet in a pink minidress and a now severely dated 'do with mounds of dark hair piled atop her head. The article teasers on the cover included "Marijuana—Assassin of Youth?" "Horse racing—the Million-dollar Tip," and "How to Attack the Establishment on a Shoestring." On the inside, it was all heavily youth and guy oriented.

Now for the real historical footnote and the potential scandal. A shocking confession. If the truth be known, "They Come Only in Dreams" was not wholly my own work. I had a collaborator, sorta. Harlan Ellison. I can hear the gnashing of teeth all across the land as bibliographers and literary historians go berserk.

Here's what happened.

The morning I was heading down to the offices of Sirkay Publications with my first intended submission in hand, Harlan thought to check out my effort in advance. He quickly skimmed my dark fantasy of succubi and temptation and shook his head. Then he gently suggested that maybe I might have a better shot if I raised the heat of the story a few degrees.

I probably looked as dull and uncomprehending as one of the lesser rocks at Stonehenge. Harlan sighed, shook his head, grabbed my typescript (this *was* the old days), and started changing a few passages, marking out some particularly inept prose, adding the occasional *bon mot*. When your read the story, I'll confide in you that "She kissed him there and her tongue went for a silken stroll" is Harlan's. Ditto "Insanely, he

70

thought of the total area of the state of Texas: 267,339 square miles, including inland water." I won't divulge the others. Some things should remain a mystery.

Suffice it to say, I received a valuable editing and writing lesson. The story had a few tingly moments. And the commercial current of my writing career was off and . . . hopping.

So here it is, "They Come Only in Dreams" with its warts, dated attitudes, *faux* hipness, and all the rest. As I said earlier, I'm not at all ashamed of it and I'm delighted it's creaked back into the light of day here in this anthology. We've all got to start somewhere.

For me, it's like stumbling onto a forgotten carton of old newspapers stashed in the attic. It's nostalgia time. But let me close with one caution. Whatever you do, don't track down this story in some moldering archive of men's magazines, then present the issue of *Adam* to Harlan at a convention and badger him to sign it. Both of us, we'd have to kill you.

THEY COME ONLY
IN DREAMS

by Edward Bryant

"HELLO, lover," said the succubus.

Martin Wintergreen didn't know she was a succubus, or even what a succubus was. He had led a circumscribed life. Martin saw a naked girl lying beside him in his bed, and his first reaction was complete confusion.

What are you doing in my bed? Martin thought. What he actually stammered was, "Who—how did—you?" The whole situation had a nightmare surrealism about it, yet Martin had the sickening feeling he was awake. He shut his eyes and massaged them fiercely with his fingertips. Even with eyes closed, he saw her afterimage; the girl's skin was a healthy pink in the dim glow from the night-light; her body was incredibly curved, almost as plump as the Rubens nudes Martin had surreptitiously lusted after during his Sunday afternoon visits to the County Museum; her face was—sweet, Martin's atrophic imagination described it, yet with sensual overtones—like a debauched angel.

Martin lay on his back with eyes screwed shut and frantically hoped he'd awaken. Then he felt the moist, warm hand of the dream lightly brush the thin hairs on his stomach; she began to caress him.

His eyes snapped open and he sat upright. "What

are you *doing*?" There was a rising note of hysteria in his voice; "circumscribed life" was perhaps not specific enough: cloistered was closer. Not on-the-button, but closer.

The girl drew back, apparently startled by Martin's panicky indignation. Then she leaned forward, pushed him gently but firmly down against the pillow and let her long blonde hair tickle across his face.

"I'm seducing you," she said matter-of-factly in a breathless, little-girl voice. Martin identified it with TV situation-comedy caricatures of Hollywood actresses. She snuggled against him and in his agitation Martin wondered how much skin area she possessed. Insanely, he thought of the total area of the state of Texas: 267,339 square miles, including inland water. His entire body seemed to be kissed by pulsing, moist flesh.

"Stop!" Martin pushed the girl away roughly. She lay propped on one elbow, her expression surprised. She had marvelous breasts, very firm. He thought he saw anger flash across her features, anger and something else—something too quick to recognize. Too quick or— "Who are you?" asked Martin, making a valiant effort to appear calm.

The girl smiled, and for a moment Martin could see the pink tip of her tongue. "My name is Dulcinea, Martin."

"How did you know that?"

"Your name? I know everything about you, Martin. I was given a complete dossier. You're thirty-one years old and you've never been married. You work

73

as a quality control sub-inspector in the Chemié de Burbank Works. You hate it."

"I don't hate it," said Martin. "It's just—well, dull."

"You hate it. Let's see—oh yes, you had your first and last affair seven months short of ten years ago. You were a college senior. It was an unsatisfactory act performed on the folddown passenger's seat of a 1958 Rambler American."

Martin blushed. "Now wait a—"

Dulcinea kissed him. "Don't worry about it, Martin. I'm very glad you saved yourself for me. I'll make you forget about those long years of—"

Martin wrenched away from her passionate embrace. "Hold on," he pleaded. "What in hell—"

She interrupted him. "Nowhere in hell, Martin. Here. In your bed. And I want to hold on. To you." She tried to demonstrate, but Martin hastily grabbed her wrists. They were surprisingly slender, considering her otherwise statuesque proportions. "Martin," she said, "you protesteth too much. Now let me fuck you."

"I knew I shouldn't have had cheese blintzes," Martin said. He flung his legs over the side of the bed and sat up. The clock on the bedside table indicated twenty minutes past midnight. "All I wanted was to get to sleep early. Periodontist appointment tomorrow."

"Don't mumble, darling," Dulcinea whispered, her lips lightly brushing like butterfly wings against Martin's ear. She kissed him there and her tongue went for a silken stroll.

He twisted his head aside. "Will you *kindly* stop that!"

Dulcinea shrugged, appearing somewhat daunted. "Sorry. Did it tickle?"

"What?"

"Tickle. In your ear."

Martin said nothing. Dulcinea let her own legs slide off the bed and sat up beside Martin. Her shoulder and hip touched him.

"Something's bothering you," said the succubus.

"Bothering me! What could be bothering me? My God. I'm awakened out of a sound sleep in my own bed in my own apartment by a—a naked person I've never seen before—a person who—who—" He swallowed. "Who makes advances to me! And you guess that something's bothering me?" Martin stood up, swayed, steadied himself by grabbing the headboard.

"I need some coffee," he said.

"Do you have any tea?" asked Dulcinea.

"Only instant with lemon and artificial sweetener."

"That will be fine."

This isn't happening, Martin thought. He weaved slightly as he walked across the plush carpet to his closet. "Here," he said. "Wear this. Please." He tossed Dulcinea a charcoal-gray dressing gown without looking at her.

She donned it but left the top three buttons undone. Martin turned at the sound of fabric on skin and counted the buttons as Dulcinea slipped them through their respective eyelets. "Do you mind buttoning it to the top?"

"Yes." She smiled ingenuously. "I wouldn't be comfortable. It would crush my lovely—"

Martin blushed again.

"May I have my tea now, darling?"

"God, if I'm sleeping through my periodontist's—" His eyes focused on the Wyeth print hanging behind her right shoulder. "Milk? Sugar?"

"Both, please," she said. "Dear, don't worry about your appointment. You'll sleep very well if you'll just let me help you."

"Milk," said Martin hopelessly.

"Sugar." He turned and started for the kitchen. Dulcinea grasped the limp fingers of his left hand and followed him demurely.

She sat quietly, the dressing gown fallen open to reveal crossed, silken legs, watching his reflection in the surface of the Formica tabletop. Martin set a pot of water to boiling on the gas range.

"Here," he offered. He set a box of oatmeal cookies on the table.

"If I can have one from your hand."

"Oh, my God," Martin said, trembling.

Reluctantly, he picked an oatmeal cookie out of the package and proffered it to Dulcinea. She smiled and took it from him, allowing her fingers to slide against his. She devoured her prize and Martin found himself mesmerized like a rabbit before a cobra. He had never seen a cookie eaten more sensually.

"Darling, would you like to kiss the crumbs off my lips?"

There was a spatter and hiss as the pot of water boiled over. Martin turned to the stove, then whirled back to face the girl. "Why are you doing this to me?"

Dulcinea smiled again, sweetly. "There's something I want. A need I have."

"What do you want?"

"You, darling. Your kisses. Your—affection."

He stared at her. "You're crazy."

"No, no I'm not. I'm—" she paused. "I'm hungry. Could I have my tea, please?"

"Oh, you're hungry?" Martin pushed the box of cookies in front of her.

"Thanks, darling. But a succubus doesn't thrive on a diet of oatmeal cookies."

"A what?"

"Don't be wearisome, darling. You really don't know? What are the schools teaching these days?"

Martin looked blank. He poured the water onto the waiting instant tea.

Dulcinea sighed and recrossed her legs. Martin noted in his peripheral vision that the *bottom* three buttons of the dressing gown had somehow come undone. The girl sipped gingerly from her teacup.

"Didn't you take mythology courses in college?"

"No," said Martin. "I didn't have any time."

"A succubus," said Dulcinea, "is a female demon who tempts men in their sleep. Just as my brother, the incubus, tempts young girls. We generally center our efforts on the young and impressionable, the virgins, the—"

Martin's blush, which had been steadily fading, returned with a vengeance. "But I'm not—"

"Close enough." She smiled sympathetically. "It's a sad comment on the times. There aren't as many virgins to tempt as there once were. Humans are becom-

ing too liberated. We've had to extend our scope."
She sighed. "Sorry, I didn't mean to sermonize."

"This is crazy," said Martin. "Insane."

"You've said that."

"All right, if you're real, what do you really want?"

"That you *also* asked."

"But you didn't answer me."

"I did so. I said I was hungry."

"Not for cookies?"

"No, darling." She leaned toward him, and Martin
noted that none of the dressing gown's buttons were
now fastened. Dulcinea gently clasped Martin's hand.
"Your soul, dearest. That's what I want."

"Oh." Martin looked nonplussed. "My, uh, soul."

"Well, not exactly your soul. That sounds a bit
melodramatic. I should have said something like soul
energy, um, charismatic residue. Synergistically speaking. Does that help?"

"No," said Martin.

"Psychic vibrations, then? My masters and I receive a—
a certain nourishment from your innermost emotions."

"My soul," Martin mused. "I didn't really think I had
one. It's been years now—souls and trading with the Devil
and Daniel Webster and all those things are supposed to
be pretty passé, even for bad movies, aren't they?"

"Oh don't be silly, baby. This isn't trading with
Satan or anything like that. Do I look like the sort of
girl who'd run with *that* gauche crowd?"

Martin looked at her smile, saw how white and
sharp her teeth were and felt a chill of apprehension.
"What do I get out of the trade?" he asked.

"Could I have some more tea, please?" She spooned fresh instant from the jar of tea.

"You're not answering me!"

"Don't shout, darling. Please?" Her tone was conciliatory, gentle. Martin's hand shook slightly as he poured her another cup of hot water.

"That's better," she said, daintily placing two sugar cubes in the tea. "You've got to realize that we demons aren't malevolent, dear. There's nothing sinister about this. Just accept me as I am, please." She looked down at the oatmeal cookies. "I'm just a succubus who likes you very much, Martin. I want to give you pleasure and take pleasure in return."

"Dulcinea." She didn't look up, didn't meet his eyes. "I don't think you're telling the truth."

Martin shoved back his chair and stood. "Whoever you are, whatever you are, I'm tired. I want to sleep. My gums ache and I have to rest. Do you mind?"

She shrugged.

He turned to the telephone. "I'll call you a cab." There was no dial tone. He clicked the cradle up and down. Still no tone. He looked back and Dulcinea was laughing—but softly. Martin strode purposefully into the living room.

The succubus heard him trying the door. She called, "No good, darling. It isn't locked, but you won't be able to open it." Martin reappeared in the kitchen doorway.

"Resign yourself, sweetheart. You can't get rid of me. Oh, you could fast, pray and go to confession— that's the old way, Martin—but in your case I don't think it would be too effective."

"Listen, this is insane."

"Third time's the charm, dear. Don't be a bore." She had taken off the bathrobe and draped it carelessly over a kitchen chair. She pressed herself against Martin; at the same time she flipped the light switch and Martin had a final glimpse of her face.

My God! What's happening? He thought. The room became night and Martin felt Dulcinea's skin, smelled a strange, musky perfume, listened as the succubus whispered strange soft things in his ear that seemed more obscene than any words he had ever heard. Finally, he felt fear—the gut-level, wrenching, visceral thing; the desperate struggling trap he could remember from his other nightmares; the falling helplessly; the sensation of being pursued through musky swamps where muck clung in in endless possession to every running footstep. Fear. And he screamed.

"Oh baby, poor baby," she whispered, holding him like a child, kissing his face and his neck, comforting him. "Come here."

She led him to his bedroom and undressed him as he began to cry; then she lay beside him.

He wept on the outside and struggled within. He stared through dilated pupils at the darkness of the bedroom—the night-light seemed to have gone out.

Above him—up there? Martin could no longer trust his sense of equilibrium. Up there where the ceiling ought to be was a deeper darkness, a blacker-than-black shadow, a penumbra that pulsed in and out in and out in. Mostly in.

No! Martin knew he was screaming only in his mind.

Screaming, hating what was happening, screaming, fearing, fearing—what?

Dulcinea was skilled. She drew upon all her vast experience, all the myriad women's tricks distilled and refined since Lilith.

She spun dreams for Martin. He swam with her in a warm, ice-green lagoon. They crawled out onto the grassy bank and she lay lazily before him, begged him to make love to her.

No!

They sat opposite one another across a rough board dinner table and watched each other's eyes. They consumed huge quantities of aphrodisiac delights. Before dessert, Dulcinea leaned forward, whispered something as her lace bodice fell away—

No!

Scenes from harems and ski lodges and sensual seascapes and small boats rocking and a plush carpeted stair landing in a New Orleans gaming house and a sunny mountain meadow and—

No! No! Nononono!

He fought and found strengths he'd never suspected were inside. No! I don't want you or need you! Get out get away go!

And he won. Somehow, someway he pushed the darkness back. He felt it recede until it hung sullenly just below the ceiling again and he felt Dulcinea move away from him. Startled, he realized he was looking at a pair of blue eyes—hers. The night-light was glowing again. He could see Dulcinea and the maple bedside table and the rest of the bedroom.

The succubus closed her eyes and seemed to capitulate. "Martin, dearest, I don't believe you. Never before, in eleven thousand years has someone so frustrated me. My lord, Belial, I'm horny!"

"Maybe like you said, it's the times." Martin was very weary. He realized he was covered with six different kinds of sweat. "Maybe people are different now."

"We're desperate," said Dulcinea. "Believers seem to be fewer each decade, even each year."

"Sorry," said Martin. "No."

"I wasn't pleading." Dulcinea shook her head and let a smile soften the hard set of her mouth. "We'll make it. Survive, that is. We can adapt."

"Good luck," said Martin. He felt he could afford to be magnanimous.

Dulcinea only smiled again, this time rather ferally, and silently vanished.

Martin rolled onto his back among the sweat-soaked sheets and stopped, shocked. The faint umbra of the black cloud was still up there, pulsing perceptibly.

Something cleared its throat. Something beside Martin in the bed.

Martin slowly raised his head. He looked, then stared, toward the deep baritone voice. At the close-cropped dark hair, the hard-muscled truck-driver's body. The family resemblance was undeniable.

Martin suddenly felt like shouting for Dulcinea to reappear, but he couldn't; his vocal cords were frozen.

"Hello, lover," said the incubus.

INTRODUCTION TO
"THE CLEANING MACHINE"

by F. Paul Wilson

This is the fifth publication of "The Cleaning Machine," but only the third I've been paid for. I got stiffed on the first two.

I wrote "The Cleaning Machine" (now *there's* a gripping title) in 1969 during medical school. I thought of it as a science-fiction horror story. I mean, it had a weird machine, so that made it science fiction, right? And bad things happened to people, so that made it horror, sort of. Whatever the genre, it was the best thing I'd written so far.

And I couldn't *give* it away.

The story earned form-letter rejections from every science fiction and fantasy periodical I could find an address for. Only John W. Campbell (Yes, I sent a horror story to *Analog*! What was I thinking?) had the courtesy to tell me why it did not suit his editorial needs at that time. (He always told me why he was rejecting my stories, and I always will revere him for that. When he'd accept one, however, he sent only a check.)

He wrote: "It's not a story because it doesn't go anywhere. (The tenants do but the story doesn't!) It's a vignette."

Cool. I'd written a vignette, whatever that was—sounded like those sugary things they serve at Café du Monde in the French Quarter. But I still didn't have a sale.

And Campbell was right, as usual. "The Cleaning Machine" didn't work as science fiction, but I had faith in it. Vignette or not, I felt it was a decent piece of quiet horror. Trouble was, hardly anyone was publishing horror in 1969. I'd tried Joseph Payne Brennan's *Macabre;* he liked it but wrote back that he was overstocked and not accepting new material.

But then in 1970 I stumbled on a pair of magazines Robert A. W. Lowndes was editing for Health Knowledge, Inc.: *The Magazine of Horror* and *Startling Mystery Stories.* Lowndes wrote informative editorials that he followed with reprints of hoary yarns from *Weird Tales, Strange Tales, Argosy,* and other Depression-era pulps. But he also published one new story per issue by newcomers with names like Stephen King and Greg Bear. Hey, if these nobodies could sell to Lowndes, so could I.

So I sent him "The Cleaning Machine" . . . and a few months later he wrote back to say he was taking it for *Startling Mystery Stories.* This was my second sale in a month; a few weeks earlier John Campbell had bought "Ratman" for *Analog*. The big difference was that Campbell had sent a $375 check on acceptance. Lowndes' company paid on publication.

So I waited. Even though it was my second sale, "The Cleaning Machine" became my first published story, appearing in the March 1971 issue of *Startling Mystery Stories* (#18)—with my name on the cover, no less.

I had arrived!

Unfortunately, the check never did. Health Knowledge Inc. folded *Startling Mystery Stories* with that issue. I contend that this was pure synchronicity. "The Cleaning Machine" had nothing to do with the failure of the magazine. Nothing.

But that's not the end of the story. Fifteen years later I'm signing books at a convention and here comes a reader with the August 1971 issue of an illustrated science fiction magazine called *Galaxy Mission*. I ask him what he wants me to do with it. He says a signature on the title page of my story would be greatly appreciated. What story? I've never even heard of *Galaxy Mission,* let alone sold to it. So he opens to the only text piece in the issue, and there's "The Cleaning Machine" under my byline.

The story I initially couldn't give away had been pirated and reprinted within months of its first publication, and I still hadn't seen a penny for it.

And people wonder why so many writers die drunk or mad.

THE CLEANING MACHINE

by F. Paul Wilson

DR. Edward Parker reached across his desk and flipped the power switch on his tape recorder to the "on" position.

"Listen if you like, Burke," he said. "But remember: she has classic paranoic symptoms; I wouldn't put much faith in anything she says."

Detective Ronald Burke, an old acquaintance on the city police force, sat across from the doctor. "She's all we've got," he replied with ill-concealed exasperation. "Over a hundred people disappear from an apartment house and the only person who might be able to tell us anything is a nut!"

Parker glanced at the recorder and noticed the glowing warm-up light. He pressed the button that started the tape.

"Listen."

". . . and I guess I'm the one who's responsible for it but it was really the people who lived there in my apartment who drove me to it—they were jealous of me.

"The children were the worst. Every day as I'd walk to the store they'd spit at me behind my back and call me names. They even got other little brats from all over town and would wait for me on corners and doorsteps. They called me terrible names and said that I carried awful diseases. Their parents put them up to it, I know it! All those people in my apartment building laughed at me. They thought they could hide it but I heard it. They hated me because they were jealous of my poetry. They knew I was famous and they couldn't stand it.

"Why, just the other night I caught three of them rummaging through my desk. They thought I was asleep and so they sneaked in and tried to steal some of my latest works, figuring they could palm them off as their own. But I was awake. I could hear them laughing at me as they searched. I grabbed the butcher knife that I always keep under my pillow and ran out into the study. I must have made some noise when I got out of bed because they ran out into the hall and closed the door just before I got there. I heard one of them on the other side say, 'Boy, you sure can't fool that old lady!'

"They were fiends, all of them! But the very worst was that John Hendricks fellow next door who was trying to kill me with an ultra-frequency sonicator. He used to turn it on me and try to boil my brains while I was writing. But I was too smart for him! I kept an ice pack on my head at all hours of the day. But even that didn't keep me from getting those awful headaches that plague me constantly. He was to blame.

"But the thing I want to tell you about is the

machine in the cellar. I found it when I went down to the boiler room to see who was calling me filthy names through the ventilator system. I met the janitor on my way downstairs and told him about it. He just laughed and said that there hadn't been anyone down in the boiler room for two years, not since we started getting our heat piped in from the building next door. But I *knew* someone was down there—hadn't I heard those voices through the vent? I simply turned and went my way.

"Everything in the cellar was covered with at least half an inch of dust—everything, that is, except the machine. I didn't know it was a machine at that time because it hadn't done anything yet. It didn't have any lights or dials and it didn't make any noise. It just sat there being clean. I also noticed that the floor around it was immaculately clean for about five feet in all directions. Everywhere else was filth. It looked so strange, being clean. I ran and got George, the janitor.

"He was angry at having to go downstairs but I kept pestering him until he did. He was mighty surprised.

" 'What *is* that thing!' he said, walking toward the machine. Then he was gone! One moment he had been there, and then he was gone. There was no blinding flash or puff of smoke . . . just gone! And it happened just as he crossed into that circle of clean floor around the machine.

"I immediately knew who was responsible: John Hendricks! So I went right upstairs and brought him down. I didn't bother to tell him what the machine had done to George since I was sure he knew all about it. But he surprised me by walking right into the circle and disappearing, just like George.

"Well, at least I wouldn't be bothered by that ultra-frequency sonicator of his anymore. It was a good thing I had been too careful to go anywhere near that thing.

"I began to get an idea about that machine—it was a *cleaning* machine! That's why the floor around it was so clean. Any dust or *anything* that came within the circle was either stored away somewhere or destroyed!

"A thought struck me: Why not 'clean out' all of my jealous neighbors this way? It was a wonderful idea!

"I started with the children.

"I went outside and, as usual, they started in with their name-calling. (They always made sure to do it very softly but I could read their lips.) There were about twenty of them playing in the street. I called them together and told them I was forming a club in the cellar and they all followed me down in a group. I pointed to the machine and told them that there was a gallon of chocolate ice cream behind it and that the first one to reach it could have it all. Their greedy little faces lighted up and they scrambled away in a mob.

"Three seconds later I was alone in the cellar.

"I then went around to all the other apartments in the building and told all those hateful people that their sweet little darlings were playing in the old boiler room and that I thought it was dangerous. I waited for one to go downstairs before I went to the next door. Then I met the husbands as they came home from work and told them the same thing. And if anyone came looking for someone, I sent him down to the cellar. It was all so simple: in searching the cellar they had to cross into the circle sooner or later.

"That night I was alone in the building. It was wonderful—no laughing, no name-calling, and no one sneaking into my study. Wonderful!

"A policeman came the next day. He knocked on my door and looked very surprised when I opened it. He said he was investigating a number of missing-persons reports. I told him that everyone was down in the cellar. He gave me a strange look but went to check. I followed him.

"The machine was gone! Nothing was left but the circle of clean floor. I told the officer all about it, about what horrible people they were and how they deserved to disappear. He just smiled and brought me down to the station where I had to tell my story again and they sent me here to see you.

"They're still looking for my neighbors, aren't they? Won't listen when I tell them that they'll never find them. They don't believe there ever *was* a machine! But they can't find my neighbors, can they? Well, it serves them right! I told them I'm the one responsible for 'cleaning out' my apartment building but they don't believe me. Serves them *all* right!"

"See what I mean?" said Dr. Parker with the slightest trace of a smile as he turned the recorder off. "She's no help at all."

"Yeah, I know," Burke sighed. "As loony as they

come. But how can you explain that circle of clean floor in the boiler room with all those footprints around it?"

"Well, I can't be sure, but the 'infernal machine' is not uncommon in the paranoid's delusional system. You found no trace of this 'ultra-frequency sonicator' in the Hendricks apartment, I trust?"

Burke shook his head. "No. From what we can gather, Hendricks knew nothing abut electronics. He was a short-order cook in a greasy spoon downtown."

"I figured as much. She probably found everybody gone and went looking for them. She went down to the boiler room as a last resort and, finding *it* deserted, concluded that everybody had been 'cleaned out' of the building. She was glad but wanted to give herself the credit. She saw the circle of clean floor—probably left there by a round tabletop that had been recently moved—and started fabricating. By now she believes every word of her fantastic story. We'll never really know what happened until we find those missing tenants."

"I guess not," Burke said as he rose to go, "but I'd still like to know why we can find over a hundred sets of footprints approaching the circle but none leaving it."

Dr. Parker didn't have an answer for that one.

INTRODUCTION TO
"AGONY IN THE GARDEN"

by Thomas F. Monteleone

After having been invited into this anthology, I pulled down an archival copy of the March, 1973, issue of *Amazing Science Fiction Stories* to peruse the story that follows. It was the first time I'd read it in at least twenty-five years and I noticed several salient facts regarding its place in the History of English Literature:

1. it wasn't all that *amazing,* and
2. there wasn't much *science* in it; but
3. it *was* fiction, and
4. it wasn't so damned bad a job . . .

At least not half as bad as I was expecting it to be. Now, maybe I say this because I'm writing about my first creation to knuckle-drag itself into the public arena, my firstborn, my first professionally published story. Or, maybe I'm saying it because it's true. . . .

You'll have to judge for yourself, but the story now strikes me as ambitious in scope, if not length, and original in concept. I found the execution stilted, and more than a little self-conscious, but not the purple, bloated excess I'd expected. Interestingly, the thematic wrestling with religion and its icons would be one I would revisit on more than one occasion during my career.[1] My formative years as a Roman Catholic, underpinned by four years of Latin and philosophy at a Jesuit high school, get my votes as major reasons for that.

Now, although I bought my first typewriter when I was twelve, and started writing sporadic and derivative stories[2] from that point on, I officially began writing on a regular basis (with the objective of becoming a working pro) in January 1970. My first rejection slip came from an outfit called "The Broome Agency," who used to advertise in *Writers' Digest* that they would sell new writers' work. I sent them three stories, and they told me they didn't think they could sell them. End of *that* tune.

So I figured, hey, I don't need an agent to sell short stories anyway, and started sending out my stuff with trusty SASEs attached. For the next two and half years,

---

[1] The most remarkable instance being *The Blood of the Lamb,* my "religious thriller" that copped the 1993 Bram Stoker Award. That novel and its sequel, *The Reckoning,* is forthcoming from Overlook Connection Press in a single volume entitled *Benediction.*

[2] Inspired in large part by EC Comics and others.

I probably wrote thirty stories, none of which ever sold or managed to get published.[3] I kept them circulating through a hierarchy of markets which always began with *Playboy* (because they paid several *thousand* dollars for short fiction), then notched ever downward through *Penthouse, Esquire,* a few anthology series like Damon Knight's *Orbit* and Terry Carr's *Universe,* and finally filtering out to *The Magazine of Fantasy & Science Fiction, Analog, Galaxy, Worlds of If, Fantastic Stories, Alfred Hitchcock's Magazine of Suspense, Ellery Queen's Mystery Magazine,* and finally *Amazing Science Fiction.* I would also send my tales to places like *Argosy* and the B- and C-level skin-mags with titles such as *Dude, Gent,* and *Nugget,* but with less regularity because I didn't always think my stories were thematically what this last group was looking for.

And the stories kept coming back. My mailbox was always jammed with manila envelopes and I had this file folder stuffed like an overripe kielbasa with rejections slips—more than *two hundred* of them. Almost all the standard form-letter stuff. I would actually get excited when some slush pile[4] reader would scribble a "Sorry,"

---

[3] I wrote them mainly at night between the hours of 10:00 P.M. and 2:00 A.M. on the dining room table of my very small apartment. I remember the guy on the first floor was a supermarket manager who had to get up at 4:00 every morning; he complained to the landlord—the ratcheting of my typewriter was waking him up! At that stage of my life, my writing mode could easily be described as driven, and more likely *feverish.* My response was therefore to advise my neighbor to do something to himself that would be anatomically challenging.

[4] That's what all the publishers called the mailbags full of unsolicited manuscripts that weekly cluttered their offices. The term persists to this day.

or a "Thanks for thinking of us!" or the extremely rare "Not bad, but not for us," because it was a sign of human contact, a shard of evidence that another human being had actually *read* my work. I remember being happy to receive a personal reply from Joseph Payne Brennan, who used to edit a very small press magazine—even though it was a large, black "No!" scribbled in large block print across my cover letter.[5]

There were plenty of reasons my stories weren't selling. Primary among them were my lack of consistent skill in storytelling, my overwritten, man-I'm-so-in-love-with-language style, and my lack of originality of story ideas. I knew I had to come up with stories that no editor had already read ten times that week, and for the first couple years, I just wasn't doing it.

The following story was sparked from reading I was doing at the time by psychoanalyst Carl Jung and his theory of what he termed the collective unconscious of our entire species. I had written a question in a notepad where I kept a huge list of possible story ideas: "What happens to the gods when no one believes in them anymore?" I kept thinking about that concept and figured I might be onto something. I struggled through several drafts of "Agony in the Garden,"[6] and sent it off to Damon Knight, who had be-

[5] Yeah, he really did that. Either the story was sensationally putrid, or I happened to hit him up when he was having a Very Bad Day.

[6] The title is a double entendre, with a direct reference to Christ's bad night in Gethsemane and the metaphor of the "garden" meaning the world. I thought I was being clever, erudite, and all that

come something of a mail-correspondence mentor to me. He'd taken an interest in my work, and had always been brutally honest about how much work I needed to do to become a good writer. He didn't buy the story for *Orbit,* but he told me it was "head and shoulders" above anything else I'd ever written, and with some rewriting, had a chance of getting itself sold.

Not being a touch-typist in the pre-computer days, I was loath to do third and fourth drafts, but I knew I had to do it with this story. And when it finally started making its rounds, I received quite a few personal notes on my rejection slips. I knew this one was better than anything I'd previously submitted. I *knew* this one had a chance. I just had to keep it out there circulating, and I saw an interesting possibility in a mimeographed newsletter called *Locus,* which was a pipeline to what was going on in the science fiction publishing world, and I saw a notice in there for a short story contest sponsored by something called "N3F," which I discovered later stood for the National Fantasy Fan Foundation. The contest was for nonprofessionals only and the judge was none other than Edward L. Ferman, the editor of the prestigious publication, *The Magazine of Fantasy & Science Fiction*. I entered "Agony in the Garden," and waited.

Months went by, and finally I got this form letter from Howard Devore of N3F, who told everyone who entered the short story contest there had been 160

sort of thing. Maybe I was . . .

entries, the quality of the submissions had been very high, the winners were listed below, and better luck next year if your name wasn't down there. Well, I looked down the page, and the second place winner was "Agony in the Garden." I forget what the prize was, but I do remember feeling like a very big, high-struttin' frog in a very small pond. I immediately sent off a photocopy of the story to Ed Ferman, reminding him he'd given me second prize, and supremely confident I'd be ringing up my first sale.

Three weeks later, it came back from *F&SF* with a form rejection slip. I felt as I often do when the world sucker punches you: stunned, but *never* crushed. I kept the story out there, collecting its rejections, but getting noticed in some small fashion. In the summer of 1971 I wrangled an invitation to this weekend gathering in Baltimore called the Guilford SF Writers Workshop. You had to have two stories to submit for public dissection and I brought "Agony in the Garden" and something else that still crackles with age in my file cabinet. The other attendees were either unpublished writers like me or guys who'd just sold their first few stories. We were all in our twenties and all sporting lean, hungry looks.[7] I was the stone-cold rookie in the group, and the level of criticism was just this side of evisceration. When "Agony in the Garden" came up for discussion, I had no idea what to expect—they might love it or hate it.

---

[7] The other guys were Jay and Joe Haldeman, Jack Dann, George Effinger, Gardner Dozois, Bob Thurston, and Ted White, who was the editor of *Amazing SF*.

Actually, they did neither. They all agreed it was a good story, but needed various tweaks and adjustments. They were all impressed with it enough to accept me as one of their own, as somebody who *belonged* there, and that was all I needed. So I was really knocked out when Ted White came up to me after that Saturday afternoon session and told me he'd buy the story if I made some of the revisions suggested during the workshop. I smiled and said I'd be happy to do whatever it took. The rest of that weekend I savored my triumph. I'd made a vow to myself I would become a professional writer, and I'd done it.

Then I waited for that first check, which came several months later from a guy named Sol Cohen, who turned out to be the publisher living in Flushing, New York. I'd been paid the outrageous sum of a penny per word, and that $30.00 draft could have been gold bullion—that's how good it felt to be holding it in my hands.

Then I waited for the publication date in March, and I believe I lived through the longest six months of my life. I was watching the calendar like I hadn't done since I was nine years old and counting off the days in December until Christmas. When my contributor copies finally showed up, and upon ripping them out of the envelope, I saw my name on the cover, I felt a mixture of elation and wonder and shock. It was one of those signal moments in my life, at once unforgettable, yet almost indescribable.

And here's something kind of weird: the lead story

that issue was part one of a serialized novel by Jack Vance. As I looked at the suitably psychedelic seventies cover art, I was struck by utter irony of the whole thing. When I was seven, my parents had given me for Christmas my first "grown-up people's" hardcover book. It was one of the Winston Science Fiction titles called *Vandals of the Void* by . . . Jack Vance. So you can see where I'm going with this. Each life contains its share of strange ironies and surprising symmetries; and this is one of mine. How oddly wonderful the guy who wrote the book that helped instill in me a sense of wonder and an urge to write my own stories would be the *same* guy sharing pages of a publication containing my first published work.

Life, as they say, is good.

AGONY IN THE GARDEN

by Thomas F. Monteleone

JESUS Christ pushed his way out of the crowd. He stepped onto an escalator and descended to the lower level of Metro station. He could hear the hum of the subway as the staircase started to move. When he reached the bottom, a man was standing in front of him, blocking his path.

"Fool!" yelled Christ, even though he knew the man couldn't hear him. "Get out of my way!"

The man continued to stand in the way, smoking a cigarette. Christ raised his arm and jammed the point of his elbow into the back of the man's neck. The man seemed to move in slow-motion as he careened forward, arms outstretched, his face expressionless. He hit the concrete headfirst, the rough surface scraping away his skin.

Damn you, thought Christ. Then looking out at the crowd: *You all deserve the same thing.*

He stepped over the fallen man; but before he could walk away, the man had gotten up, and resumed smoking his cigarette as if nothing had happened.

Nothing had.

Always the same, thought Christ. *They've forgotten everything. Wasting my time.*

He turned from the escalator and walked toward the waiting subway car. It was filled with perspiring passengers, but he forced his way in between two faceless riders. He stepped on their feet, elbowed their ribs; they didn't feel a thing. Their insensitivity to him served to augment his contempt for them. There had been a time in the past when he had wished for some permanent contact with them, an end to the deathless coexistence. He had tried so hard. How foolish he had been.

Some passengers left at the next stop, giving him

some room. He looked at his reflection in the glass of the car's window. His leather jeans waxed blackly, wrapped around his hips and legs, making him appear taller than he actually was. The silk shirt shimmered with a cool smoothness, its long collar flapping over his leather coat. He was pleased with his appearance. He might even—

A villager dressed in brown, ragged clothing turned a street corner and threw a molotov cocktail at the phalanx of British troops. The soldiers scattered as the gasoline ignited, a few of them rolling in the dust to extinguish their flaming uniforms. Two others shouldered their automatic rifles and their bullets stitched the attacker to a half-standing wall. The man remained attached to the wall for a split second before crumpling to the dirt, leaving a red-stained smear on the wall that followed his descent. Two other soldiers sprayed a volley of rounds into the surrounding houses, ripping out windows and frames, exploding brick and mortar. At the end of the street grain bags were piled to form a barricade. Men and women huddled behind the barrier shooting and throwing rocks at the troops. A Catholic priest ran across the street away from the barricade and was struck down by a Protestant sniper's bullet. In the dim sky above the battle, crosses stood out like blackened, outstretched corpses.

—Jesus blinked his eyes and found himself leaning against the side of the subway car. He wiped some sweat from his forehead, staining the leather sleeve of his coat. Another attack. Those damned visions, more frequent, more vivid each time. His brain was being dissected, each convolution uncurled, each fissure probed by some metaphysical scalpel. And with every flash of the blade, another nightmare was cut loose from the tissue to go screaming.

He left the subway at St. Catherine station, sickened by the motion of the train. The escalator took him to the upper level and the maze of slidewalks that crisscrossed the avenue of shops. He rode one to the end of the block, where a massive geodesic dome dwarfed the other buildings. It was the Phylatron, a multileveled structure with each level glowing from the light of a different sun. Inside it was the plant life of every known world that the Starships had reached.

Christ entered the main gate, ignoring the robot turnstile that was not programmed to detect such beings as he. He walked among the different levels of the dome, absorbing the vivid explosions of color and form that comprised the galaxy's plant life. The plants seemed trapped, strangled by the glass that surrounded them. Yet they flourished in the controlled climates and the carefully blended atmospheres.

How could they do it? thought Christ. *The very things that gave them life for millions of years.* All killed when they didn't need them anymore. What wasn't dead they put under glass to be gawked at.

He stopped before a sign that read: *Last Living Olive Tree, Earth.* The tree was old, gnarled. Its limbs flowed outward from the trunk in complex patterns, finally ending in tender, green buds. Jesus noticed that there were no olives on the branches. It was possible that it wasn't the right season for them but he chose to think otherwise. *What's the use,* he thought, *in growing fruit that nobody will ever eat? Or seeds that would never be planted?*

The Phylatron was filled with prisoners—each one doomed to outlive its captors. It was a cruel punishment for the crime of existence.

Christ leaned over the railing and spit into the artificial soil. Then he turned and squeezed through the crowd, looking for the exit gate. *Screw this place,* he thought. *Don't know why I ever come here. Better to just get away. Somewhere else. Just get away.*

As he left the dome, he saw the buildings of the city slowly dissolve, the people in the streets melt into waxen blobs. The city became a village of huts with thatched roofs, the people on the sidewalks turned into naked, black-skinned natives. There was a white man standing in their midst; he wore a beige straw hat and steel-rimmed glasses. His features were sharp and his face was narrow—a small bloodless pair of lips, gray, flaccid eyes, and a pointed nose. He looked like a heron standing among them. The man was holding a cross in his upraised hand, gesturing with it, and pointing at it while he spoke. Their god was false, he said. Believe in mine, he said. They would burn if they did not believe. He told them all those things in a furious, quivering voice. And the dark people listened to his entire speech before they killed him.

Christ staggered back from the slidewalk access.

103

The vision faded and the familiar structures of the city reappeared. He'd seen that one before. The faces were different, the place, the time: but the results were always the same. *Not exactly,* he thought. But did it really matter *who* was killed? He was sick of the damn nightmares. They were constant reminders of what he was to them.

He had tried so hard to be unlike them, unlike what they had said he was. He watched their faces as they glided by him on the slidewalk and he tried to pick out a face and examine it. He looked for something in one of them that could be interpreted as living; there was nothing. He looked out across the vista of the city and saw that it was filled with an endless stream of fleshed-out golems—dead in life.

He walked past the slidewalk, refusing to ride their machinery. The heels of his boots clicked on the glassphalt road surface. He liked the sound they made as he walked. It gave him a feeling of accomplishment to be able to do something that no one else could do, even if he was the only person who heard it or appreciated it. He passed under the stanchions of a monorail system just as the train was passing overhead; he recognized the colorcode of the cars. It was going to the Yards. He remembered the Yards as a massive expanse of steel and concrete, a place where the men left for the stars.

The Yards were not far away because he could hear the scream of the Starships' engines leaving the surface. He began walking down the dim streets of an industrial sector toward the Yards, when he heard an odd sound. A human cry came to him, weak and plaintive, and threatening to be engulfed by the shadows.

Christ turned a corner and saw an old man lying crumpled next to a recycling pit. A mound of trash served as his pillow. He was derelict, dressed in rags, and he labored with each liquid breath. Christ smiled and almost laughed when he saw him. He could smell the wine before he even got close to the old man. Strangely enough, he felt a kind of affinity for the drunk; for Christ had often wished that *he* could have a way to escape his own torment.

But he also hated the man.

You scum, he thought, looking at the man. *You deserve to die in that stinking pile of shit. Thousands of years. For this?*

Christ stood over the man clenching and unclenching his fists. One of the old man's eyelids fluttered open revealing a swollen, yellow eye. The one eye stared up at Christ and he felt a tingling sense of awareness touching his brain.

So, thought Christ. *You think you see me, do you? You must be one of the reasons that I'm still around this rotten place! Why I've had to hang on and watch all the others go. You filth!*

Christ kicked the old man in the ribs with the point of his boot and the man's chest erupted in a spasm of choking, oily coughs. A trickle of blood appeared at the corner of his mouth.

Suddenly the man began to change. Christ watched him as his features coalesced until they became those of a dark-skinned, bearded man. The man was stretched out upon a large wooden machine; his hands were tied to one end and his feet were bound to a large wheel at the other end. There was a theologian dressed in hierarchical robes asking the tormented man questions; and each time the man could not answer, the theologian would look at the three hooded judges seated above him, and then turn the wheel another inch. The man on the rack screamed with each turn as the muscles in his limbs were slowly ripped apart. Another question. Another turn. Then the theologian whipped the man with savage fervor, cutting deep grooves into his back.

Christ had stepped back from the old man as the dark images disappeared. The attacks were becoming more frequent, more punishing than ever. He looked down at the unconscious derelict and kicked him again. The man coughed up some blood and it spilled onto Christ's boot. He saw the blood and he jumped on the man, crushing his chest into the mound of trash. The man's breathing finally stopped.

Killed him, thought Christ. *And only because he knew me.* He looked at the body, half-buried in the trash, envious of the escape he had given the man. The ultimate escape that had been denied him by the collective unconscious of man. Spawned and sustained by man's fears and desires, and then forgotten. Almost forgotten. Man evolved but Christ could not change with him. Myths don't evolve, they die. Slowly he turned from the old man's body and walked toward the Yards.

He heard the wailing of the Starships as he grew

closer; and he knew what he would now do. There would be no more endless wandering, no more stolen clothing, stolen images. And there would be an end to the nightmarish attacks, the gut-tearing reminders of his reason for being. There was no hope of survival for there was no evolution to match the shifting thoughts of the thoughts of the human mind.

He walked up the stairs to the entrance of the Yards where a Starship waited to take him away. He had thought of leaving many times in the past; but he had always been afraid. Afraid that he might have been overlooking some slight possibility. But it no longer mattered. Maybe he would find another world, light-years from here, that held love, as well as warmth and life, within its atmosphere. He had seen enough death, felt enough hate.

At the top of the concourse, Christ looked down upon the Yards, an immense steel plain reaching out to the horizon. The fading sunlight turned the sky to a soft purple at the point where it joined edges with the Yards. As he looked out upon the Starships, hunched like great insects ready to rise up humming on invisible wings, he thought of all the years that he had endured before coming to this moment. He recalled the others that once shared his Jungian existence—Dis, Pan, Vishnu, all of them, gone. And now he must also go.

Once past the embarkation terminal, Christ selected the S. S. *Gamow* for his rite of passage. Soon it would be free of Earth's atmosphere, and its FTL drive would hurl it silently into hyperspace. Christ would enter a region where the things of man were unknown, except for the fleeting intrusions of the ships.

The crew of the *Gamow* did not see him or hear him as he walked among them. Each one was performing his last duties prior to the liftoff. Christ watched the main scanner, which showed the purple glow of the Yards at sunset. He saw the onboard signal lights flashing, he heard the intercom crackle out its jargon. Then the ship trembled slightly from the vibrations of the engines and leaped into the approaching night.

On the scanner the Yards shrank into nothingness, swallowed by the vastness of the continent. Minutes later the Earth itself was reduced to a small sphere cleaved by a hemisphere of darkness. Diagrams flickered on the information grids and the crew prepared for the FTL jump.

Christ felt a giddy, light-headedness in his skull. Another vision! No! Not now! But the vision didn't come. Instead he continued to feel a numbed, drunken sensation in his brain. A dull throb grew in his temples until it increased to jackhammer intensity.

He looked at the scanner as if to find an explanation for the pain and he saw a long cord stretching out from the Earth, reaching through the darkness of space to touch the ship. A tenuous umbilical, wispy and ephemeral, pulling at his very being as the ship increased its distance from the Earth. The strain was sapping his vital energy, draining him of his awareness. While his consciousness was rushing away from him,

Christ felt feeble pulses of racial memory ebbing into him, trying to reverse the flow of his being.

The ship convulsed as it made the hyperspace jump.

Christ's brain exploded into a million fragments and they flickered strobelike before him. Time became compressed, losing all meaning for him. The umbilical had snapped, ruptured in the darkness.

The last perception was the scanner—a black hole where the stars were winking out.

INTRODUCTION TO

"THE CASE OF THE FOUR AND TWENTY BLACKBIRDS"

by Neil Gaiman

As a ten-year-old boy, I decided to read a book of quotations from cover to cover. I didn't get very far, but I did get all the way through the letter *A*. This was a good thing, as *A* contained all the quotations attributed to Anonymous, a tireless member of the writing community responsible for many fine and memorable lines. In addition to writing poems and songs, Anonymous also, it turned out, wrote some of the best lines of graffiti on the walls and restrooms of the world.

This was one of his:

Humpty Dumpty was Pushed.

It was one I remembered a decade later, when I sat

down one morning to be a writer. I wanted to write—
I was, what, twenty? Twenty-one?—and I had nothing
to write about. I thought pastiche might be a good
way to begin, as I wasn't sure enough of my narrative
voice. This was because I didn't have a narrative voice
at that point. But I did have (and it's served me well
over the years) an ear for other people's styles.

(You'll probably think this is me doing Chandler or
Hammett, but I wasn't to start reading either of them
for another year. Actually this is me doing Woody
Allen doing Chandler.)

If you're going to have a hard-boiled detective investigating something, you need a murder. I didn't
know much about murders, not back then. But there
was one thing I knew.

Humpty Dumpty was Pushed.

It seemed as good a place to start as any. . . .

THE CASE OF THE FOUR AND TWENTY BLACKBIRDS

by Neil Gaiman

I SAT in my office, nursing a glass of hooch and idly cleaning my automatic. Outside the rain fell steadily, like it seems to do most of the time in our fair city, whatever the tourist board says. Hell, I didn't care. I'm not on the tourist board. I'm a private dick, and one of the best, although you wouldn't have known it; the office was crumbling, the rent was unpaid, and the hooch was my last.

Things are tough all over.

To cap it all the only client I'd had all week never showed up on the street corner where I'd waited for him. He said it was going to be a big job, but now I'd never know: he kept a prior appointment in the morgue.

So when the dame walked into my office I was sure my luck had changed for the better.

"What are you selling, lady?"

She gave me a look that would have induced heavy breathing in a pumpkin, and which shot my heartbeat up to three figures. She had long blonde hair and a figure that would have made Thomas Aquinas forget

112

his vows. I forgot all mine about never taking cases from dames.

"What would you say to some of the green stuff?" she asked in a husky voice, getting straight to the point.

"Continue, sister." I didn't want her to know how bad I needed the dough, so I held my hand in front of my mouth; it doesn't help if a client sees you salivate.

She opened her purse and flipped out a photograph—a glossy eight by ten. "Do you recognize that man?"

In my business you know who people are. "Yeah."

"He's dead."

"I know that too, sweetheart. It's old news. It was an accident."

Her gaze went so icy you could have chipped it into cubes and cooled a cocktail with it. "My brother's death was no accident."

I raised an eyebrow—you need a lot of arcane skills in my business—and said "Your brother, eh?" Funny, she hadn't struck me as the type that had brothers.

"I'm Jill Dumpty."

"So your brother was Humpty Dumpty?"

"And he didn't fall off that wall, Mr. Horner. He was pushed."

Interesting, if true. Dumpty had his finger in most of the crooked pies in town; I could think of five guys who would have preferred to see him dead than alive without trying.

Without trying too hard, anyway.

"You see the cops about this?"

"Nah. The King's Men aren't interested in anything to do with his death. They say they did all they could do in trying to put him together again after the fall."

I leaned back in my chair.

"So what's it to you? Why do you need me?"

"I want you to find the killer, Mr. Horner. I want him brought to justice. I want him to fry like an egg. Oh—and one other *little* thing," she added, lightly. "Before he died Humpty had a small manila envelope full of photographs he was meant to be sending me. Medical photos. I'm a trainee nurse, and I need them to pass my finals."

I inspected my nails, then looked up at her face, taking in a handful of waist and Easter-egg bazonkas on the way up. She was a looker, although her cute nose was a little on the shiny side. "I'll take the case. Seventy-five a day and two hundred bonus for results."

She smiled; my stomach twisted around once and went into orbit. "You get another two hundred if you get me those photographs. I want to be a nurse *real* bad." Then she dropped three fifties on my desktop.

I let a devil-may-care grin play across my rugged face. "Say, sister, how about letting me take you out for dinner? I just came into some money."

She gave an involuntary shiver of anticipation and muttered something about having a thing about midgets, so I knew I was onto a good thing. Then she gave me a lopsided smile that would have made Albert Einstein drop a decimal point. "First find my brother's killer, Mr. Horner. And my photographs. *Then* we can play."

She closed the door behind her. Maybe it was still raining but I didn't notice. I didn't care.

There are parts of town the tourist board don't mention. Parts of town where the police travel in threes if they travel at all. In my line of work you get to visit them more than is healthy. Healthy is never.

He was waiting for me outside Luigi's. I slid up behind him, my rubber-soled shoes soundless on the shiny wet sidewalk.

"Hiya, Cock."

He jumped and spun around; I found myself gazing up into the muzzle of a .45. "Oh, Horner." He put the gun away. "Don't call me Cock. I'm Bernie Robin to you, Short-stuff, and don't you forget it."

"Cock Robin is good enough for me, Cock. Who killed Humpty Dumpty?"

He was a strange-looking bird, but you can't be choosy in my profession. He was the best underworld lead I had.

"Let's see the color of your money."

I showed him a fifty.

"Hell," he muttered. "It's green. Why can't they make puce or mauve money for a change?" He took it, though. "All I know is that the Fat Man had his finger in a lot of pies."

"So?"

"One of those pies had four and twenty blackbirds in it."

"Huh?"

"Do I hafta spell it out for you? I . . . *Ughh . . .*"

He crumpled to the sidewalk, an arrow protruding from his back. Cock Robin wasn't going to be doing any more chirping.

Sergeant O'Grady looked down at the body, then he looked down at me. "Faith and begorrah, to be sure," he said. "If it isn't Little Jack Horner himself."

"I didn't kill Cock Robin, Sarge."

"And I suppose that the call we got down at the station telling us you were going to be rubbing the late Mr. Robin out. Here. Tonight. Was just a hoax?"

"If I'm the killer, where are my arrows?" I thumbed open a pack of gum and started to chew. "It's a frame."

He puffed on his meerschaum and then put it away, and idly played a couple of phrases of the *William Tell Overture* on his oboe. "Maybe. Maybe not. But you're still a suspect. Don't leave town. And Horner . . ."

"Yeah?"

"Dumpty's death was an accident. That's what the coroner said. That's what I say. Drop the case."

I thought about it. Then I thought of the money, and the girl. "No dice, Sarge."

He shrugged. "It's your funeral." He said it like it probably would be.

I had a funny feeling like he could be right.

"You're out of your depth, Horner. You're playing with the big boys. And it ain't healthy."

From what I could remember of my schooldays he was correct. Whenever I played with the big boys I always wound up having the stuffing beaten out of me. But how did O'Grady—how *could* O'Grady have known that? Then I remembered something else.

O'Grady was the one that used to beat me up the most.

It was time for what we in the profession call "legwork." I made a few discreet enquiries around town, but found out nothing about Dumpty that I didn't know already.

Humpty Dumpty was a bad egg. I remembered him when he was new in town, a smart young animal trainer with a nice line in training mice to run up clocks. He went to the bad pretty fast though; gambling, drink, women, it's the same story all over. A bright young kid thinks that the streets of Nurseryland are paved with gold, and by the time he finds out otherwise it's much too late.

Dumpty started off with extortions and robbery on a small scale—he trained up a team of spiders to scare little girls away from their curds and whey, which he'd pick up and sell on the black market. Then he moved onto blackmail—the nastiest game. We crossed paths once, when I was hired by this young society kid—let's call him Georgie Porgie—to recover some compromising snaps of him kissing the girls and making them cry. I got the snaps, but I learned it wasn't healthy to mess with the Fat Man. And I don't make the same mistakes twice. Hell, in my line of work I can't afford to make the same mistakes once.

It's a tough world out there. I remember when Little Bo Peep first came to town . . . but you don't want to hear my troubles. If you're not dead yet, you've got troubles of your own.

I checked out the newspaper files on Dumpty's death. One minute he was sitting on a wall, the next he was in pieces at the bottom. All the King's Horses and all the King's Men were on the scene in minutes, but he needed more than first aid. A medic named Foster was called—a friend of Dumpty's from his Gloucester days—although I don't know of anything a doc can do when you're dead.

Hang on a second—*Dr. Foster!*

I got that old feeling you get in my line of work. Two little brain cells rub together the right way and in seconds you've got a twenty-four-carat cerebral fire on your hands.

You remember the client who didn't show—the one I'd waited for all day on the street corner? An accidental death. I hadn't bothered to check it out—I can't afford to waste time on clients who aren't going to pay for it.

Three deaths, it seemed. Not one.

I reached for the telephone and rang the police station. "This is Horner," I told the desk man. "Lemme speak to Sergeant O'Grady."

There was a crackling and he came on the line. "O'Grady speaking."

"It's Horner."

"Hi, Little Jack." That was just like O'Grady. He'd been kidding me about my size since we were kids together. "You finally figured out that Dumpty's death was an accident?"

"Nope. I'm now investigating three deaths. The Fat Man's, Bernie Robin's, and Dr. Foster's."

"Foster the plastic surgeon? His death was an accident."

"Sure. And your mother was married to your father."

There was a pause. "Horner, if you phoned me up just to talk dirty, I'm not amused."

"Okay, wise guy. If Humpty Dumpty's death was an accident and so was Dr. Foster's, tell me just one thing.

"Who killed Cock Robin?"

I don't ever get accused of having too much imagination, but there's one thing I'd swear to. I could *hear* him grinning over the phone as he said: "You did, Horner. And I'm staking my badge on it."

The line went dead.

My office was cold and lonely, so I wandered down to Joe's Bar for some companionship and a drink or three.

Four and twenty blackbirds. A dead doctor. The Fat Man. Cock Robin . . . Heck, this case had more holes in it than a Swiss cheese and more loose ends than a torn string vest. And where did the juicy Miss Dumpty come into it? Jack and Jill—we'd make a great team. When this was all over perhaps we could go off together to Louie's little place on the hill, where no one's interested in whether you got a marriage license or not. "The Pail of Water," that was the name of the joint.

I called over the bartender. "Hey. Joe."

"Yeah, Mr. Horner?" He was polishing a glass with a rag that had seen better days as a shirt.

"Did you ever meet the Fat Man's sister?"

He scratched at his cheek. "Can say as I did. His sister . . . huh? Hey—the Fat Man didn't have a sister."

"You sure of that?"

"Sure I'm sure. It was the day my sister had her first kid—I told the Fat Man I was an uncle. He gave me this look and says, 'Ain't no way I'll ever be an uncle, Joe. Got no sisters or brother, nor no other kinfolk neither.'"

If the mysterious Miss Dumpty wasn't his sister, who *was* she?

"Tell me, Joe. Didja ever see him in here with a dame—about so high, shaped like this?" My hands described a couple of parabolas. "Looks like a blonde love goddess."

He shook his head. "Never saw him with any dames. Recently he was hanging around with some medical guy, but the only thing he ever cared about was those crazy birds and animals of his."

I took a swig of my drink. It nearly took the roof of my mouth off. "Animals? I thought he'd given all that up."

"Naw—couple weeks back he was in here with a whole bunch of blackbirds he was training to sing 'Wasn't that a dainty dish to set before *Mmm Mmm*.'"

"Mmm Mmm?"

"Yeah. I got no idea who."

I put my drink down. A little of it spilled on the counter, and I watched it strip the varnish. "Thanks, Joe. You've been a big help." I handed him a ten dollar bill. "For information received," I said, adding, "Don't spend it all at once."

In my profession it's making little jokes like that that keeps you sane.

I had one contact left. I found a pay phone and called her number.

"Old Mother Hubbard's Cupboard: Cake Shop and Licensed Soup Kitchen."

"It's Horner, Ma."

"Jack? It ain't safe for me to talk to you."

"For old time's sake, sweetheart. You owe me a favor." Some two-bit crooks had once knocked off the Cupboard, leaving it bare. I'd tracked them down and returned the cakes and soup.

". . . Okay. But I don't like it."

"You know everything that goes on around here on the food front, Ma. What's the significance of a pie with four and twenty trained blackbirds in it?"

She whistled, long and low. "You really don't know?"

"I wouldn't be asking you if I did."

"You should read the Court pages of the papers next time, sugar. Jeez. You are out of your depth."

"C'mon, Ma. Spill it."

"It so happens that that particular dish was set before the King a few weeks back. . . . Jack? Are you still there?"

"I'm still here, ma'am." I said, quietly. "All of a sudden a lot of things are starting to make sense." I put down the phone.

It was beginning to look like Little Jack Horner had pulled out a plum from this pie.

It was raining, steady and cold.

I phoned a cab.

Quarter of an hour later one lurched out of the darkness.

"You're late."

"So complain to the tourist board."

I climbed in the back, wound down the window, and lit a cigarette.

And I went to see the Queen.

The door to the private part of the palace was locked. It's the part that the public don't get to see. But I've never been public, and the little lock hardly slowed me up. The door to the private apartments with the big red heart on it was unlocked, so I knocked and walked straight in.

The Queen of Hearts was alone, standing in front of the mirror, holding a plate of jam tarts with one hand, powdering her nose with the other. She turned, saw me, and gasped, dropping the tarts.

"Hey, Queenie," I said. "Or would you feel more comfortable if I called you Jill?"

She was still a good-looking slice of dame, even without the blonde wig.

"Get out of here!" she hissed.

"I don't think so, toots." I sat down on the bed. "Let me spell a few things out for you."

"Go ahead." She reached behind her for a concealed alarm button. I let her press it. I'd cut the wires on my way in—in my profession there's no such thing as being too careful.

"Let me spell a few things out for you."

"You just said that."

"I'll tell this my way, lady."

I lit a cigarette and a thin plume of blue smoke drifted heavenward, which was where I was going if my hunch was wrong. Still, I've learned to trust hunches.

"Try this on for size. Dumpty—the Fat Man—wasn't your brother. He wasn't even your friend. In fact he was blackmailing you. He knew about your nose."

She turned whiter than a number of corpses I've met in my time in the business. Her hand reached up and cradled her freshly powdered nose.

"You see, I've known the Fat Man for many years, and many years ago he had a lucrative concern in training animals and birds to do certain unsavory things. And that got me to thinking . . . I had a client recently who didn't show, due to his having been stiffed first. Doctor Foster, of Gloucester, the plastic surgeon. The official version of his death was that he'd just sat too close to a fire and melted.

"But just suppose he was killed to stop him telling something that he knew? I put two and two together and hit the jackpot. Let me reconstruct a scene for you: You were out in the garden—probably hanging out some clothes—when along came one of Dumpty's trained pie-blackbirds and *pecked off your nose.*

"So there you were, standing in the garden, your hand in front of your face, when along comes the Fat Man with an offer you couldn't refuse. He could introduce you to a plastic surgeon who could fix you up with a nose as good as new, for a price. And no one need ever know. Am I right so far?"

She nodded dumbly, then finding her voice, muttered: "Pretty much. But I ran back into the parlor after the attack, to eat some bread and honey. That was where he found me."

"Fair enough." The color was starting to come back into her cheeks now. "So you had the operation from Foster, and no one was going to be any the wiser. Until Dumpty told you that he had photos of the op. You had to get rid of him. A couple of days later you were out walking in the palace grounds. There was Humpty, sitting on a wall, his back to you, gazing out into the distance. In a fit of madness, you pushed. And Humpty Dumpty had a great fall.

"But now you were in big trouble. Nobody suspected you of his murder, but where were the photographs? Foster didn't have them, although he smelled a rat and had to be disposed of—before he could see me. But you didn't know how much he'd told me, and you still didn't have the snapshots, so you took me on to find out. And that was your mistake, sister."

Her lower lip trembled, and my heart quivered. "You won't turn me in, will you?

"Sister, you tried to frame me this afternoon. I don't take kindly to that."

With a shaking hand she started to unbutton her blouse. "Perhaps we could come to some sort of arrangement?"

I shook my head. "Sorry, Your Majesty. Mrs. Horner's little boy Jack was always taught to keep his hands off royalty. It's a pity, but that's how it is." To be on the safe side I looked away, which was a mistake. A cute little ladies' pistol was in her hands and pointing at me before you could sing a song of sixpence. The shooter may have been small, but I knew it packed enough of a wallop to take me out of the game permanently.

This dame was *lethal.*

"Put that gun down, Your Majesty." Sergeant O'Grady strolled through the bedroom door, his police special clutched in his hamlike fist.

"I'm sorry I suspected you, Horner," he said dryly. "You're lucky I did, though, sure and begorrah. I had you trailed here and I overheard the whole thing."

"Hi, Sarge, thanks for stopping by. But I hadn't finished my explanation. If you'll take a seat I'll wrap it up."

He nodded brusquely, and sat down near the door. His gun hardly moved.

I got up from the bed and walked over to the

Queen. "You see, toots, what I didn't tell you was who did *have* the snaps of your nose job. Humpty did, when you killed him."

A charming frown crinkled her perfect brow. "I don't understand . . . I had the body searched."

"Sure, afterwards. But the first people to get to the Fat Man were the King's Men. The cops. And one of them pocketed the envelope. When any fuss had died down the blackmail would have started again. Only this time you wouldn't have known who to kill. And I owe you an apology." I bent down to tie my shoelaces.

"Why?"

"I accused you of trying to frame me this afternoon. You didn't. That arrow was the property of a boy who was the best archer in my school—I should have recognized that distinctive fletching anywhere. Isn't that right," I said, turning back to the door, ". . . 'Sparrow' O'Grady?"

Under the guise of tying up my shoelaces I had already palmed a couple of the Queen's jam tarts, and, flinging one of them upward, I neatly smashed the room's only light bulb.

It only delayed the shooting a few seconds, but a few seconds was all I needed, and as the Queen of Hearts and Sergeant 'Sparrow' O'Grady cheerfully shot each other to bits, I split.

In my business, you have to look after number one.

Munching on a jam tart I walked out of the palace grounds and into the street. I paused by a trash can, to try to burn the manila envelope of photographs I had pulled from O'Grady's pocket as I walked past him, but it was raining so hard they wouldn't catch.

When I got back to my office I phoned the tourist board to complain. They said the rain was good for the farmers, and I told them what they could do with it.

They said that things are tough all over.

And I said, Yeah.

SURPRISE FALL: REVISTED

by Yvonne Navarro

Sometimes the smallest of what a person does is the biggest indicator of what she will become.

"Surprise Fall"—I never thought this story would see print again. In fact, it never occurred to me to offer it anywhere and I seldom think about the tale. Looking back, "Surprise Fall" seems more like a small, timid experiment—full of possibilities but not necessarily potential, the desire for something bigger but hardly the stepping stone to a career. Yet it was exactly that, and more.

I say this, oddly, because I don't recall disliking the cold so much. Seventeen-plus years ago I wanted a perpetual summer as much as any semi-sun-worshiping young woman, but winters were what they were and they didn't seem to make me nearly as mis-

erable as they do now. Reading this short short story
so many years after it was written is undeniable evidence that the seeds of yearning for heat had already
been planted, and looking back, I realize now that the
same year "Surprise Fall" was published was also the
same year I first uttered the words *"I'd love to move
to Phoenix!"* I never dreamed I'd grow to crave the
heat, the sun, and the southwest as much as I do, so
much so that I've spent months at a time visiting Arizona and a day doesn't pass where I don't indulge in
my perpetual dream of relocating there.

That "Surprise Fall" was also the first of dozens of
published stories also astonishes me. Who would have
thought my career would keep on growing, that I possessed the ability to learn this craft, the willingness to
listen to those much wiser than I, and the determination (stubbornness?) not to give up in the face of
rejection . . . especially when I didn't see a second
story published for more than four years? Who I was
then is as different from who I am now as a Chihuahua is from a golden retriever—I was even too shy
and afraid of ridicule to read "Surprise Fall" aloud at
a gathering of close friends and fellow writers during
the summer of 1988. Now, of course, I'm always
searching for a reading slot at conventions or time at
a bookstore so I can subject an unsuspecting audience
to the latest of my personal slices of darkness.

As Freud or Jung might have interpreted a dream,
perhaps a writer's first story is merely a clue about
what truly lies within the subconscious and the soul.

SURPRISE FALL

by Yvonne Navarro

THERE is a time each year when every person wakes in the morning and realizes suddenly that fall has arrived. Certainly the days have gradually cooled, but this goes unnoticed, like the gentle growing of a plant. Then—look! It's here!

In bed, your eyes open before the alarm sounds; there is no need to force your body awake though you snuggle under the blanket. Instinctively your eyes seek the window above the cafe curtains, or the split where the draperies don't quite meet, and you see cold gray. Not ominous gray summer storm clouds or dirty gray carbon monoxide smog, but the sullen stone gray of October sky.

Within your warm, nighttime cocoon, you feel a cold, crisp nip, not only in the room, but outside. (How could you know *that*? You aren't even out of bed yet.) It creeps uninvited, biting at your ankles and raising the hair on your legs, cold fingers stroking unprotected ears and nose.

The alarm switches on and a voice in the black box explains the unseasonable weather—*It will pass quickly,* he says, *there is a low pressure front.* . . . Safe and warm, you wonder if there wasn't a slight hint of doubt in the weatherman's voice. . . .

You dress for work, drawing on a coat and staring

at commuters who ignore the obvious signs of fall. But then, who would think of fall? Fall? Why, yes! You can even *smell* the coming cold on the wind that stings your eyes and face.

Exiting the train, you slip into a doorway to listen intently as a ragged man totes a sign and becries the world's doom. *Hark!* he wails. *Feel the weather! The end has started and none will but take the time to see! Pray . . .*

It is the third day. The temperatures have dropped steadily. Others goggle in amazement as their breath fogs beneath their noses and their fingers redden and ache should they forget the simple protection of gloves. But then, who would think of gloves?

Each morning you shiver in the cold room (heat's not required by the building code yet, your landlord insists), and listen to the boxed voice of the weatherman. Yesterday he still sounded hopeful. Today he resignedly predicts even colder weather.

At work they laughed when you declared fall had arrived. So, of course, winter will soon follow. Some chuckled, others smirked, all disbelieved. No longer laughing, they frown with hooded eyes, resentment bubbles in their voices. Why should they resent you? You only tried to warn them.

There is no laughter, on this third day of fall. They stare out windows at trees ablaze overnight with fall's magnificent yellows, bright oranges, dark, fiery reds, and forbidding purples; dead leaves are blown by cold, surging breezes.

Like the others, you glance at your calendar. The

difference is you can accept, because, of course, you know. You've known for three days.

And like you, a few (but oh not enough) will remember the moaning voice of the tattered crier of doom.

The end has started . . .

The calendar.

July 5th.

INTRODUCTION TO

" DREAMERS "

by Kim Newman

In late 1982, after two years or so of postgraduate unemployment—during which I wrote plays, song lyrics, and job application letters, and performed with an interlinked theater group and a cabaret band—I read in the book review pages of *Starburst,* then written by Christopher Evans, that there were two new British science fiction magazines starting, *Interzone* and the Irish-based *Extro,* taking up where the departed *New Worlds* left off. I'd just started selling nonfiction film pieces and had been writing fiction for years, publishing a few things in the magazine associated with the theater group (*Sheep Worrying*—if you're after back issues, good luck).

The arrival of these markets prompted me to start writing for and submitting to them. I quickly put four pieces in circulation: "The Terminus," which had been in *Sheep Worrying* and eventually appeared in *Fantasy Tales* after an encouraging near-acceptance from *Interzone* (I noticed that when the manuscript came back

133

with a "not quite right for us but submit again" letter that it had editorial changes penciled on it); "D and D," which finally appeared in yet another short-lived UK science fiction magazine, *The Edge;* an untitled novella that was a first draft of what became my first novel *(The Night Mayor);* and "Dreamers." Written the week after I finished the novella, "Dreamers" was a pendant that shared its future-world backdrop, and was one of a clutch of stories from about that time with science-fictional backgrounds but noir or horror themes. Here, I was trying to do something along the lines of those Roald Dahl or Stanley Ellin ironic-twist murder stories that were dramatized on *Alfred Hitchcock Presents.* It may be that the plot nugget came while I was working on the longer piece, and just didn't fit but decades on I can't actually remember.

I sent the novella to *Interzone* and "Dreamers" (then, I think, called "Review Copy") to *Extro;* it took *Interzone,* which was then collectively edited, almost a year not to take the novella (too long for them, but not long enough for its premise). By then *Extro* was out of business and had returned "Dreamers," which I then sent to *Interzone* and which they published in 1984. Colin Greenland was the collective member who did the fine edit, and the sale more or less brought me into the field socially and professionally. I was— along with Paul McAuley, Steve Baxter, Ian MacLeod, Eric Brown, Alex Stewart, Scott Bradfield, and Geoff Ryman, among others—part of a wave of new or new-ish writers who helped *Interzone* establish an identity separate from that of *New Worlds,* perhaps because we all enjoyed narrative as much as experiment. "Dreamers" appeared in book form in *Interzone: The First Anthology,* which brought me to the attention of Antony Harwood, who is still my agent, and Robyn Sisman, an editor who asked to see a novel from me and bought *The Night Mayor,* shortly before leaving the business.

Looking again at the story, written nearly half my life ago, I notice the bits of 1982 woven into it: Richard and Carol Horton are named after neighbors in the low-rent rooming house I was living in, whom I had a grudge against because they sometimes stole my dole (welfare) checks, and the future of the story is informed by the Thatcherite individualism of the year and my own shut-in-a-cold-bedsit circumstances at the time. I understand some readers think of me as a promising science fiction writer who got sidetracked by horror (though I've probably written as much science fiction as anything else). I think that what I was really doing, in an extension of my theater work, was satire, and that's still where I think most of my work lives.

DREAMERS

by Kim Newman

ELVIS Kurtz was dreaming. He dreamed he was John F. Kennedy, former president (1960—Lee Harvey Oswald) of the former United States of America. The dream was a riot of pornography; involving enormous wealth, extreme power, intermittent ultra-violence, and sex with Marilyn Monroe. It was a pre-sold success. An inevitable Iridium Tape. An inescapable quinquemillion-seller.

Kurtz was dybukking, a passenger in the mind. Kurtz was aware of what John Yeovil thought it felt like to be John Fitzgerald Kennedy in August 1961. He had access to a neatly arranged file of memories, plus a few precog glimpses carried over from waking life. He would have to pull out before Dallas. The JFK similie was not aware of Kurtz. Actually, the JFK similie hardly seemed to be aware of anything.

Yeovil had had JFK plump his mistress' bottom on the edge of the presidential desk, and penetrate the former Norma Jean Baker (1926—next year) standing up. A pile of authenticated contemporary documents were scrunched up beneath their spectacular copulation.

Kurtz trusted Yeovil had got the externals right. Through the JFK similie he was perceiving the Oval Office precisely as it had been. Marilyn's squeals were done in her actual voice, distilled from over three hundred hours of flatty soundtracks and disc aurals. Yeovil would have had a computer assist handle that. Sometimes Kurtz envied the man's resources.

Marilyn and the president were sexing like well-oiled flesh robots. The dreamership liked their sexing pristine, with all the mess and pain taken out. Kurtz seared his overlay onto the dreamtape, burning a semi-apocalyptic series of multiple climaxes.

This was standard wet-dream stuff. The sort of thing Kurtz could do in his sleep. Kurtz's dybbuk overmind left the internals to his experienced subconscious and skimmed through the similie's memory. He ignored the story-so-far synopsis and picked a few random sensations.

The Pacific, WW II: the smell of burning oil and salt water, all-over sun heat, repressed fear, an aural loop of "Sentimental Journey." His father throwing a tantrum: the usual mix of shame, terror, and embarrassment. Prawns at Hyannis Port. The inauguration; January chill, tension, incipient megalomania: ". . . ask not what your country can do for you . . ."

Kurtz wondered who had written that speech. Yeovil did not know; all the question got out of the similie was a momentary whiteout. Damn, an extraneous thought. It would bleed onto the tape. Yeovil had taken the trouble to insert a 1961 image: Kennedy ejaculated like an ICBM silo; a thermonuclear chain reaction inside Marilyn took her out.

Yawn. Kurtz was an orgasm specialist. He topped the metaphor (too literary, but what did he expect) with a jumble of cross-sensory experiences. He translated the aural stimuli of the "Saint Matthew Passion" into a mass of tactiles. The dream shadow could take it, although a real body would have been blown away.

Marilyn lay facedown, exhausted, her hair fanned on the pile carpet. JFK traced her backbone with the presidential seal. Yeovil had Catholic guilt flit through JFK's mind.

"Jack," breathed Marilyn, "did you know there's a theory that the whole universe got started with a Big Bang?"

Kennedy parted Marilyn's hair and kissed the nape of her neck. Kurtz felt a witty reply coming. Something hard at the base of the president's skull. A white hot needle in his head. A brief skin-and-bone agony, then nothing.

Damn Yeovil. Oswald was early.

Like most of the *haut ton* that year John Yeovil was devoted to Victoriana. The tridvid sages said the craze was a reaction to the acid smogs that had taken to settling on London. Usually Yeovil affected to despise fashions, but this one suited him. Frock coats and stiff collars became his Holmesian figure, a beard usefully concealed his slash mouth, and the habitual precision of his gestures was ideal for consulting a half-hunter, taking a pinch of snuff, or casually slitting a footpad's nose with an iridium-assist swordstick.

At thirty-nine Yeovil was rich enough to indulge himself with opium-scented handkerchiefs, long case clocks, and wax wreaths under glass. Three of his dreams were in the current q-seller listings. The *JFK* advance had accounted for the complete redecoration of his Luxborough Street residence.

Awaiting his guest, Yeovil adjusted the pearl pin in his gray cravat. Exactly right. Exact rectitude was all Yeovil asked of life. That and wealth and fame, of course. He sighted his one-sided smile in the mirror. The smile which, flashed during a tridvid interview or frozen on a dustjacket could cost him one million pounds *perannum* in lost sales alone. A definitive figure would have to take personal appearances, merchandizing, and graft into consideration.

The smile was Yeovil's little secret. The mark of the submarine part of his mind he rigidly excluded from his dreams. John Yeovil had come to terms with his character. He lived with himself in relative comfort, despite the fact that he was easily the most hateful person he knew.

He had the dreaming talent, but so did hundreds of others. He had the patience to research and the skill to concept, but any raw Dreamer with funding could buy access to the D-9000 for those. Success in the dream industry was down to depth of feeling. Any feeling.

Great Dreamers were all prodigies of emotion. Susan Bishopric: empathy; Orin Tredway: imbecile love; Alexis St. Clare: paranoia. And John Yeovil had hate. It did not come through as such in the dreams, but he knew that it was his great reservoir of hate that gave weight to his conjuring of excitement, joy, pain, and the rest.

The doorbell sounded. Yeovil had sent an in to

Elvis Kurtz. The Household admitted him. A few tendrils of smog trailed the guest. The Household dispelled them.

"Mr. Kurtz?"

"Uh. Yes." Kurtz was muffled by his outdoor helmet. He pulled out of it. His eyes were watering profusely. Yeovil was familiar with the yellowish stream of tears. "Sorry about this. I have a slight smog."

"My sympathies," said Yeovil. "You can leave your things with the Household."

"Thanks." Kurtz ungauntleted and de-flakjacketed. Underneath he wore a GP smock. Yeovil led his guest through the hall. The Household offed the hallway lamps, and upped the gas jets and open fire in the drawing room.

"You were difficult to find, Mr. Kurtz."

"I'm supposed to be." He had a trace of accent. Possibly Lichtenstein. "I've been out."

"Of course." Yeovil decanted two preconstituted brandy snifters. "Piracy or pornography?"

"A little of both." Kurtz accepted the drink, smeared his tears, and sagged into a heavy armchair. He was not at ease. As well he might be. Kurtz decided to hit him now, and cover later.

"Mr. Kurtz, prior to your incarceration you produced bootleg editions of my dreams which made a sizable dent in my income. I can now offer you the opportunity to repay me."

"Your pardon?" Kurtz was trying not to look startled. Like most Dreamers he was rotten at that sort of thing. Most, Yeovil reminded himself, not all.

140

"Don't worry. I'm not going to tap you for money. I'll even pay you."

"For what?"

"The use of your talent."

"I don't think you understand . . ."

"I'm well aware of your limitations, Mr. Kurtz. Like myself you are a Dreamer. In many ways you are more powerful than I. You are capable of taping sensations far more intensely than I can. Yet I am successful and well regarded," (by most at least) "and you are reduced to aping my dreams. Or producing work like this."

Yeovil indicated a stack of tapes. Inelegant under-the-counter dreams with clinical titles: *Six Women With Mammary Abnormalities, The Ten Minute Orgasm.* They were badly packaged, with lurid artists-imps on the dustjackets. There was no Dreamer by-line, but Kurtz recognized his own stuff.

"I'm too strong, Yeovil. I can't control my dreams the way you can. My mind doesn't just create, it amplifies and distorts. I wind up with so many resonances and contradictions that the dream falls apart. That's an advantage with one-reel wet dreams, but. . . ."

"I don't require of you that you justify yourself, Mr. Kurtz. I am an artist. I have no capacity for moral outrage. We have that much in common. Our position is at odds with those of the judiciary, the critical establishment, and the British Board of Dream Censors. Come with me."

The dreaming room was different. Most of the house was a convincing, dark, stuffy, and uncomfortable recreation of the 1890s. The dreaming room was what people in 1963 had expected the future to look like. All the surfaces were a glossy, featureless white.

Kurtz was impressed. He touched his fingertips, then his naked palm, to the glasspex wall. He started away, and a condensation handprint faded.

"It's warm. Is that eternity lighting?"

"Partly. I have the dreaming room kept at womb temperature."

"You dream here?"

"Of course. The surroundings have been calculated exactly. Psychologically attuned to be beneficial to the dreaming talent. The recording equipment is substantially what you are familiar with."

"You have computer assist?"

"My Household has a library tap for research. I don't use it much, though. I actually read books. I'm not one of the D-9000's troop of hacks. I don't think we should be the glorified amanuenses of a heuristic pulp mill."

"I don't like the machines either. They hurt." Kurtz was irritated. Good, that should keep him off balance. "What is all this about?"

"Would you be surprised to learn that I am an admirer of your work?"

Kurtz cleared an unconvincing laugh from his throat. "Would you be prepared to say that on the dustjacket of *Sixth Form Girls in Chains*?"

Yeovil tapped his ID into the console. The Household extruded a couch from the floor. It looked sculpted. Out of vanilla ice cream.

"Beside yours my talent is lukewarm. I want to make use of your capacities to underline certain aspects of my work in progress."

"Uh-huh."

"I am dreaming a historical piece, focusing on the character of John Kennedy, martyred president of the United States of America. Kennedy was known to be a man with a highly passionate nature. I think it not inapt that your touch with erotica be applied."

Kurtz sat on the couch, trying to find the loophole. "What about the certification?"

"I plan on sidestepping the BBDC. They have no real authority, and I am supported by my publishers and the vast public interest in my work. The Board owes its precarious existence to its claim that it represents the desire of the majority. Once that is disproved, they will fall. *JFK* has been concepted as a radical dream."

"How is this going to work?"

"I've dreamed a guideline. The sequence you'll work on is fully scripted. The externals are complete. However the first person is blank."

"Kennedy?"

"Yes. He is emerging as a very strong figure in the dreaming. But in this scene he's empty. I want you to amend the internals as he sexes with his mistress."

"Same old wet dream stuff?"

"Essentially. But in this case the explicit material is crucial to the concept. The character of Kennedy is seminal to an understanding of the twentieth century. All of his drives must be exposed. The underlying . . ."

"Yeah. Right. Let's talk about the money."

*　　*　　*

Yeovil balanced the newly-discharged needle gun on his fingertips as he walked across the room, and dropped the weapon into the Household Disperse. Kurtz lay face down on the dreaming couch with a three-inch dart in his brain. The tape was still running, although the Kurtz input was zero. Yeovil sucked his burned fingers. He would smear them better when he was finished with Kurtz.

He had never killed anyone before. He sadly discovered that R was better than actual. Like sex. He stored the minor rush of emotions for future use.

The tape clicked through. The Household offed the recorder. Yeovil picked the subcutaneous terminals out of Kurtz's head and dropped them into their glass of purple. The whirlpool rinse sucked particles of Kurtz out of its system.

Yeovil went through Kurtz's smockpocks. A few credit cards and a bunch of ins. A couple of five-pound bits. They all went into the Disperse, along with Kurtz's outdoor gear, porno tapes, and finger-printed brandy glass. Do it, then clear up afterwards—the secret of criminal success.

The Household presented Yeovil with his outdoor kit: a visored hat, and a padded Inverness. The tailors boasted that their garments were proof against a fragmentation charge. That was true: in the event of such an unlikely weapon being turned on the cape, it would be unmarked. Anyone inside it, however, would find his torso turned to jelly by the impact. Most footpads used needle guns, anyway.

Yeovil hauled Kurtz out to his armored Ford. On the street he fitted an outmoded breather. It kept the smog out of his lungs as well as a more stylish domino, and disguised him.

Yeovil pressed his car in, and tapped his ID into the automatic. The smog lights upped. The streets were deserted.

Yeovil drove around central London for fifteen minutes before chancing upon a suitable dump. He slung the body over several twist-tie rubbish bags in the forecourt of a condemned high-rise. It would look like an ordinary waylaying. There were probably five similar corpses within walking distance. If the Black Economists got to Kurtz before the Metropolitans, the body would be stripped of any usable organs. The incident would not rate a mention on the local.

Back at Luxborough Street Yeovil reprogrammed his Household to forget Kurtz's visit. He fed in a plausible dull evening at home, and wrote off the energy expenditure to various gadgets.

Then he slept. The next stage was complicated, and he did not want to deal with it late at night after his first murder. He felt a twinge of insomniac excitement, which he countered by backgrounding a subliminal lullaby.

The Household woke him early with a call. It was Tony, Yeovil's chief editor at Futura. Tony looked harrassed.

"You've overreached another deadline, John. I wanted the *JFK* master back yesterday. We're committed to a production start. And we have marketing to consider. It's a q-seller on advance sales, and you haven't delivered yet."

"Sorry." Yeovil stretched his mind around the problem. "I've still got a few more amendments."

"You're a trekkiehead, John. Leave it alone. I told you it was finished last week. I'm satisfied as is. And I'm supposed to be a bastard tyrannical editor. We're all expletive deleted here. The copiers are primed."

"You have my word as a gentleman that a definitive master will be on your desk tomorrow morning."

"Tomorrow morning? I get into the office Kubricking early, John." Tony looked dubious. "Okay, you've got it, but no more extensions. No matter how many errors slip through the fine-tooth. You can have Oswald miss, and reelect the randy bugger for all I care. The next John Yeovil hits the stands Friday. Does that scan?"

"Of course. I apologize for the delay. I'm sure you understand. . . ."

"If that means: will I forgive you for being an iridium-plated prick, no way. However, my slice of your sales buys you a lot of tolerance. Ciao."

Tony over-and-outed. He was getting near termination. There were other publishers. Offers tapped up in Yeovil's slab every morning.

The Kurtz-assist master was still slotted. Yeovil pulled it, primed the duplicator, and cloned a copy. The master tape was too recognizable as such for his purpose. Too many splices and scribbles. Plus he would need it later. His plan did not include writing off the work done on *JFK*. The dream would be worth a lot of money. Yeovil doled himself out a shiver of self-delight.

He printed on the clone's spine: *JFK* by John Yeovil. And under that he scrawled: review copy.

Review copy. Yeovil backgrounded an aural of Richard Horton's review of his last dream. Just to remind himself what this was about.

Yeovil is lucky that his publishers have the clout to buy off his heroine's heirs, 'cause *The Private Life of Margaret Thatcher* is quite as unnecessary and unsavory as his previous efforts. Yeovil is genned up on period externals, and has an insidious knack for concepting his dreams so you zip through without being too annoyed. But once the headset is off, you know you've had a zilch experience. A few critics praise the man for his high-minded moral tone, but even they will find the lip-smacking prurience of *Margaret Thatcher* difficult to get their heads around. Yet again Yeovil bombards the captive mind with an endless round of sensuality—enormous state banquets, thrilling battles, ichor-drenched "tasteful" sexing—and finally condemns all the excesses he has dragged us through with such gloating relish. He is at his worst when his heroine submits to what he has her anachronistically think of as "a fate worse than death" under the well-remembered, much-maligned Idi Amin in order to save a planeload of hostages. One symphathizes with the feminist group who have petitioned for Yeovil's judicial castration under the anti-sexism laws. Finally, the man's dreams are a far less interesting phenomenon than his publicity machine. If you're out there taking a rest from adding up the profits, John, pack it in and join the Rural Reclamation Corps. With relief we turn to a new dream from Miss Susan Bish-opric, who has made such an. . . .

Richard Horton was as smug a little shit as ever there was. Listening to his middle-aged parody of the adjectival overkill of a comput-assessor made Yeovil's fingers twist his watch chain into flesh-pinching knots.

Yeovil could not decide which made him hate Richard Horton more. The Carol business, or his tridvid defamations. Carol Horton had been Yeovil's mistress for three months. Before he had elected to sever the bond, Carol had taken it upon herself to return to her husband. Moreover she had instituted a civil lawsuit against Yeovil, alleging that he had drawn upon copyrighted facets of her personality for Pristine, the protagonist of his *The Sweetheart of Tau Ceti*. When he thought about her Yeovil still disliked Carol, but only to prove a point. Deep down it was Horton's insulting reviews that lifted Yeovil's loathing into the superhate bracket.

Before leaving the house Yeovil vindictively erased all his Horton tapes.

Richard Horton was dreaming. He dreamed that he was John F. Kennedy. Or, rather he dreamed that he was John Yeovil jacking off while dreaming that he was John F. Kennedy. If Kennedy had been like the similie no one would now be around to review the dream. The Ivans would have nuked the world in desperation.

So far it had been the typical John Yeovil craptrap.

The man never missed a chance to be cheap and obvious.

In the Oval Office JFK was sexing Marilyn Monroe. Why was it always Marilyn Monroe? Every dream set in the mid-twentieth century found it obligatory to have the hero sex Marilyn Monroe. The girl must have had a crowded schedule. The semiologically inclined comput-assessors called her an icon of liberated sensuality. Richard Horton called her a thundering cliché.

It was the regulation wet-dream stuff, a little harder than Yeovil's usual hypocritical lyricism. At least there were no butterflies and gentle breezes here. Just heavy-duty sexing. Another depiction of woman as a hunk of meat. Kubrick knows what Carol ever saw in Yeovil.

Horton's attention strayed around the scene. Perhaps he should feed the dream through the British Museum Library's researcher. It might catch Yeovil out on an external. It was probably not worth it. Yeovil was the kind of Dreamer who got every wallpaper tone and calendar date right and then hit you with a concept that would make a computer puke.

Yeovil had peppered the sexing with memories. The lanky git was pathetically pleased with himself. Look how much research I did, screamed a mass of largely irrelevant facts. WW II, Holy Joe Kennedy, Hyannisport.

Who wrote Kennedy's inaugural address? That was out of character. Horton's dybbuk flinched from the whiteout. There was another mind crowding in, superimposed on the Kennedy similie. It was not Yeovil, he was working overtime on having JFK remember who was topping the bill at the Newport, Rhode Island, jazz festival in 1960. There was someone else. A strong mind Horton could not place. It was a contributory Dreamer. Was Yeovil trying to pirate again? Eclipsing a collaborator on the credits was not beneath him.

Horton felt himself getting lost in the dream. The fiction was broken, and he was disconcerted. For an instant he thought he actually was sexing Marilyn Monroe. The woman was screaming in his ear. After all these years, the real thing.

Then it was cartoon time. The JFK similie body stretched impossibly. The return of Plastic Man. There was a playback fault. That was it. Whoever had last dreamed through this copy had left an accidental overlay. Horton fished around for a name, but was dropped into a maelstrom of explosion imagery.

Was Yeovil experimenting with hard core? At least that would make a change.

Then the dream came together again, and Horton was locked in. Wedged between the minds of Yeovil, Kennedy and the mysterious Mr. X.

Marilyn lay face down, exhausted, her hair fanned on the pile carpet. JFK traced her backbone with the presidential seal. Horton was disgusted to feel Catholic guilt flit through JFK's mind. Yeovil was piling cant upon cliché as per usual.

"Jack," breathed Marilyn, "did you know there's a theory that the whole universe got started with a Big Bang?"

Yeovil's dialogue was always the pits.

Kennedy parted Marilyn's hair and kissed the nape of her neck. Horton felt a trekkiehead reply coming. Something hard at the base of the president's skull. A white hot needle in his head. A brief skin and bone agony (what was that about Oswald?), then nothing.

Horton was not Horton anymore. Horton was not anybody anymore. His mind had been wiped. Completely, as an erase blanks a tape. Yeovil watched as the former Horton rolled on his side, retracting his arms and legs, wrapping himself into an egg.

The dreamtape was still running. Yeovil offed the machine, and pulled the clone tape. Elvis Kurtz had been unknowingly generous. He had shared his death.

Yeovil freed Horton from his headset, and gently popped his contact lenses. They had been making him cry. No point in keeping up enmities from a previous incarnation.

Yeovil wondered how Carol would take to motherhood. She always had shown an inclination to sentiment over gurgling infants. Now she had a chance to be closely acquainted with one. Horton had a lot of growing up to do.

Yeovil dropped the tape into Horton's Disperse, and used the critic's in to gain access to his Household. He wiped the whole day. As an extra flourish, he wiped the entire Household memory. A little pointless mystification to obscure his involvement.

Now all he had to do was get back to Luxborough Street, wipe Kurtz off the master tape, give that to

Tony, and wait for the returns. Do it, then clear up afterwards.

Tony had messaged in the Household tridvid.

"I had a merry hell of a time overriding your Household, you bastard. But we didn't lend you company programs for nothing. So you were spending the day putting a few final touches to the masterpiece were you? If so, you must be doing it in another dimension because the master is here and you aren't. Where the Jacqueline Susann are you? Actually, don't bother to tell me. I don't give a damn. I now have the *JFK* master, and that fulfills your contract. You can start looking for a new publisher. By the time you play this back we'll have a million copies in distribution, with an expected second impression on Monday. Don't worry, though. You won't have to sue us to get what's coming to you. Ciao."

INTRODUCTION TO

A FEW WORDS ON "OPTIONAL MUSIC FOR VOICE AND PIANO"

by Poppy Z. Brite

I wrote "Optional Music for Voice and Piano" during a Young Writers' Workshop at the University of Virginia in the summer of 1985. I don't know how much about writing was "taught" at this workshop, but I found it incredibly valuable because it gave me a chance to meet other young, weird people who wanted to write, something I hadn't experienced before. Unfortunately, on the first day of the workshop I fainted in a restaurant and was taken to the emergency room, where I was prodded, pierced, and left to sit in the hall for three hours after being told that I could have an ectopic pregnancy and might need surgery right away to avoid sudden death.

It turned out to be a nasty case of pelvic inflammatory disease, also known as Female Trouble, and I was put on a course of antibiotics that made me dizzy and light-headed for the entire first week of the workshop. At the end of the week I wrote this story on my old manual typewriter (gone now—I don't know where). It was the first thing I'd ever written that felt as if it came from elsewhere, came *through* me rather than *from* me. In *Misery,* Stephen King calls this "getting an idea," as opposed to "trying to have an idea."

I was eighteen then, and I'd been trying to sell stories since I was twelve. One is never certain until the contract comes in the mail, but as soon as I typed the last lines of "Optional Music," I felt pretty sure that this was going to be my first sale. I sent it to David B. Silva at *The Horror Show,* from whom I'd got a few encouraging rejection slips. A few weeks later, I rode the bus home from my crappy candy-making job and found the acceptance letter and contract waiting on my mom's dining room table. "Optional Music for Voice and Piano" was published in the Winter 1985 issue of *The Horror Show.*

Over the years, readers have tried to identify the model for the story's nameless singer. Guesses have ranged from Michael Stipe of R.E.M. to Peter Murphy of Bauhaus, neither of whom I'd ever heard of when I wrote it. The singer's voice, costumes, and ability to "fly" onstage were all inspired by Peter Gabriel, particularly his years with Genesis. I should qualify this by saying that, as far as I know, listening to Genesis has never killed anyone (though I wouldn't swear it for their later stuff).

OPTIONAL MUSIC FOR VOICE AND PIANO

by Poppy Z. Brite

1960

WHEN the hand snaked out and dragged him into the alley, the boy's only emotion was a sick sense of I-told-you-so. He'd known he couldn't make it home safely.

There had been a new book about magic at the library. Reading it, he'd lost track of time, not knowing how late it was until Mrs. Cooper reminded him that she had to close up in fifteen minutes. His parents would be furious. He'd rushed out of the reading room and down the stone steps that led to the sidewalk, having taken only the time to close the book reverently and slide it back into its own space on the shelf.

Even in a hurry, he had loved the newness of the red leather against the older, more faded cloth covers.

He had never been out by himself so late at night. Somehow the night allowed familiar things to change their forms. Bats swooped around streetlights; they seemed too low, almost brushing the top of his head with their skittery wings. Two bristling, pointy-eared things darted across his path, and he jumped back and made an involuntary little sound in his throat. That was when the hand closed around his neck.

It dragged him into the alley and held him tightly against itself. His face was buried in the folds of a dress or cloak. A pungent, musty smell squirmed up his nostrils. He was unable to cough the dust away. He began to choke. Then the hand was at his mouth. The fingers, hard, dry, and impossibly sharp, scrabbled at his mouth. It was trying to force his lips apart.

He twisted his face away, clamping his lips tighter than he had thought possible. The fingers dug into his face, wrenching his head back into the folds of the cloak. Something tiny and delicate snapped in his neck. A soft cry escaped him—the pain was sickening.

There were two hands then; one pinched his nose, drawing blood. Finally, unable to hold his breath any longer, he opened his mouth and gulped great gasps of mercifully cool air. The other hand slapped down over his mouth. Something soft and slimy slid past his lips and spread over his tongue. He felt as if a salted slug had dissolved in his mouth. The stuff tasted the way the cloak had smelled, tangy and bitter.

He wanted to spit, but the hand was still clamped

painfully across his face. The glob warmed his throat
as it slid down. That part almost felt good. The
warmth began to spread through him. He went won-
derfully limp. His toes and fingers tingled. The hands
let him go and he slithered to the ground.

The cool bricks felt good against his cheek. His neck
was twisted at an awkward angle, but he no longer
noticed the pain. Between the tops of the buildings
that soared up on either side of him, he could see a
sliver of darkness sprinkled with pinpoint stars. A
night breeze brushed over his face and ruffled his hair
as he stared up. The sky was incredibly beautiful. He
wanted to sing to it.

1980

The piano keys were bone-smooth and cold under his
fingers. He loved the starkness of them, black on white
against the deeper black lacquer of the piano. The
room was stark too, purposely so. The piano and its
bench were the only objects in the room. The floor
was of dark polished wood with a honey-golden undertone that made it seem to glow.

He sat with his back to the long window which
nearly filled the rear wall of the room. His house sat
on a cliff overlooking the sea. When he stood at the
window, he could look down at waves crashing and
disintegrating on jagged rocks. But he sat on the far
side of the room. If he had turned to face the window,
he would have seen only a long expanse of gray-blue

sky broken by the three heavy crossbars of the window.

It might have been an early morning sky or an early evening sky or a sky about to storm; he neither knew nor cared. He slept whenever he was tired and spent most of his waking hours at the piano. His face, bent over the keys, was serene and nearly expressionless. At thirty, he was almost as boyish as he had been at ten: his body was slim and compact, his unlined pale face overhung by a soft mop of dark hair, eyes like limpid black pools, a serious, sad mouth.

He let his hands wander across the piano keys. The notes rose, clustered, broke away from each other and drifted back down to melt into the golden floor. As they touched his ears, he smiled faintly. It had taken him so long to realize he could make this kind of music.

1960

His neck wasn't broken. Having it wrenched so sharply had pulled a muscle, and while he was in the hospital he had to lie flat on his back, as nearly motionless as possible, with a thick metal-and-foam collar holding his neck immobile. He learned the position of every crack and speck on the ceiling. At times the boredom was almost tangible.

He learned not to cry because the tears would trickle down the sides of his head and make the hair behind his ears unpleasantly damp; he couldn't lift his hands high enough to wipe the tears away.

After the first two days he discovered that singing relieved his boredom. Even better, it made him forget his pain and his experience in the alley.

One night a nurse heard him. He stopped when she came into the room, but she asked him to go on, and after a bit of coaxing he sang her a song. He had composed the words and the tune himself, while lying in the hospital bed. He could see trees and a piece of sky through his window, and he longed to be outside. He had rhymed "trees" with "breeze." It was the work of a ten-year-old, although the poetry showed promise.

What mattered, though, was his voice. His neck was strained and padded; by all rights his voice should have sounded stifled, weak. Instead, it was glorious. He sang high and hoarse and sweet, the voice of a child, but hidden in his song were hints of darkness, intimations of fear and pain.

As the nurse held his hand and listened to him, tears started in her eyes. She had remembered a night nearly forty years ago, when her parents had gone on a shopping trip to the city and forgotten to leave the front door unlocked for her. They were three miles away from their nearest neighbors, and she had huddled in a corner of the front porch, tiny and sick with terror, until the familiar car had finally turned into the driveway. Nothing in the boy's pretty little song had suggested this, yet she recalled it so vividly that her stomach twisted with childish dread.

The memory hurt her, but the boy's voice was so beautiful that she called the other nurses in to hear him sing. They held their breaths until he had finished. One of them, a girl barely twenty-one, ran out of the room sobbing. She explained later that she didn't know what had come over her; she supposed she just felt sorry for the poor child, lying there so pale and thin.

The boy listened to the nurses whispering outside the door, and tears pooled in his eyes too. He blinked them away, remembering that he couldn't cry. Instead he began to sing softly to himself.

1970

He stood with his forehead pressed against the cool glass of the small window that wouldn't open. Behind him, in the dressing room of the club, the other members of the band were milling about; tuning guitars, running nervous fingers through their ratty hair, getting ready to do a show. He could see faint reflections of their movements in the glass.

He looked past the phantom images at the sky. Evening was stealing over the city. The sky was a gradually intensifying blue, deeper than eggshell but not yet azure; swirled through the blue were pale pink clouds as fluffy and ethereal as cotton candy. He couldn't look away from it until PJ came over and clapped a hand onto his shoulder. "How are you doing, man? All set?"

He turned to face PJ. The drummer blinked, then grinned. "I love it," he said. "You look great."

He was dressed entirely in black: leotard, tights, a

long scarf tied around his head. His face was painted white, and around his eyes and eyebrows he had smudged black kohl, making them look sunken and veiled. His face was framed by his dark hair, which fell nearly to his shoulders. He looked ghoulish; he looked beautiful.

"I love it," PJ said again.

"Thanks." He turned away from the window.

"It's pretty crowded out there. I looked." PJ grinned again, nervous. This was the band's first real performance, the first time they were to be paid for making music.

"Great," he said with an effort. He didn't want to talk; he could feel the anticipation building up inside him. Right now he didn't want to use his voice for anything but singing.

The dressing room door opened and a head popped in. "Guys? You about set?" The other three grimaced at each other. He closed his eyes, feeling a shiver begin in the pit of his stomach and go through him in two directions; it slid down his legs, making his knees lock; it tingled up through his chest into his throat, trying to push his voice out. He was ready.

At the first thrill of his voice, the crowd's conversations dwindled. By the time he had sung the opening lines of the first song, everyone in the club was staring at him, some pushing forward to get closer to the stage, some breathing the smoke-swirled air a little more shallowly.

Their set was not long, but time stopped for him; the show might have gone on a moment or an aeon.

At the highest notes his voice hoarsened and seemed as if it must break; the sound brought tears to a few listeners' eyes.

By the last song, some of the crowd sang along with the chorus. Others sat absolutely still, eyes fixed on his face. Several were crying openly as they sang or listened.

In the back of the club, a heavy man in a business suit shuddered and put his hand over his eyes. He scouted for a record label, and he had come to ferret out marketable talent, not to have his emotions ravaged by the music. But the singer's voice had brought to his mind a soft, sweet lullaby his mother had sung to him years ago. His mother had died swiftly and messily in a highway accident when he was fifteen. The memory was nearly unbearable.

The man shuddered again, then froze and pressed his hand to his chest. He felt his heart miss a beat. He started to get up with the vague idea of finding a phone, finding a doctor, asking someone, anyone, for help. The pain slammed him back into his chair. He wanted to loosen his collar, but when he raised his arm, a bolt stabbed at his heart.

The last thing he saw was the singer staring confusedly toward the back of the club, then, as people realized what was happening and moved to help, bowing his head as if in shame.

1973

She was a pretty girl, though wan and fair-cheeked, with shiny black hair in two ponytails and a battered metal boom box in her arms. An earplug cord ran from the box up to her shoulder and disappeared beneath her right ponytail.

The girl stood on the roof of a gray stone office building and stared down at the cars roaring through the grubby streets, the people milling eleven stories below. She imagined being in the middle of that crowd, smelling the people's bodies, their hot stale breath. She hoped she would land on one of them.

This wasn't the way it was supposed to be. In cartoons or on TV shows a crowd of people always gathered below, half of them trying to save the person, the other half yelling, "Jump!" No one had even noticed her on the edge of the roof. No one would see her go off.

A gust of wind startled her, and she stumbled for her balance. She wasn't even sure whether she had the nerve to jump yet; she certainly didn't want to be pushed off. She pressed a button on her cassette player. The tape began, hissing its silence into her ear; then the voice filled her head. Her band, her singer, her love—the only person she loved. None of her poems expressed the agony of her life as well as the darkness and pain in his voice. He had known the same pain, she thought—not worse pain, nothing could be *worse* than her pain, but he knew. He understood. The excruciating beauty of his singing told her so. Yes, he understood. If she died, she would die for him. She was glad she had written him that note.

The music controlled her entire body now. It would lift her off the edge of the roof. If she was meant to live, it would carry her away; she would fly. If not, she would fall.

Now his voice filled the world. "In the fire—in the center of the fire—I am pure," he wailed. His voice crested on the word "pure."

She leaped. His voice followed her down. The boom box shattered when she hit the sidewalk.

1974

"I don't want to," he said. It was a half-hearted protest.

"Yes you do. You say you don't, but I can hear what you really mean. You mean you want to," Killner told him. Killner was the band's manager. He hated Killner's voice. Unpleasantly dry and papery, it got into his ear and skittered around until he lost track of his thoughts and ended up agreeing to whatever it was Killner wanted him to do.

Killner kept talking. He took the phone away from his ear and stared at it, half-smiling at the buzz of unintelligible words. Eventually he put the phone back to his ear.

"Besides, you're not the only member of this band," Killner was saying. "I already talked to PJ and Toby and Mack. They all want to do it. You're crazy to pass this up. You haven't done anything in six months—no recording, no gigs. Do you want everybody to forget about you?"

"Yes."

"Well, that's great. You know this band is nothing without your voice. Do you want to let everybody down? Those fans? PJ and Toby and Mack?"

"Look," he told Killner. "Singing is my life. I sing to myself every day; there's no way I could stop. I love it more than anything else in the world. But I told you before, I don't want to do any more records and I especially don't want to do any more live shows. Something always happens. I don't know why it is, but something always happens. Remember the guy who died at our first gig?"

"That guy had a history of heart trouble."

"Right. What about the people who've died in car wrecks when they just happened to be heading home after one of our concerts? What about that girl who tried to stab her lover in the parking lot after a show? What about the guy who started screaming during the last concert? Guys came to get him, Killner. Guys in white coats.

"I thought that only happened in the funny papers. They took him to the hospital. I heard later that all he would say for three days was, 'His eyes.' *His eyes.* They thought he was talking about *my* eyes, Killner. That was the night I wore the black robes and the green Day-Glo paint around my eyes. My eyes looked like they were glowing. What about that?"

"It was your costume, not—"

"I'm not finished. What about that suicide note, Killner? What about the note? Remember the fifteen-year-old girl who sent me her suicide note and threw herself off a building? Remember 'I love only you and I'm doing what your voice tells me to do?' What about that, Killner?"

"Do you hold yourself accountable for all the crazy people in the world?"

"Only—when—they're—crazy—because—of—my—voice."

"Look . . ." Killner's voice turned oily, seductive. "This is an incredible opportunity. It's amazing that they even want you to play there. Rock bands never play there."

"We're not a rock band."

"What's wrong with being a goddamn rock band? Never mind—don't start. They know you're an artist. You know what they want you to do? They want you to do the flying bit."

He closed his eyes, remembering the glinting Peter Pan wire, the stomach-dropping sensation of soaring.

"Like in '72. Remember how you loved that? The first time you did it, you told me it was the most glorious performance you'd ever given—soaring above the stage, singing your everloving heart out in midair. You want to miss that?"

He kept his eyes closed. He had always imagined that flying would be nearly as incredible as singing. Doing both at once had been almost too much to bear.

"So what do you say?"

"No," he whispered. "I told you no and I still say no. I can't hurt any more people."

Killner gave up then and said goodbye in aggrieved tones. Ten minutes later the phone rang. That would

166

be PJ. When Killner couldn't convince him to do something, he always enlisted PJ to give it another try. PJ had a way of making things sound so simple and appealing that one felt like a fool for ever having refused them. He wanted this so much; he wouldn't be able to say no again. He wasn't going to answer the phone.

It rang again.

If he picked it up, he was lost.

The phone screamed at him.

He had to answer it.

He mustn't.

He had to.

He snatched the receiver off its cradle. "All right," he yelled into the phone. "All right, all right, I'll do it, all right, only leave me alone."

"What?" said PJ's voice as he choked back a sob.

He was wearing his oldest costume: black, pure black, with white face and dark, hollow eyes. It had always been his favorite, the simplest yet the most powerful, and the black flying harness blended well with it.

He thought about flying. It had been so long—

PJ's hand was on his shoulder. "I realize this is rough for you," PJ told him. "You know we really wanted to do this show. Thanks for agreeing to it." He nodded at PJ, didn't speak. The others were used to his pre-concert silence; it no longer fazed them. They thought he was saving his voice for the show. They didn't understand that when he was going to sing, speaking just wasn't worthwhile.

It hardly seemed to matter now.

He pushed aside the window curtain and looked out at the sky. No cotton candy clouds this time; tonight he saw only a small cold moon floating high in the sky, haloed and partially obscured by clouds.

One of the stage technicians came up behind him. "Listen, I wanted to remind you about the harness wires once more. Be careful. Make sure the wires are well away from your neck before you give the signal that you're ready to go up, because I can't see what you're doing. That wire's sharp. If I pull you up while one of them's looped around your neck, it could cut your head half off. Just take your time and give me the signal when you're ready."

The tech patted him on the back, between the straps of his harness. He smiled madly and waved the guy away, wanting nothing more than to end the stream of chatter. He didn't need a briefing on those wires. He knew everything about them.

There were ten minutes to go, then five, then none. They were onstage before he really knew what was happening. PJ and Toby and Mack pranced a bit, happy to be performing again. He stood still at center stage, staring out at the crowd.

He could see faces in the first few rows; they were watching him, wanting him, wanting the deepest part of him. Who would he hurt tonight? Who would go home and put a gun to his forehead—who would hurt a person she loved—who would lose his mind?

No one.

No one at all, if he knew what he was doing.

He sang the first song. He threw himself into it so hard that by the end of the song he was on his knees, clutching the microphone with both hands, pushing every bit of air in his body into the notes. His glory had reached its crescendo. If anyone noticed the wetness on his cheeks, they thought it was sweat. He held the last note of the song for a full minute.

The crowd went wild.

It was time to fly.

He eased himself up, trembling, and went to the rear of the stage where the wires dangled. They glinted gold and silver and all the colors of the stage lights, thin as hairs but strong enough, together, to support a hundred and thirty-five pounds of him. He began attaching them to the hooks on his harness. When he came to the last wire, the one that supported the largest part of his weight, he glanced into the wings. The tech nodded, ready to pull him up.

He looped the wire around his neck and gave the signal.

1980

He got up and walked away from the piano to the window. Fine mist from the crashing of the waves on the rocks was hitting the glass—there would be a storm soon. He might sit by the long window and watch its glorious fury.

He returned to the piano and played a little more, a sprinkling, dancing tune that skipped across the polished floor. He rested his cheek on the top of the piano, loving its sleek coolness against his skin. His hand strayed to his throat and stroked the tight, shiny scar that stretched nearly from ear to ear. His fingers traced the jagged line of it. He remembered the relief he'd felt, waking after the hours of impossibly delicate surgery, when the doctor told him his vocal cords had been severed and he would never talk—let alone sing—again.

He sat at his piano for a while. Then, when the long, sweet sound of serenity had completely filled him, he went to the window to watch the storm.

INTRODUCTION TO

"AMYMONE'S FOOTSTEPS"

by Gary A. Braunbeck

Though by no means a great story, "Amymone's Footsteps" is nonetheless a very important one for me; not only because it was my first professional sale, but because it marked a turning point in my evolution as a writer.

It came to be published in the Fall 1986 issue of *Twilight Zone's Night Cry*, then under the keen editorial eye of Alan Rodgers—whom I had not intended to see it, so his buying it (and subsequently three other stories from me) was a happy accident.

To whit: Over the first half of the eighties, I fought tooth-and-nail to get a story accepted by T.E.D. Klein for *Twilight Zone*. Over the course of five years, I collected something in the area of forty rejection slips from the redoubtable Mr. Klein. I still have all of them. Read in order, they're very entertaining. (I

never once received a "standard" rejection from *TZ*.)
The basic gist of each rejection goes like this:

Dear Gary:

I really liked this story. In fact, I liked it even better
than your last one—and you *know* how much I liked
that one. Terrific stuff. Poignant. Creepy. First-rate.
I'm not going to *buy* it, but, man, was it good!

Please send more.

T.E.D. Klein

This went on for several years, until I submitted
"Amymone's Footsteps." Mr. Klein just *loved* it. In
fact, that's what he said—"I *loved* this one!"

The thing was, he was about to step down as editor
at *TZ*, so he couldn't buy it ("I would if I could," he
wrote). Instead, he was going to pass it along to Michael Blaine, the new editor, with a very strong recom-
mendation to buy. Somehow, Blaine thought the story
hadn't been read yet, and so passed it on to one of
the first readers, who in turn passed it on to someone
else . . . on and on, until it somehow wound up in
Alan Rodgers' hands. Alan dug it, asked me for a
revision, and then bought it. He then bought three
more stories in the Myth cycle—none of which ever
saw print, because *Night Cry* folded in early '88. So I
not only made my first professional sale at *Night Cry*,
but was paid my first professional "kill" fees.

There is another reason that this story—as much as

it makes me cringe in several places now—is an important one for me. It is the story in which, after nearly five years of writing, my own narrative voice began to emerge. Oh, it's a squeaky voice here, no doubt, cracking every other sentence as a voice passing through adolescence is cursed to, but it's most definitely *there*. Readers familiar with my latter works will be able to recognize the emerging voice. In fact, there are a couple of passages in "Amymone's Footsteps" that, even now, I wouldn't want to change.

I resisted the temptation to "fix" anything for its appearance here, aside from some glaring misspellings. What you read here—as awkward, forced, and (in paces) overwritten as it is—is exactly how it first appeared sixteen years ago. I was younger and much more impatient. Keep that in mind.

AMYMONE'S FOOTSTEPS

by Gary A. Braunbeck

DEBRA Bishop stood alone on the night beach and watched as the ocean returned the pebble she'd thrown out only moments before. Kneeling to pick up the tiny stone she wondered if everything she ever tried to share or give of herself would be tossed back in her face with the same efflorescent carelessness, but self-pity was never a land in which she journeyed for long, so she stood erect, arched her back, and heaved the stone out into the damp night. She pulled a handful of change from her pockets, then—in a superstitious act of honor to the ancient Egyptian Trinity of Osiris, Isis, and Horus—bowed three times to the moon while making the loneliest of her lonely wishes. Half covered by the sand at her feet she saw the moldering remains of a very small starfish, and she found herself wondering if the creature had been washed ashore against its will, or if it was waiting for others like itself to rise from the depths and join it. Somehow the night here made her think this way, and she was beginning to hate it.

"Are you coming in? I gotta get goin'." It was David.

"In a minute."

"The tide will be coming in pretty soon. You're not waiting to try and outrun *that,* are you?"

"Oh, *God,* no. I'm just . . . you know, *thinking.*"

"About me?"

"Among other things."

"Among other things," he mimicked playfully. "That doesn't make me feel very much wanted."

As if I don't know the feeling, she thought.

She stood hugging herself under the moon, looking at the dead starfish, waiting for David to come out and join her before he left. Sea spray lapped her feet. The starfish remained anchored to its spot. There was something so ethereal to the scene she couldn't take her eyes from it. It was a beautiful spot, she had to admit, and she had, after all, told David she didn't mind his leaving her here at nights, but that was before . . . *don't think about it, honey.*

She watched as a line of foam crept onto the sand, nearly reaching her feet. The sight made her jump inside so she took a step back and turned, nearly running face-first into David.

"Figures," he said. "I come out and you decide you want to go in. Does wonders for my ego."

"Are you sure you have to go tonight?"

"Come on. You know the only reason we came down here was to see the clubs. If Jim decides to tour the band down here—"

"I know, I know; you'll know which places to try and book. I know how important this is to you and the band, really I do, but we've been here six days and you've only spent one night with me."

175

"You said you didn't want to come along—"

"And I don't. I know this is technically a business trip, but it would be nice if you could mix it with a little pleasure . . . preferably mine."

"Please, Debbie? I know you have to feel bad about staying here alone at night, but I hadn't planned on you coming along in the first place." She smiled and turned back out to face the sea. He was right; her coming along had been a last-minute decision, so she had no right to feel resentment, but she did. One night, was that too much to ask? Just talk to him about it, you can still talk to him about things. He's the same David, the same guitar player in a rock'n'roll band, talk to him. About love. About loneliness.

About fear.

"Look, this place is really starting to scare me at night. Please don't leave."

"Why don't you come along tonight? I promise you this club has no strippers."

"I promise you this house *will* have a stripper if you stay."

"You don't give up, do you?"

"No, because if I give up I'm going to get angry and you don't like me when I'm angry."

"You're not the same person when you're mad."

"Then stay here and build a fire and tell me stories and get me drunk. I don't make this offer too often, so you'd better jump. Yammer about the trouble you used to get into when you were in the navy, do your stupid W.C. Fields imitation, and then make love to me in whatever room you want, I don't care. Just don't leave." He didn't say anything for a moment, and that's when she noticed that he'd dropped something large and silver behind him.

"What's that?" He gave a small, nervous laugh.

"Something that wouldn't help if . . . *why* does this place scare you at night? I think it's beautiful."

"Then why don't you stay here?"

"That's not an answer." That's because there *was* no answer; at least not one he'd accept. What could she say? That after twenty-nine years of living, thirteen of them on her own, she'd suddenly discovered that she didn't like being alone at nights? That wouldn't hold water . . . so to speak. Why not the truth? Why not just turn full face toward him and say, "I think the tide is trying to get me!"?

Because he'd laugh in your face, that's why.

"You'd never believe me," she said. "Now, what in the hell is that thing?"

"You don't want to know."

"If I didn't want to know I wouldn't have asked. 'Fess up." He looked at her, shrugged, then walked over and retrieved it.

"It's something I read about in one of your Mark Twain books." He came close and offered it to her. It was a loaf of the zwieback she'd baked the other day, only he'd wrapped it in aluminum foil and stuck a thermometer in it.

"I give up," she said.

"Twain said that if you put some quicksilver in a loaf of bread and float it out on the water, it will stop over the place where a drowned body is. I was going to ask you about it, trying it out, I mean. I thought it might be kind of fun."

Debra shrank away from him *and* it. "Christ, David! That's morbid!"

He turned to face the ocean. "I told you you wouldn't want to know."

Please don't do what I think you're going to do.

He arched back and threw the zwieback loaf out to the water. It soared like a metallic football for what seemed a mile, then splashed down far from shore, but not so far that Debra couldn't see it under the moonlight.

"Why did you *do* that?"

"Why not?" He moved close to kiss her. She turned her head and pushed him away. Revulsion and fear merged as one within her, and there was no longer any room for false tenderness.

"If you care anything about me, please stay."

"Don't pull that number on me. I've seen you out here when I leave at nights. You walk up and down this beach like it's your own private island and personal domain. Don't you dare pull something so petty as 'If you love me' because it won't work! Now . . . I'm going. Are you coming along this time or not?"

"Go to hell."

David said nothing for several moments, then whirled around and began walking away.

"If you really get scared call the club down the road and have me paged. I'll be there all evening." He vanished up the dune by their cabin, leaving her alone on the night beach with the moon above, the tide only thirty minutes away, and his horrible corpse finder still floating in the distance. Just as she turned to walk back to the cabin she caught sight of something squirming in the sand a few feet away from her and took three hesitant steps toward it. What she saw struggling in the sand made her want to call out after David, but another, stronger part, a part that was in the process of giving itself over to fear's silent fascination, would not allow her to make a sound.

There were now two starfish lying on the beach.

She walked hurriedly back to the cabin, slammed shut the sliding glass doors, and leaned against the frame. Her heart was trying to squirt through her ribs and bounce off the far wall, but through some buried reserve of self-control she prevented herself from giving over to her fear. She pressed her weight against the door, her barrier from the waves, and took several deep breaths. Maybe this was just overreaction, a delayed paranoia from childhood, a budding, warped form of xenophobia . . . maybe it was just her imagination, which was more than capable of playing a few tricks on her.

This was ritual. Try and be convincing. Always the same, always very reasonable, always a dismal failure. She turned and looked into the ocean.

The corpse finder still shone brightly under the moon, but now it had stopped drifting. The waves didn't seem to be touching it at all; it simply rose above them like a high jumper in slow motion and waited for them to pass under, as if it were irrevocably anchored to the spot.

Which was roughly a hundred yards from shore.

Debra ground her teeth. *Terrific, David. It worked. You're out getting stewed to the gills and I'm standing vigil over a drowned body. You bastard.*

Her heart tried squirting again, but still she looked. The waters were churning, gearing up for the explosion of foam and power that would soon come pounding, it seemed, right to the back door, beckoning. White froth like a rabid animal, shattering shells, shedding the seaweed that would wrap itself around the sand-killed trees, a subterranean serpent and she its water-logged Eve. There was something hideous about the night tides, something dark and unthinkable, yet she, at times, could well understand why lemmings marched unblinking into the oceans and seas; the sheer *force* of the tide was enough to overwhelm any living creature. They had been the first to emerge from the waters of the Earth and touch land, the tides, and they kept going back only to return six hours later, as if some huge beast lay sleeping under the ocean floor, inhaling for six hours then, after it tired, releasing its breath; a reminder to the two-legged creatures on land that things bigger than themselves controlled the real forces of existence and always would.

Clumps of algae clung to rocks nearby, stunned swimmers hanging on for dear life in hopes of a speedy rescue and return home. The sand was white and duned, cluttered by skeins of kelp, hunks of driftwood, skeletal remnants of surfboards and skis, drenched and moldering reminders of those fallen to the waves and tides.

Gary A. Braunbeck

She felt something prickling at her side.

The tides.

More than their sight, their froth, their power, it was their sound that most frightened her. The lapping and churning and crashing all merged somewhere far above the sand to take on the sound of mighty wings, the moon-pull simply an exponential doorway into this world, the rhythm of the waters a pulsing, sententious flow of eternity, calling, singing, approaching closer every night. The tides gave life to her own personal deathbird, constantly circling over the cabin, looking for food to carry back to its nest, feeding its young until they, too, could fly in the night and search out their own Debra ... throbbing, brewing, rising, calling, coming closer, closer, teasing, then pulling back, promising to come closer the next time. Tides. The first conundrum. Lonely siren singing. Embrace me. Let me caress you, cleanse you, awaken in you sensations never before felt. Come closer, that's it, a little more, dance with me, cascading, dance over here, touch, experience, there—

I have you now.

Debra snapped her head to the side and closed her eyes. This was definitely overreacting. It was just water, with no consciousness, no reason, nothing along those lines. So *what* if David's little device had worked? There were probably thousands of drowned bodies in the water; after all, wasn't something like seventy-three percent of the world's surface covered by it? Good reason . . . good as any. She looked toward the silver corpse finder.

Was it closer?

No, uh-uh. It was still anchored to its find, and to the best of her knowledge there hadn't been a drowned body washed up here in some time, so why worry, right?

Right.

So why was she worried?

She checked her watch; a little more than twenty minutes until tide. Enough time to gather some driftwood and get a fire started. She walked across the room and tripped on the corner of an upturned rug, stumbled into the bookshelf and knocked one of its volumes to the floor. It landed on its spine and fell open to a random page, something no human being can resist looking at. Debra picked up the book and saw it was her copy of Edith Hamilton's *Mythology*. Her eyes scanned to the top of the page and saw 288, and just below that, one word:

AMYMONE

She read on:

She was one of the Danaïds. Her father sent her to draw water and a satyr saw her and pursued her. Poseidon heard her cry for help, loved her, and saved her from the satyr. With his trident he made in her honor the ring which bears her name.

She thought that was very sweet, until she flipped back to read who and what the Danaïds were. She then, *very* quickly, closed the book and crammed it back onto its place on the shelf, her thoughts wandering back to David and why he chose to leave her here, knowing that she was half comatose with fright, be it real or imagined. Why did love always have to carry with it the threat of emotional violence? Why, when you cared about someone enough to want to be an irreplaceable part of their life, why were there times when you really wanted to kill them? The Danaïds—fifty sisters who married their fifty cousins and then murdered their husbands in the wedding bed—had acted on this impulse, and for their act they marched forever in hell, eternally filling jars with water from a spring, jars that were riddled with holes so the water leaked out, causing them to again and again return to refill their pathetic containers. The brides of Sisyphus. Debra shook her head. You didn't want to kill them just with words, the one you loved, but literally wrap your hands around their throat and squeeze until the last ounce of life dripped from their flesh, leaving a crumpled and cold mass of rubbery skin drooped over useless bones. Maybe the Danaïds had something after all.

Maybe she was rapidly starting to walk in Amymone's footsteps.

With that cheerful thought she donned her plastic parka and went outside to gather driftwood for the fire. She had about fifteen minutes if she hurried.

She descended the dunes, lost her footing, and tumbled down to the beach in a tangle of sand clouds and curses. The beach was, of course, deserted, one of the reasons they'd chosen to come here during the off season. During the day only a few dozen people roamed the sands, and at night there was virtually no one around.

No one.

Everything was stitched in crescent-shaped shadows under the moon, shadows that hinted at the things which lie outside the reach of the murky yet ethereal glow from the sky. In the distance, somewhere between the waters and the tidemarks in the sand, a buoy clanged out its metallic canticle to a world that couldn't hear it for musical, a world that muffled its echo like a scream down a tunnel. The deserted lifeguard tower, monolithic and forbidding, stood pointing toward the moon like a giant, skeletal finger. A foghorn sounded somewhere far, far away. A lighthouse that stood off in the night, its exterior decayed and crumbling, offered no reply to the pitiful outcalling. If there had ever been any doubt in Debra's mind that she was alone, it was now erased.

She jaunted around the beach, quickly snatching up the pieces of kelp and driftwood that offered themselves up to her, and within minutes her arms were full enough to return to the cabin.

A sharp stab of light pierced her eyes and she dropped the firewood at her feet. She tried shielding her eyes from the intense light, but even closed the brightness penetrated them. She finally turned away, but in the instant before her back was to it, she saw that the light emanated from the flood lamp on top of the lifeguard tower. She took a series of deep, angry breaths.

"Very funny, David! Now you can just get your ass down here and help me pick all this up!"

There was no answer, save that of the blowing wind.

"All right, that's enough! Get down here . . . please? I'm sorry that I was so unpleasant earlier."

No answer. She turned and began picking up her wood, and then she saw.

Her pair of discarded starfish had been joined by others now, only they weren't scattered randomly about as they should have been. They were lying in a perfect line that extended all the way across the beach and climbed the dune, nearly reaching the back door of the cabin. She remained unmoving.

"Goddammit, *please* come down," she whispered.

The light snapped off.

There was no sound from the blackness of the tower and, somehow, she knew with the absolute certainty that the darkness and its fear always provides, that it wasn't David in the tower.

There came to her the sound of massive wings, fluttering, soaring, then flapping ever closer. The tide spray was already spattering in her face, its icy wetness only adding to her fear. She climbed the dunes, trying desperately to ignore the line of starfish, and darted back into the cabin, then closed the glass doors and locked them tight. She dumped the wood down in front of the glowing fire and proceeded to lock every door and window in the house. If there was some creep running around out there trying to get his jollies by scaring the holy bejeezus out of her, she'd just wait it out in here. She never gave in to panic without a fight, and she refused to do so now anymore than she already had. She poured herself a glass of wine, popped a cassette into the player, and sat in front of the crackling fire as the soothing chords of Vivaldi's *Le Quattro Stagione* filtered majestically into the air.

It wasn't until the end of the first movement that she realized there was a fire burning in front of her, a fire that hadn't been burning when she left, and when she *did* realize this she leaped to her feet, spilled the wine, and grabbed the poker. Through the rear window she saw that the tide was bouncing off the dunes in a springlike fashion, which meant that its power would increase more and more until she could literally feel the force under her feet, even though the cabin was almost a hundred feet above the beach.

She turned up the music to a point that neared distortion, checked every door and window again to assure herself she'd locked them all, then inspected every room to make sure she was alone. The idea that this creep, whoever he was, had been in here made her feel sick inside.

Damn you.

I know you're out there and I know you're watching me, but just try it, fucker. Just try anything and I'll pound your brains right out of your ears. Just try it. You and your goddamn trick with the starfish. That was pretty good, though, I'll give you that. You must have been watching me for quite some time now.

Damn you. Look what you're doing to me.

She found herself recalling the time David had let himself into her apartment with the spare key and left a nice little note for her on the kitchen table. Now, she trusted David, more so than she had any other man, and she knew that he'd probably never go snooping about her place, but it was that *probably* that stayed with her; privacy was damned important to her, an aftereffect of a childhood that held not one moment of blissful isolation or secrecy. That afternoon when she found his note, Debra realized just how violated a person could feel about something like that; as if some alien thing had oozed into her life while she wasn't looking, touched everything she had to touch, then skulked out before she could do anything about it, leaving behind its scent, its traces, its calling card that read: You will never be alone again after this; I am always watching and I am always here.

That feeling was with her now. Violation. Some jerk-wad beach dweller had dragged himself in here and left a fiery calling card right in front of her, a calling card that was intended, obviously, to unnerve, and had achieved its desired effect. Like the floodlight. But that was all right because she was in here and that fucker, whoever he/she/it might be, was out there with the foam, the tide, the flapping deathbird in all its power and hunger. She turned to walk back over and sit in front of the fire, but her eyes wouldn't let her relax. She saw small black spots out of the corner of her eyes, spots that would loom over objects on the other side of the room and then snap back to hide behind things when she turned to face them. The music seemed to be too sharp then too flat in her ears, shaking loose parts of her spinal column. She took a few sips of wine but it tasted like swallowed smoke. Outside the deathbird foamed and flapped, its talons reaching forth to scrape across the roof with every bouncing of the foam. The violins were screeching now, and she reached over to turn the music down, but the screeching continued. Low, almost guttural howls raced around the windows, slashes of water flung themselves into the glass, and shadows split under the moonlight to spread themselves across the darkening sand.

Calm down, she thought. Take it the hell easy or you'll go nuts. It's no big thing, right? If mother were here breathing down your neck she'd tell you what a hopeless child you were, frightened of a little wind and water, and she'd be right. Stop injecting such malevolent undertones into everything, that's how paranoia starts and that's the last thing you need right now.

She closed her eyes and took several deep breaths, then poured herself another glass of wine.

The screeching continued from outside, and in some equidistant part of herself, Debra knew that it wasn't *just* the wind. She shook her hair out of her face and began to take her place back in front of the fireplace when another dark spot made its presence known to the corner of her eye, but, unlike the others, this one did not run and hide when she turned to face it; it simply hovered for a few moments and then threw itself into the window as the screeching reached its crescendo.

Debra rose and crossed to the window, counting the steps as she did so. Nine. Nine steps from the window to the fireplace, the distance across her island. And it would be; for the next five hours, or however long it took for David to return, this would be her island, these nine steps, nothing more. Maybe it was boxing herself in, but the cabin seemed to be shrinking anyway, so it was best to be prepared.

She stared out the window, and was surprised to find that it wasn't all that difficult to see out into the ocean.

But five seconds later she wished that it had been.

The screeching wasn't *just* the wind. And there were reasons. The wind couldn't anchor itself to one spot. The wind couldn't maintain the same pitch constantly . . .

And the wind couldn't wave its arms for help.

Debra unlocked the doors and flung them open. She hoped that maybe, just *maybe* she'd imagined the figure in the water screaming and thrashing. What if her late night boogeyman decided to take a dip and had gone out too far? But it wasn't a boogey*man,* because the screaming was definitely female to Debra's ears. She tried focusing her eyes again but could discern nothing in the ocean, and whatever it was hadn't been that far away. She darted to the kitchen table and pulled her parka off the seat of a chair, then dropped it when she saw what had been hidden beneath.

David's corpse finder, thermometer still intact.

The screaming started again. The foam bounced back, leaving her deathbird a marked target.

She stared at the loaf for several moments before her shock was replaced by anger. Dammit! She'd *let* it frighten her! Whoever put it here knew it would make her jump out of her pants. . . .

So why didn't you see it when you threw your parka down there? It's a big goddamned loaf of zwieback wrapped in aluminum foil with a thermometer sticking out of it! A little hard to miss so *why didn't you see it?*

Answer, dummy: *Because it wasn't there.*

Something large and heavy careened off the glass doors from outside, spiderwebbing a large crack in its wake and causing Debra to shriek and jump back. Acting on impulses born of anger and fear she snatched up the corpse finder and ran over to the window, arching back to heave it out to where it belonged. In the instant before she saw what thrashed in the water screaming she realized, for some obscure, incomprehensible reason, that her watch had stopped.

She dropped the zwieback loaf and stood watching herself drown.

She heard the creature with her face scream for David who wasn't there because he had better things to do than sit around with her on her nine-step island where corpses delivered their own tombstones and starfish marched from the sea and birds of foam flung themselves through spiderweb cracks that looked more and more like eyes with the passing of each stilled moment. She tried to stop her hands from shaking but couldn't. She folded them, rubbed them together, made them into fists and pounded then against the sides of her legs, but their dissociated trembling continued, as did the shouting and struggling of the creature that wore her face in the water. She turned away for only a moment and saw the reflection of a pair of headlights in the window, then sprinted over just in time to see David running for the dunes. She ran back over to the glass doors and saw him as he jumped into the roaring waters, screaming her name, pumping his legs in a furious effort to get to her, only it wasn't her he was swimming toward. She threw open the doors and jumped back as the tide threw seemingly dozens of starfish in at her feet, but she quickly jumped over them and lunged out toward the dunes, toward the tides, the sound of wings beating louder and louder in her ears, the cries of the deathbird pulsing through her chest in glorious expectation. She skidded to a halt just below the base of the dunes and opened her mouth to scream, but sharp talons dug into her side, deep into her flesh, and tore away part of her, lifted it, mangled and tormented it, then carried it out over David and dropped it in the spot where the creature with her face and body came into full being, having been given that part of itself Debra had long denied to herself and those she cared for. On the beach Debra collapsed into the sand and tried to shout a warning to David, but then, even though she was on land, she could see only through the eyes of the creature in the water, and what she saw with these eyes was the vision of a well lighted cabin on the beach while merciless and angry waters latched onto her limbs and tried to drag her under, laughing. But just ahead, just in the distance, she saw something which gave her hope, because there was a figure, a familiar figure, coming toward her through the slashing droplets, a determined figure that was calling to her not to be afraid, a figure that promised her warmth and dry land and other things she could not imagine. The waters pulled down on her and again she tasted

bitter, stinging salt, but then she was up and there was
air, her lungs spewing out the vile coldness that was
trying to weigh them down for eternity . . . fight it . . .
and still the figure of David kept pushing its way
toward her, still calling, still promising safety and
peace. She pushed upward with her legs and waved
her arms away from her chest, pushing back the waves
that were trying to snuff out her life like rain would
a candle flame. Things below brushed by her legs,
causing them to buckle and jerk her down, but she
saw the lights from the warm shelter on the beach and
found still new reserves of strength. Overhead there
were night clouds that tried to force themselves over
the moon to ease the pull of the tides for her, but
these clouds were too slow and the foam too powerful.
She tried to call out again but the talons were still in
her side, drawing out her life's blood with every
bouncing back of the waters, of the blue, the foam,
the pulse-beat of infinity. The figure suddenly reached
her and she felt its strong and loving arms enfold her,
but then some sleeping creature below said, *No, it's
not the way I want it,* and lurched up to sink its teeth
into her legs, and the pain was great, angry fire within
her strained and agonized muscles, and in desperation
she grabbed the saving figure by the hair, then the
ears, then the eyes, anywhere she could secure some
kind of grip to stay above the surface. She clawed,
suddenly, then scratched and screamed and struggled
against the beast below, but the figure, her David,
didn't know that she was fighting something other
than itself because it tried to slap her, tried to shock

her into lifeless submission. She arched her back and prayed for the power of the great wings, a power that would enable her to shoot upward and fly above it all to land on the soft beach like the gulls in summertime did, but the pull was too great, too monstrous for her to comprehend, so she slammed down into the saving figure of her David and began clawing at the torn and bleeding flesh on its face, finally reaching for its eyes as a fist walloped into her mouth, causing no pain, leaving no impression. Nothing but the water left impressions now. She sank her fingers into one of the eyes and pulled it out as new cries filled the air. Black liquid ran through her clenched fingers and into the savior's gaping mouth as the hungry beast reached up to pull them both down into the murky blue beyond the swirling foam. She looked down to see a sloping canyon that opened itself full before her, filled with dark green leaves, black sea urchins, and small flowerlike white algae where fingerlings browsed. She reached out to touch them, her chest full of peace, just as a school of silvery sars, the goat bream, round and flat as saucers, swam by in rocky chaos. Bubbles escaped from her mouth and swelled on their way up through the pressure layers, flattening out like mushrooms when they pressed against the medium. The surface of the ocean shone down to her like the reflection of a defective mirror, and soon the arms of the savior, her David, soon its arms slumped to its side, a small school of fish burrowing their way into its skull through the open eye socket. She closed her eyes and heard no sounds, save for that of a mild

stream that flowed gently through her brain, a stream
where so many maidens dipped into its waters with
decaying and leaking jars, jars that returned the waters
to this stream, so serene and cool and rewarding, like
the wind from the wings that flapped over the shore
of dreams and demons . . .

A trident was offered up to her . . .

The maidens looked to her and smiled . . .

She felt David's loving arms pull away . . .

. . . bubbles broke against the surface.

Sometime later Debra sat up on the beach and opened
her eyes, watching as the heavy clouds began breaking
up and allowing some sunlight to ripple through. She
turned and watched the headlights of David's car fizzle
out. Beside her there lay one starfish, and next to it
a shoe she recognized as being David's. The tide was
running far, far away, and Debra smiled. Yes, my
Amymone. Love is born of fear, and this fear is manifested in our loneliness. Maybe now David knew how
she'd felt all this time, and maybe, maybe *soon*, as
soon as the sleeping monster below began to release
its breath, maybe then she'd know how David had felt
during those last few moments, and then the two of
them would be together at last, united forever there
within the waves. . . .

Which was all she'd ever wanted; probably since the
moment of her birth.

She smiled, crossed her legs, and turned to face the
figure kneeling next to her. So beautiful was this
stranger, who was not a stranger at all.

"I'm waiting for David," said Debra. "He'll be coming back soon."

"They all come back," said the figure. Debra smiled at her newfound sister, stood erect, and picked up her jar.

There was much to be done, here by the waters.

INTRODUCTION TO

" COLT . 24 "

by Rick Hautala

Writing this introduction may be more difficult than I thought, especially since I've always been the kind of person who has trouble remembering what he had for supper last night. But writing and selling your first short story is (or should be) a little like witnessing the birth of your first child. Even though "Colt .24" is *(gasp!)* more than fifteen years old, there are some things about it—besides being my first published short story—that make it memorable for me.

The conventional wisdom, at least as far as I've experienced it, is that writers have to work their way up—they must earn their stripes, as it were. Colleges and universities in particular are guilty of fostering the misconception that, in order to become a "real" writer, you *must* start with the "easier" stuff—you know, poems and short stories, honing your skills until you have what it takes (if you have it at all) to begin work on that ultimate achievement, your first novel. In keeping with the anti-pedantic attitudes expressed in the following short story. I'll say flatly—that's bullshit!

Okay. I'll moderate myself: that isn't necessarily true. I know I'm not the only writer who is an exception to that rule. I had two published novels, and two more under contract before I sold my first short story. Oh, I had tried a few times. Besides a half dozen or so aborted attempts, I may have completed three or four short stories, one or two of which I sent out to magazines where they garnered their (deserved and humiliating) rejection. There was one particularly scathing—perfectly accurate—rejection from Ben Bova at *Analog* for a story called "The Path of My Birthing." He said that, at the core, the idea for the story was "cute," but it didn't quite work.

"Cute!"

When I stared thinking seriously about writing, my first impulse was to tackle a novel head on. Maybe I was too foolish to realize the folly of that, but that's a discussion best saved for another time. In the summer of 1976, I rolled up my sleeves and began work on the werewolf novel that became my first published novel, *Moondeath*. I'd had ideas and inner drives to write stories ever since I can remember, but the only difference between the (eventually) published writer and someone who "has always wanted" to write is that the (eventually) published writer applies the seat of his or her pants to a chair with a typewriter or keyboard within reach.

So I took two years to write *Moondeath* on a manual typewriter, and it took two years beyond that finally to sell it. Pretty fast, when you think about it, but I did have Stephen King (who had read and liked the manuscript) sending it around, recommending it to editors and, eventually, his agent. (Thanks, Steve!) After a while, the book found a home. Not the home I expected, and not for anywhere near the money I had wanted, but a home.

I was a published novelist.

Moondeath (not my original title, by the way) was followed a year later by *Moonbog* (most *definitely* not my original title). The books and I got some attention, at least locally. That's where that "other horror writer from Maine" business began. (Sorry, Steve!) My next book, *Nightstone* (again not my title) came out in 1986, and it sold well over a million copies. It's been the life of a freelance novelist ever since then, with all its requisite ups and downs.

As I said, I consider myself primarily a novelist, and I expected to be writing novels for the rest of my life. My uncle George Pistenmaa was a carpenter his whole life. Although he was a wizard who could make just about anything from a house to a finely detailed chair or spice rack out of wood, he used to say that he liked rough-framing houses because he could make so many little mistakes that the big ones wouldn't show.

That idea seemed to apply to writing as well. I avoided writing short stories because, like fine furniture, the short story form was so demanding that, one little slip within its ten or twenty pages, and you were lost. I liked the room, the freedom to roam that writing novels gave me. I also liked the money. It was—

and still is—extremely difficult (read: pretty much impossible) to make a living exclusively as a short story writer. I was working on my next novel and never even considered writing short stories until I got a call from Charles Waugh. Charles had edited several anthologies with Martin Greenberg, and he was calling to ask if I'd be interested in contributing a story to an anthology he was preparing with Marty and Isaac Asimov.

Isaac Asimov!

I had read Asimov since . . . forever. He was one of the gods, along with Heinlein, Clarke, Burroughs, and Bradbury. I was dizzy and thrilled that I had been asked to write a story that Isaac Asimov would not only read, but might even consider good enough to publish. I was also scared and intimidated because my (two—count 'em boys and girls, *two*) published novels, while written with all the heart and head and skill I could muster at the time, seemed a bit like flukes to me. (Yes, to be honest, at times I *did* think that they had been published only because Steve had helped me. It took me another half dozen novels to get over that idea. Another discussion for another time.) Being asked for a short story, I realized, was taking at least one more step up into the ranks of the "real" writers who were capable of producing on demand. The thought scared the beejezus out of me.

The parameters were simple enough as Charles explained them. The editors wanted a "deal with the devil" story. Since my masters degree from the University of Maine was in English Literature with a concentration in Renaissance Literature, I figured a variation of the Doctor Faustus story would do. Of course, I needed a twist. I have no idea how I came up with the idea of a gun that . . .

Wait a second.

I don't want to give anything away. Suffice it to say that, after a phone conversation or two with Charles, he and I came up with the "McGuffin" for this story. I remember working hard on the story, writing draft after draft until I was satisfied, and then writing draft after draft until Charles was satisfied.

The story was published in 1987, in *Isaac Asimov's Magical Worlds of Fantasy #8: Devils*. I remember being as thrilled seeing my story in that book as I had been when I saw my first novel in print. It marked a true watershed for me: I had published novels *and* a published short story. That—and nothing else—made me a "real" writer.

Since then, I've had well over fifty short stories published. I don't mean to sound like a snob about it, but I still consider myself primarily a novelist who only writes a short story when asked to by an editor or publisher. The form is too difficult, too demanding. To think just because you can write an adequate novel means you can also write an adequate short story (or vice versa) is another fallacy I've often heard in academic circles . . . usually propounded by someone who has been unable to complete, much less sell, anything of *any* length!

So it's fitting and satisfying and just plain cool that Marty is reprinting my first published short story in

Horrible Beginnings. I'm thrilled to see it get another run around the track where people who haven't read it before will see how I've modernized the Doctor Faustus legend. And I'm glad that, once again, I can dedicate "Colt .24" to:

> Charles Waugh, Marty Greenberg,
> and in memory of Isaac Asimov.

COLT . 24

by Rick Hautala

DIARY *entry one:* approximately 10:00 A.M. on Valentine's Day—*hah!* What irony!

If you've ever spent any time in academic circles, you've no doubt heard the expression "Publish or perish." Simply put, it means that if you intend to keep your cushy teaching position, at least at any decent college or university, you've got to publish in academic journals. I suppose this is to prove you've been doing research, but it also contributes to the prestige of your school.

My experience, at least in the English department here at the University of Southern Maine, is that the more obscure and unread the periodical, the more prestige is involved. I mean, if you write novels or stories that don't pretend to art, you can kiss your tenure good-bye. A good friend of mine here did just that—wrote and sold dozens of stories and even one novel, but because it was seen as "commercial" fiction, he didn't keep his job. After he was denied tenure, a few years back, he and I used to joke about how he had published *and perished!*

I have reason to be cynical. The doctor who talked with me last night might have a fancier, more clinical terms for it, but I might be tempted to translate his conclusions about me to something a little simpler: let's try "crazy as a shit-house rat."

That's crazy, all right; but just read on. I'm writing this all down as fast as I can because I know I don't have much time. I'm fighting the English teacher in me who wants to go back and revise and hone this all down until it's perfect, but if I'm right . . . Oh, Jesus! If I'm *right.* . . .

Look, I'll try to start at the start. Every story has a beginning, a middle, and an end, I've always told my students. Life, unfortunately, doesn't always play out that way. Sure, the beginning's at birth and the end's at death—it's filling up the middle part that's a bitch.

I don't know if this whole damned thing started when I first saw Rose McAllister . . . Rosie. She was sitting in the front row the first day of my 8:00 A.M. Introduction to English Literature class last fall. It might have been then that everything started, but I've gotta be honest. I mean, at this point, it doesn't matter. I think I'll be dead . . . and *really* in Hell within . . . maybe four hours.

So when I first saw Rosie, I didn't think right off the bat: God! I want to have an affair with her.

That sounds so delicate—"have an affair." I wanted to, sure; but that was after I got to know her. We started sleeping together whenever we could . . . which wasn't often, you see, because of Sally. My wife. My dear, departed wife!

I guess if I were really looking for the beginning of this whole damned mess, I'd have to say it was when we started our study of Marlowe's *Doctor Faustus*. Your basic "deal with the devil" story. I didn't mention too much of this to the police shrink because . . . well, if you tell someone like that that you struck a deal with the devil, sold him your soul—yes, I signed the agreement with my own blood—you expect him to send you up to the rubber room on P-6. If I'm wrong, I don't want to spend my time writing letters home with a Crayola, you know.

I'm getting ahead of myself, but as I said, I don't have much time . . . at least, I don't think so.

Okay, so Rosie and I, sometime around the middle of the fall semester, began to "sleep together." Another delicate term because we did very little "sleeping." We got whatever we could, whenever we could—in my office, usually, or—once or twice—in a motel room, once in my car in the faculty parking lot outside of Bailey Hall. Whenever and wherever. The first mistake we made was being seen at the Roma, in Portland, by Hank and Mary Crenshaw. The Roma! As an English teacher, I can appreciate the irony of *that,* too. Sally and I celebrated our wedding anniversary there every year. Being seen there on a Friday night, with a college sophomore ("young enough to be your daughter!" Sally took no end of pleasure repeating), by your wife's close (not best, but close) friend is downright stupid. I still cringe when I imagine the glee in Mary's voice when she told Sally. Hell! I never liked Mary, and she never liked me. Hank—he was all right, but I always told Sally that Mary was *her* friend, not mine.

So, Sally found out. Okay, so plenty of married men (and women) get caught screwing around. Sometimes the couple can cope—work it out. Other times, they can't. We couldn't. I should say, Sally couldn't. She set her lawyer—Walter Altschuler—on me faster than a greyhound on a rabbit. That guy would have had my gonads if they hadn't been attached!

But I'm not the kind of guy who takes that kind of stuff—from *anyone!* And, in an ironic sort of way, I'm getting paid back for that, too. If someone sics a lawyer on me, I'm gonna fight back.

Now here's where it gets a little weird. If I told that police shrink all of this, he'd bounce me up to P-6 for sure. I said we were reading *Faustus,* and that's when I decided to do a bit of—let's call it research. I dug through the library and found what was supposedly a magician's handbook—you know, a grimoire. I decided to try a bit of necromancy.

Look, I'm not crazy! I went into it more than half-skeptical. And I want to state for the record here that I . . .

Diary entry two: two hours later. Times's running out for sure!

Sorry for the interruption. I'm back now after wasting two hours with the shrink again. He ran me over the story again, but—I think—I held up pretty well. I didn't tell him what I'm going to write here. I want this all recorded so if I'm right . . . If I'm right. . . .

Where was I? Oh yeah. Necromancy. A deal with the devil. Yes—yes—*yess!* Signed in *blood!*

The library on the Gorham campus had a grimoire. Well, actually a facsimile of one, published a few years ago by Indiana University Press. It's amazing what's published these days. I wonder if the person who edited that text—I can't remember his name—kept his job. I looked up a spell to summon the devil and— Now I *know* you're gonna think I'm crazy! I did it! I actually summoned up the devil!

Laugh! Go ahead! I'll be dead soon—in Hell!—and it won't matter to me!

I have a key to Bailey Hall, so I came back to my office late at night—sometime after eleven o'clock, so I could be ready by midnight. After making sure my door was locked, I started to work. Pushing back the cheap rug I had by my desk (to keep the rollers of my chair from squeaking), I drew a pentagram on the floor, using a black Magic Marker. I placed a black candle—boy, were they hard to find—at each of the five points and lighted them. Then, taking the black leather-bound book, I began to recite the Latin incantation backwards. Actually, I was surprised that it worked—my Latin was so rusty, I was afraid I'd mispronounce something and end up summoning a talking toadstool or something. But it worked—it *actually* worked! In a puff of sulfurous fumes Old Nick himself appeared.

Looking around, he said, "Well, at least you're not another damned politician! What do you want in return for your soul?"

With his golden, cat-slit eyes burning into me, I had the feeling he already knew—more clearly than I did at that moment. Anyway, I told him. I said that I wanted an absolutely foolproof way of killing my wife and not getting caught. I told him I was willing to sign my soul over to him—yes! Dear God! In *blood!* If I could somehow get rid of Sally and be absolutely *certain* I wouldn't get caught.

I'm writing this, you must know by now, in a jail cell. I'm the prime suspect, but I haven't been charged with anything. I have a perfect alibi, you see, and there are other problems, too; but if you read the *Evening Express,* you'll know soon enough that I didn't get away with it.

What the devil did was hand me a revolver; he called it a Colt .24—a specially "modified" Colt .45—and a box of nice, shiny, brass-jacketed bullets. He told me all I had to do, after I signed the agreement, of course, was point the gun at Sally—he suggested I sneak home sometime before lunch someday—pull the trigger, throw the gun away, and make *sure* I went to work as usual the next day. If I did what he said, he guaranteed I'd go free.

Sounded okay to me. At this point, I was well past rationally analyzing the situation. I was under a lot of pressure, you've got to understand. My wife's lawyer had stuck the end nozzle of his vacuum cleaner down into my wallet and was sucking up the bucks. I'd been without sleep for nearly two days and nights running— I was getting so worked up about Sally.

And the capper was Rosie. As soon as she found out that Sally knew about us, she cooled off. Maybe— I hate to think it!—it was just the chance of getting caught that added to her excitement—her sense of adventure. Once we got caught, the thrill was gone for her. Could she have been *that* shallow?

I wasn't completely convinced this whole business with the devil had really worked, because . . . well, I must've fallen asleep after he pricked my finger so I could sign the contract, gave me the gun, and disappeared. I woke up, stiff-necked and all, flat on my back on the floor of my office just before my eight o'clock class the next morning. The candles had burned out, but in the early morning light, I could see the pentagram still there, so I knew I hadn't dreamed *everything*. I also had the gun—a Colt .24.

I'd been asleep—I don't know how long. Not more than four hours, I figure. I had started the summoning at midnight, like you're supposed to. I have no idea how long it took, but—at least for me—old Satan didn't waste any time with visions of power and glory, or processions of spirits. Nothing, really. At times, thinking about it, I could just as easily have been talking to Old Man Olsen, the janitor in Bailey Hall!

But, as I said, I also had the gun, and—damned if I didn't decide then and there that I'd use it. I had my two classes first. But after that, I was going straight home and point it at Sally and pull the trigger—even if, then and there, it blew her out through the picture window. I'd reached my limit which, I'd like to think, was considerably beyond what most men can stand.

So I did. After the second class—between classes I had time to drag the rug back and gulp down some coffee and an Egg McMuffin—I took off for home. Sally, as luck would have it, was— Damn! Here they come again!

Diary entry three: more than an hour gone—mere minutes left!

This time the police came in again. Talk about being confused. I think they'd like to charge me. But my alibi is solid and they can't get my gun to fire. So they asked me to fill them in on my relationship with Sally. They said that maybe it could give them a lead on who else might have killed her. They said I'd probably be released shortly. *Hah!* As if that might make a difference.

Well, as I was saying—Sally was home and her lawyer, old Walter-baby—was there with her. I sort of wondered why he was there—at *my* house. Maybe nosing around gave him a better idea how to skin me to the bone. Or maybe getting into her pants was part of his fee. But I couldn't afford to leave a witness, so whatever he was doing, that was just his tough luck. One more lawyer in Hell wasn't going to matter.

I walked in from the kitchen and nodded a greeting to the two of them, sitting on the couch. I said something about having forgotten some test papers as I put the briefcase down on the telephone table, opened it, and slowly took out the gun. Keeping it shielded from them with the opened top of the briefcase, I brought the gun up, took aim at him and squeezed the trigger. Not once—not twice—*three* times! Good number, three. A literature teacher knows all about the significance of the number three.

Nothing happened! There was no sound—although I had been careful to slip a bullet into each chamber before I left the office. There was no kick in my hand. There wasn't even much of a *click*. The only thing I could think was that maybe the Colt wouldn't work for someone who wasn't part of the deal. So I pointed it at her and fired off three more shots—with the same result. I do remember smelling—or thinking I smelled—a faint aroma of spent gunpowder, but I chalked that up to wishful thinking.

Sally and Walter ignored me, just kept right on talking as I gawked at them . . . so I slipped the gun back into the briefcase, shut it, and went up to the bedroom and shuffled around a bit, sounding busy while I tried to figure things out. I'd been packing to move out, but Sally—against old Walter-baby's advice, I might add— had said it was all right for me to stay at the house until the apartment I'd rented in town opened up the first of the month. Thanks, Sally. As it turned out, that was the last favor you ever did for me—except a day later, when you dropped dead!

So I left the house for my next class—with Sally and Walter sitting on the couch just as alive as they could be—feeling as though I'd been ripped off—set up or something by the devil. His gun was a dud, as far as I was concerned.

Back in my office about two that afternoon, I checked the Colt and was surprised to see six empty shells in the chamber—no bullets. Could I have been dumb enough to load the gun with empty shells? I didn't think so, but I tossed the empties and slipped in six new bullets from the devil's box. I was getting a little bit scared that I *had* hallucinated the summoning, but that still didn't explain where I had gotten the Colt.

By then I wasn't thinking too clearly, so I decided to test the gun right there in my office. I sighted along the barrel at one of the pictures on my wall—one of my favorites, actually: a silkscreen advertisement for the Dartmouth Christmas Revels—and gently squeezed the trigger. Nothing happened. Quickly, I aimed at my doctoral dissertation—now *there* was something else to hate—on the top shelf of my bookcase and pulled the trigger.

Nothing.

Again, aiming at the pencil sharpener beside the door, I squeezed the trigger.

Nada!

I pointed at the wall and snapped the trigger three more times, and still nothing happened. The tinge of gunpowder I thought I smelled couldn't have really been there, I thought . . . just my imagination, I guessed. But you shouldn't ever *guess* when the devil has your soul!

Again, though—and it struck me as really weird this time—when I opened the chamber all six bullets were spent. Maybe they were dummies or something—not really made of lead. Or maybe I was the dummy being led. I got the box, now minus a total of twelve bullets, and after inspecting them closely—they seemed real— reloaded, put the gun on the desk, and tilted back in my chair.

I'd been had, for sure, I thought, with rage and stark fear tossing me like a seesaw. I had signed my soul over to the devil for *what?* For a revolver that didn't even work!

Anyway, like I said, the next day at noon, Sally was dead. Our neighbor, Mrs. Benton, said she heard three gunshots from our house. Afraid that there was a robbery or something going on, she stayed home and, clutching her living room curtains to hide herself as she watched our house, called the Gorham police. They came shortly after that, and found Sally dead of three gunshot wounds to the head.

I, of course, didn't know this at the time. I was just coming back to my office, following a graduate seminar on Elizabethan Drama. I hadn't gone home the night before and had been forced to sleep—again— on my office floor, so I wasn't in the best of moods.

I spent the next couple of hours sitting at my desk, working through a stack of tests and pondering everything that had happened recently when there was a knock on the door. I scooped the Colt into the top desk drawer but, foolishly, didn't slide the drawer completely shut before I went to the door. Two uniformed policemen entered, politely shook hands, and then informed me that my wife had been murdered . . . shot to death by a Colt. 45.

I fell apart—wondering to myself which I felt more—shock or relief. I hadn't done it, but *someone* had! The policemen waited patiently for me to gain control of myself and explained that they wanted to know where I had been in the past three hours. Apparently Mrs. Benton had seen fit to fill them in on our domestic quarrels. They also wanted to know if I owned a Colt .45.

If this whole story has a tragic mistake—for me, at lest—it was not following the devil's advice to the letter. That's how he gets you, you know. I should have *realized* that! He had said that if I aimed the gun at Sally, pulled the trigger, and then threw the gun away, I'd never be caught.

But I didn't throw the damned thing away.

If you had asked me then, I suppose I would have said the gun was worthless. What difference would it make if I kept it or tossed it? I hadn't summoned the devil that night. I'd fallen asleep and, beaten by exhaustion and the pressure I was under, I'd had a vivid nightmare. I hadn't *really* summoned the devil. Stuff like that didn't *really* happen!

I gave the cops my alibi, and it was solid. When the

shots rang out, I was more than twenty miles from my house, on the university's Portland campus, lecturing on Shakespeare's use of horse imagery in his history plays. You can't go against the testimony of a roomful of graduate students.

About then one of the policemen noticed the revolver in the desk drawer, and, eyeing me suspiciously, asked if they could take a look at it. Sure. There was no denying that I did own a Colt .45, but after they inspected it for a moment, I took it from them.

"Look," I said, hefting the Colt. "This sucker doesn't even work. It's a model or something." I opened the chamber, showed them that the gun was loaded, clicked it shut, and, with a flourish, pressed the barrel to my temple.

"See?" I said, as I snapped the trigger three times. "Nothing happens. It's a fake."

That seemed to satisfy them. They thanked me for my cooperation and left, saying they'd wait in the hallway until I felt ready to come with them to the hospital to identify the body.

But they had no more than swung the door shut behind them when shots rang out in my office! I was just turning to pick up my briefcase when the center of the Christmas Revels poster blew away. I turned and stared, horrified, as the top row of books on the bookcase suddenly jumped. I could see a large, black, smoking hole in the spine of my dissertation. Then the pencil sharpener by the door exploded into a twisted mess of metal. Three more shots removed pieces of plaster and wood from the office walls.

With the sound of the six shots still ringing in my ears, I heard the two policemen burst back into my office. They both had their revolvers drawn and poised.

"I thought that gun didn't work," one of them shouted, leaning cautiously against the door frame. He was looking at me suspiciously, but then his expression changed to confusion when he registered that the Colt wasn't in my hand. It was lying on the desk, where I had placed it as they left.

"Man, I don't know what's going on here," the other one said. "But you better come downtown until we can check the ballistics to make *sure* this wasn't the gun that killed her."

I was in a state of near shock—I'm sure my face had turned chalky white because I felt an icy numbness rush across my cheeks and down the back of my neck. A sudden realization was beginning to sink in. It had been almost—*no!*—*exactly* twenty-four hours ago that I had aimed and shot the revolver six times in my office. Six times! And nothing had happened—until *now!*

This bit about the ballistics test had cracked my nerve. I mean, at this point I was convinced that it hadn't been coincidence. The shots I had banged off twenty-four hours earlier must have done in Sally. And I knew that, if the cops checked it out, the ballistics would match.

What about sleazy Walter Altschuler? Was he dead, too? With a sudden sickening rush, I remembered what the devil had said to me the night I summoned him . . . he said the gun was a Colt *.24!* A special, *modified* Colt .45!

I tried to force myself to appear calm. *Damn my soul to Hell!* I had pointed the gun at my head as a *beau geste* and pulled the trigger—three times! I remembered—now—that when I had done that, I *had* smelled at trace of spent gunpowder . . . like I had that morning at the house, when I had targeted Walter and Sally.

Then Joan Oliver, the department secretary poked her head—cautiously, I might add— into my office to tell the policemen they had a phone call. I fell apart completely, knowing what it would be. Walter Altschuler had been found dead in his car in the Casco Bank parking lot in downtown Portland with three .45 caliber bullet wounds in his head.

I'd been *had!* I signed that damned contract . . . in *blood!* And I *had had* that damned gun. And it *had* worked! And the devil *had* cheated me, but good, in the bargain.

So while sitting here in the cell, after coming to my senses this morning, I asked for some paper and a pen. If I'm wrong, I don't want to tell my story and be committed. But if I'm right, I want to get all of this down to leave a permanent record before those bullets from Hell blow my head off.

215

INTRODUCTION TO

"PRINCE OF FLOWERS"

by Elizabeth Hand

From the late 1970s until 1987 I worked at the National Air and Space Museum in Washington, D.C. I'd got kicked out of college in 1979, figuring this was a necessary part of my résumé as a would-be writer. Unfortunately, I hadn't actually gotten anything published yet, and was in fact spending more time killing my few remaining brain cells dancing through D.C.'s nascent punk scene than writing. My job at NASM consisted of sorting through the museum's collection of half a million photographic images, putting each photo into alphabetical order and then hand numbering it. As a career move, this was on a par with proofreading the telephone book; since I hadn't yet read *Little, Big,* I didn't know there was a literary precedent for this kind of thing. I was pretty seriously depressed.

One day I discovered a shop near the museum

called the Artifactory. It sold African and Asian imports—masks, jewelry, statuary—the kind of stuff you can find all over nowadays, but which back then was fairly unusual. I couldn't afford anything, but I liked to look; the shop was dark and it smelled nice, and the owner was friendly.

I can't remember when I first saw the puppet. It was shoved into a corner, this supernaturally beautiful wooden Balinese puppet with a jeweled batik gown and hand-painted face. I knew I had to own it. It cost fifty dollars, which was a *huge* amount of money for me in those days. I had never bought something so frivolous before, or simply because I thought it was beautiful. But I remember walking back to work, cradling it in my arms; when I got back to the cubicle I shared with my friend Greg, I showed it to him and said, "This is going to bring me luck. This is going to change my life."

I wrote this story shortly afterward. I was taking a writing workshop with novelist Richard Grant, and "Prince of Flowers" was the first thing I showed the group. Every hair on my head stood up when I read his comments on the story: I knew that I'd finally done something right.

I sent the story to Tappan King, editor of the then-thriving *Twilight Zone Magazine*. Nine months went by and I heard nothing; then the manuscript was returned with a standard rejection letter. I'd got plenty of these before (I stored them in the freezer), but this time I was crushed (and furious), because I knew damn well no one had ever looked at the story.

The happy ending came because my best friend Paul Witcover had just started working as a reader for *TZ*'s slush pile. I sent Paul the story and he passed it on to Tappan, who called to tell me he was buying it.

"Prince of Flowers" was published in February 1987. Eighteen months later I quit my job and, with no visible means of support, moved to Maine.

The puppet remains here on my desk, where it's been since I bought it.

PRINCE OF FLOWERS

by Elizabeth Hand

HELEN'S first assignment on the inventory project was to the Department of Worms. For two weeks she paced the narrow alleys between immense tiers of glass cabinets, opening endless drawers of freeze-dried invertebrates and tagging each with an acquisition number. Occasionally she glimpsed other figures, drab as herself in government-issue smocks, gray shadows stalking through the murky corridors. They waved at her but seldom spoke, except to ask directions; everyone got lost in the Museum.

218

Helen loved the hours lost in wandering the laby-rinth of storage rooms, research labs, chilly vaults crammed with effigies of Yanomano Indians and stuffed jaguars. Soon she could identify each depart-ment by its smell: acrid dust from the feathered pelts in Ornithology; the cloying reek of fenugreek and syrup in Mammalogy's roach traps; fish and formalde-hyde in Icthyology. Her favorite was Paleontology, an annex where the air smelled damp and clean, as though beneath the marble floors trickled hidden water, undiscovered caves, mammoth bones to match those stored above. When her two weeks in Worms ended she was sent to Paleo, where she delighted in the skeletons strewn atop cabinets like forgotten toys, disembodied skulls glaring from behind wastebaskets and bookshelves. She found a *fabrosaurus ischium* wrapped in brown paper and labeled in crayon; beside it a huge hand-hewn crate dated 1886 and marked WYOMING MEGOSAUR. It had never been opened. Some mornings she sat with a small mound of fossils before her, fitting the pieces together with the aid of a Victorian monograph. Hours passed in total silence, weeks when she saw only three or four people, cura-tors slouching in and out of their research cubicles. On Fridays, when she dropped off her inventory sheets, they smiled. Occasionally even remembered her name. But mostly she was left alone, sorting car-tons of bone and shale, prying apart frail skeletons of extinct fish as though they were stacks of newsprint.

Once, almost without thinking, she slipped a fossil fish into the pocket of her smock. The fossil was the

length of her hand, as perfectly formed as a fresh
beech leaf. All day she fingered it, tracing the imprint
of bone and scale. In the bathroom later she wrapped
it in paper towels and hid it in her purse to bring
home. After that she started taking things.

At a downtown hobby shop she bought little brass
and lucite stands to display them in her apartment.
No one else ever saw them. She simply liked to look
at them alone.

Her next transfer was to Mineralogy, where she
counted misshapen meteorites and uncut gems. Gems
bored her, although she took a chunk of petrified
wood and a handful of unpolished amethysts and put
them in her bathroom. A month later she was permanently assigned to Anthropology.

The Anthropology Department was in the most remote corner of the Museum; its proximity to the boiler
room made it warmer than the Natural Sciences wing,
the air redolent of spice woods and exotic unguents
used to polish arrowheads and axe shafts. The ceiling
reared so high overhead that the rickety lamps swayed
slightly in drafts that Helen longed to feel. The constant subtle motion of the lamps sent flickering waves
of light across the floor. Raised arms of Balinese statues seemed to undulate, and points of light winked
behind the empty eyeholes of feathered masks.

Everywhere loomed shelves stacked with smooth
ivory and gaudily beaded brackets and neck-rings.
Helen crouched in corners loading her arms with ban-
gles until her wrists ached from their weight. She un-
earthed dusty lurid figures of temple demons and

cleaned them, polished hollow cheeks and lapis eyes before stapling a number to each figure. A corner piled with tipi poles hid an abandoned desk that she claimed and decorated with mummy photographs and a ceramic coffee mug. In the top drawer she stored her cassette tapes and, beneath her handbag, a number of obsidian arrowheads. While it was never officially designated as her desk, she was annoyed one morning to find a young man tilted backward in the chair, shuffling through her tapes.

"Hello," he greeted her cheerfully. Helen winced and nodded coolly. "These your tapes? I'll borrow this one someday, haven't got the album yet. Leo Bryant—"

"Helen," she replied bluntly. "I think there's an empty desk down by the slit-gongs."

"Thanks, I just started. You a curator?"

Helen shook her head, rearranging the cassettes on the desk, "No. Inventory project." Pointedly she moved his knapsack to the floor.

"Me too. Maybe we can work together sometime."

She glanced at his earnest face and smiled. "I like to work alone, thanks." He looked hurt, and she added, "Nothing personal—I just like it that way. I'm sure we'll run into each other. Nice to meet you, Leo." She grabbed a stack of inventory sheets and walked away down the corridor.

They met for coffee one morning. After a few weeks they met almost every morning, sometime even for lunch outside on the Mall. During the day Leo wandered over from his cubicle in Ethnology to pass on departmental gossip. Sometimes they had a drink after work, but never often enough to invite gossip themselves. Helen was happy with this arrangement, the curators delighted to have such a worker—quiet, without ambition, punctual. Everyone except Leo left her to herself.

Late one afternoon Helen turned at the wrong corner and found herself in a small cul-de-sac between stacks of crates that cut off light and air. She yawned, breathing the faint must of cinnamon bark as she traced her path on a crumpled inventory map. This narrow alley was unmarked; the adjoining corridors contained Malaysian artifacts, batik tools, long teak boxes of gongs. Fallen crates, clumsily hewn cartons overflowing with straw were scattered on the floor. Splintered panels snagged her sleeves as she edged her way down the aisle. A sweet musk hung about these cartons, the languorous essence of unknown blossoms.

At the end of the cul-de-sac an entire row of crates had toppled, as though the weight of time had finally pitched them to the floor. Helen squatted and chose a box at random, a broad flat package like a portfolio. She pried the lid off to find a stack of leather cutouts curling with age, like dessicated cloth. She drew one carefully from the pile, frowning as its edges disintegrated at her touch. A shadow puppet, so fantastically elaborate that she couldn't tell if it was male or female; it scarcely looked human. Light glimmered through the grotesque latticework as Helen jerked it back and forth, its pale shadow dancing across the wall. Then the puppet split and crumbled into brittle curlicues that formed strange hieroglyphics on the black marble floor. Swearing softly, Helen replaced the lid, then jammed the box back into the shadows. Her fingers brushed another crate, of smooth polished mahogany. It had a comfortable heft as she pulled it into her lap. Each corner of the narrow lid was fixed with a large squareheaded nail. Helen yanked these out and set each upright in a row.

As she opened the box, dried flowers, seeds, and wood shavings cascaded into her lap. She inhaled, closing her eyes, and imagined blue water and firelight, sweet-smelling seeds exploding in the embers. She sneezed and opened her eyes to a cloud of dust wafting from the crate like smoke. Very carefully she worked her fingers into the fragrant excelsior, kneading the petals gently until she grasped something brittle and solid. She drew this out in a flurry of dead flowers.

It was a puppet: not a toy, but a gorgeously costumed figure, spindly arms clattering with glass and bone circlets, batik robes heavy with embroidery and beadwork. Long whittled pegs formed its torso and arms and the rods that swiveled it back and forth, so that its robes rippled tremulously, like a swallowtail's wings. Held at arm's length it gazed scornfully down at Helen, its face glinting with gilt paint. Sinuous vines twisted around each jointed arm. Flowers glowed within the rich threads of its robe, orchids blossoming in the folds of indigo cloth.

Loveliest of all was its face, the curve of cheeks and

chin so gracefully arched it might have been cast in gold rather than coaxed from wood. Helen brushed it with a finger: the glossy white paint gleamed as though still wet. She touched the carmine bow that formed its mouth, traced the jet-black lashes stippled across its brow, like a regiment of ants. The smooth wood felt warm to her touch as she stroked it with her fingertips. A courtesan might have perfected its sphinx's smile; but in the tide of petals Helen discovered a slip of paper covered with spidery characters. Beneath the straggling script another hand had shaped clumsy block letters spelling out the name *PRINCE OF FLOWERS*.

Once, perhaps, an imperial concubine had entertained herself with its fey posturing, and so passed the wet silences of a long green season. For the rest of the afternoon it was Helen's toy. She posed it and sent its robes dancing in the twilit room, the frail arms and tiny wrists twitching in a marionette's waltz.

Behind her a voice called, "Helen?"

"Leo," she murmured. "Look what I found."

He hunched beside her to peer at the figure. "Beautiful. Is that what you're on now? Balinese artifacts?"

She shrugged. "Is that what it is? I didn't know." She glanced down the dark rows of cabinets and sighed. "I probably shouldn't be here. It's just so hot—" She stretched and yawned as Leo slid the puppet from her hands.

"Can I see it?" He twisted it until its head spun and the stiff arms flittered. "Wild. Like one of those dancers in *The King and I*." He played with it absently, hypnotized by the swirling robes. When he stopped, the puppet jerked abruptly upright, its blank eyes staring at Helen.

"Be careful," she warned, kneading her smock between her thumbs. 'It's got to be a hundred years old." She held out her hands and Leo returned it, bemused.

"It's wild, whatever it is." He stood and stretched. "I'm going to get a soda. Want to come?"

"I better get back to what I was working on. I'm supposed to finish the Burmese section this week." Casually she set the puppet in its box, brushed the dried flowers from her lap and stood.

"Sure you don't want a soda or something?" Leo hedged plaintively, snapping his ID badge against his chest. "You said you were hot."

"No thanks," Helen smiled wanly. "I'll take a raincheck. Tomorrow."

Peeved, Leo muttered and stalked off. When his silhouette faded away she turned and quickly pulled the box into a dim corner. There she emptied her handbag and arranged the puppet at its bottom, wrapping Kleenex about its arms and face. Hairbrush, wallet, lipstick: all thrown back into her purse hiding the puppet beneath their clutter. She repacked the crate with its sad array of blossoms, hammering the lid back with her shoe. Then she scrabbled in the corner on her knees until she located a space between stacks off cartons. With a resounding crack the empty box struck the wall, and Helen grinned as she kicked more boxes to fill the gap. Years from now another inventory technician would discover it and wonder, as she had countless times, what had once been inside the empty carton.

When she crowded into the elevator that afternoon the leather handle of her purse stuck to her palm like wet rope. She shifted the bag casually as more people stepped on at each floor, heart pounding as she called goodbye to the curator for Indo-Asian Studies passing in the lobby. Imaginary prison gates loomed and crumbled behind Helen as she strode through the columned doors and into the summer street.

All the way home she smiled triumphantly, clutching her handbag to her chest. As she fumbled at the front door for her keys a fresh burst of scent rose from the recesses of her purse. Inside, another scent overpowered this faint perfume—the thick reek of creosote, rotting fruit, unwashed clothes. Musty and hot and dark as the Museum's dreariest basement, the only two windows faced onto the street. Traffic ground past, piping bluish exhaust through the screens. A grimy mirror reflected shabby chairs, an end table with lopsided lamp: furniture filched from college dormitories or reclaimed from the corner dumpster. No paintings graced the pocked walls, blotched with the crushed remains of roaches and silverfish.

But beautiful things shone here, gleaming from windowsills and cracked formica counters: the limp frond of a fossil fern, etched in obsidian glossy as wet tar; a whorled nautilus like a tiny whirlpool impaled upon a brass stand. In the center of a splintered coffee table was the imprint of a foot-long dragonfly's wing embedded in limestone, its filigreed scales a shattered prism.

Corners heaped with lemur skulls and slabs of petrified wood. The exquisite cone shells of poisonous mollusks. Mounds of green and golden iridescent beetles, like the coinage of a distant country. Patches of linoleum scattered with shark's teeth and arrowheads; a tiny skull anchoring a handful of emerald plumes that waved in the breeze like a sea-fan. Helen surveyed it all critically, noting with mild surprise a luminous pink geode: she'd forgotten that one. Then she set to work.

In a few minutes she'd removed everything from her bag and rolled the geode under a chair. She unwrapped the puppet on the table, peeling tissue from its brittle arms and finally twisting the long strand of white paper from its head, until she stood ankle-deep in a drift of tissue. The puppet's supporting rod slid neatly into the mouth of an empty beer bottle, and she arranged it so that the glass was hidden by its robes and the imperious face tilted upward, staring at the bug-flecked ceiling.

Helen squinted appraisingly, rearranged the feathers about the puppet, shoring them up with the carapaces of scarab beetles: still it looked all wrong. Beside the small proud figure, the fossils were muddy remains, the nautilus a bit of sea-wrack. A breeze shifted the puppet's robes, knocking the scarabs to the floor, and before she knew it Helen had crushed them, the little emerald shells splintering to gray dust beneath her heel. She sighed in exasperation: all her pretty things suddenly looked so mean. She moved the puppet to the window-sill, to another table, and finally into her bedroom. No corner of the flat could hold it without seeming even grimier than before. Helen swiped at cobwebs above the doorway before setting the puppet on her bedstand and collapsing with a sigh onto her mattress.

In the half-light of the windowless bedroom the figure was not so resplendent. Disappointed, Helen straightened its robes yet again. As she tugged the cloth into place, two violet petals, each the size of her pinky nail, slipped between her fingers. She rolled the tiny blossom between her palm, surprised at how damp and fresh they felt, how they breathed a scent like ozone, or seawater. Thoughtfully she rubbed the violets until only a gritty pellet remained between her fingers.

Flowers, she thought, and recalled the name on the paper she'd found. The haughty figure wanted flowers.

Grabbing her key and a rusty pair of scissors, she ran outside. Thirty minutes later she returned, laden with blossoms: torn branches of crape myrtle frothing pink and white, drooping tongues of honeysuckle, overblown white roses snipped from a neighbor's yard; chicory fading like a handful of blue stars. She dropped them all at the foot of the bed and then searched the kitchen until she found a duty wine ca-rafe and some empty jars. Once these were rinsed and filled with water she made a number of unruly bou-quets, then placed them all around the puppet, so that its pale head nodded amid a cloud of white and mauve and frail green.

Helen slumped back on the bed, grinning with approval. Bottles trapped the wavering pools of light and cast shimmering reflections across the walls. The crape myrtle sent the palest mauve cloud onto the ceiling, blurring the jungle shadows of the honeysuckle.

Helen's head blurred, as well. She yawned, drowsy from the thick scents of roses, cloying honeysuckle, all the languor of summer nodding in an afternoon. She fell quickly asleep, lulled by the breeze in the stolen garden and the dozy blur of a lost bumblebee.

Once, her sleep broke. A breath of motion against her shoulder—mosquito? spider? centipede?—then a tiny lancing pain, the touch of invisible legs or wings, and it was gone. Helen grimaced, scratched, staggered up and into the bathroom. Her bleary reflection showed a swollen bite on her shoulder. It tingled, and a drop of blood pearled at her touch. She put on a nightshirt, checked her bed for spiders, then tumbled back to sleep.

Much later she woke to a sound: once, twice, like the resonant *plank* of a stone tossed into a well. Then a slow melancholy note: another well, a larger stone striking its dark surface. Helen moaned, turning onto her side. Fainter echoes joined these first sounds, plangent tones sweet as rain in the mouth. Her ears rang with this steady pulse, until suddenly she clenched her hands and stiffened, concentrating on the noise.

From wall to ceiling to floor the thrumming echo bounced; grew louder, diminished, droned to a whisper. It did not stop. Helen sat up, bracing herself against the wall, the last shards of sleep fallen from her. Her hand slipped and very slowly she drew it toward her face. It was wet. Between her fingers glistened a web of water, looping like silver twine down her wrist until it was lost in the blue-veined valley of her elbow. Helen shook her head in disbelief and stared up at the ceiling. From one end of the room to the other stretched a filament of water, like a hairline fracture. As she watched, the filament snapped and a single warm drop splashed her temple. Helen swore and slid to the edge of the mattress, then stopped.

At first she thought the vases had fallen to the floor, strewing flowers everywhere. But the bottles remained on the bedstand, their blossoms casting ragged silhouettes in the dark. More flowers were scattered about the bottles: violets, crimson roses, a tendril rampant with tiny fluted petals. Flowers cascaded to the floor, nestled amid folds of dirty clothes. Helen plucked an orchid from the linoleum, blinking in amazement. Like a wavering pink flame it glowed, the feathery pistils staining her fingertips bright yellow. Absently Helen brushed the pollen onto her thigh, scraping her leg with a hangnail.

That small pain jarred her awake. She dropped the orchid. For the first time it didn't feel like a dream. The room was hot, humid as though moist towels pressed against her face. As she stared at her thigh the bright fingerprint, yellow as a crocus, melted and dissolved as sweat broke on her skin. She stepped forward, the orchid bursting beneath her heel like a ripe grape. A sickly smell rose from the broken flower. Each breath she took was heavy, as with rain, and she choked. The rims of her nostrils were wet. She sneezed, inhaling warm water. Water streamed down her cheeks and she drew her hand slowly upward, to brush the water from her eyes. She could move it no further than her lap. She looked down, silently mouthing bewilderment as she shook her head.

Another hand grasped her wrist, a hand delicate and limp as a cut iris wand, so small that she scarcely felt its touch open her pulse. Inside her skull the blood thrummed counterpoint to the *gamelan*, gongs echoing the throb and beat of her heart. The little hand disappeared. Helen staggered backward onto the bed, frantically scrambling for the light switch. In the darkness, something crept across the rippling bedsheets.

When she screamed her mouth was stuffed with roses, orchids, the corner of her pillowcase. Tiny hands pinched her nostrils shut and forced more flowers between her lips until she lay still, gagging on aromatic petals. From the rumpled bedclothes reared a shadow, child-size, grinning. Livid shoots of green and yellow encircled its spindly arms and the sheets whispered like rain as it crawled towards her. Like a great mantis it dragged itself forward on its long arms, the rough cloth of its robe catching between her knees, its white teeth glittering. She clawed through the sheets, trying to dash it against the wall. But she could not move. Flowers spilled from her mouth when she tried to scream, soft fingers of orchids sliding down her throat as she flailed at the bedclothes.

And the clanging of the gongs did not cease: not when the tiny hands pattered over her breasts; not when the tiny mouth hissed in her ear. Needle teeth pierced her shoulder as a long tongue unfurled and lapped there, flicking blood onto the blossoms wreathed about her neck. Only when the slender shadow withdrew and the terrible, terrible dreams began did the *gamelans* grow silent.

Nine thirty came, long after Helen usually met Leo in the cafeteria. He waited, drinking an entire pot of coffee before he gave up and wandered downstairs, piqued that she hadn't shown up for breakfast.

In the same narrow hallway behind the Malaysian artifacts he discovered her, crouched over a pair of tapered wooden crates. For a long moment he watched her, and almost turned back without saying anything. Her hair was dirty, twisted into a sloppy bun, and the hunch of her shoulders hinted at exhaustion. But before he could leave, she turned to face him, clutching the boxes to her chest.

"Rough night?" croaked Leo. A scarf tied around her neck didn't hide the bruises there. Her mouth was swollen, her eyes soft and shadowed with sleeplessness. He knew she must see people, men, boyfriends. But she had never mentioned anyone, never spoke of weekend trips or vacations. Suddenly he felt betrayed, and spun away to leave.

"Leo," murmured Helen, absently stroking the crate. "I can't talk right now. I got in so late. I'm kind of busy."

"I guess so." He laughed uncertainly, but stopped before turning the corner to see her pry open the lid

232

of the box, head bent so that he could not tell what it was she found inside.

A week passed. Leo refused to call her. He timed his forays to the cafeteria to avoid meeting her there. He left work late so he wouldn't see her in the elevator. Every day he expected to see her at his desk, find a telephone message scrawled on his memo pad. But she never appeared.

Another week went by. Leo ran into the curator for Indo-Asian Studies by the elevator.

"Have you seen Helen this week?" she asked, and Leo actually blushed at mention of her name.

"No," he mumbled. "Not for a while, really."

"Guess she's sick." The curator shrugged and stepped onto the elevator. Leo rode all the way down to the basement and roamed the corridors for an hour, dropping by the Anthropology office. No Helen, no messages from her at the desk.

He wandered back down the hall, pausing in the corridor where he had last seen her. A row of boxes had collapsed and he kicked at the cartons, idly knelt and read the names on the packing crates as if they held a clue to Helen's sudden change. Labels in Sanskrit, Vietnamese, Chinese, English, crumbling beside baggage labels and exotic postage stamps and scrawled descriptions of contents. WAJANG GOLEH, he read. Beneath was scribbled PUPPETS. He squatted on the floor, staring at the bank of crates, then half-heartedly started to read each label. Maybe she'd find him there. Perhaps she'd been sick, had a doctor's appointment. She might be late again.

A long box rattled when he shifted it. KRIS, read the label, and he peeked inside to find an ornate sword. A heavier box bore the legend SANGHY-ANG: SPIRIT PUPPET. And another that seemed to be empty, embellished with a flowing script: SEKAR MAS, and the clumsy translation PRINCE OF FLOWERS.

He slammed the last box against the wall and heard the dull creak of splintering wood. She would not be in today. She hadn't been in for two weeks.

That night he called her.

"Hello?"

Helen's voice; at least a man hadn't answered.

"Helen. How you doing? It's Leo."

"Leo." She coughed and he heard someone in the background. "It's you."

"Right," he said dryly, then waited for an apology, her embarrassed laugh, another cough that would be followed by an invented catalogue of hayfever, colds, flu. But she said nothing. He listened carefully and realized it wasn't a voice he had heard in the background but a constant stir of sound, like a fan, or running water. "Helen? You okay?"

A long pause. "Sure. Sure I'm okay." Her voice faded and he heard a high, piping note.

"You got a bird, Helen?"

"What?"

He shifted the phone to his other ear, shoving it closer to his head so he could hear better. "A bird. There's this funny voice, it sounds like you got a bird or something."

"No," replied Helen slowly. "I don't have a bird. There's nothing wrong with my phone." He could hear her moving around her apartment, the background noises rising and falling but never silent. "Leo, I can't talk now. I'll see you tomorrow, okay?"

"Tomorrow?" he exploded. "I haven't seen you in two weeks!"

She coughed and said, "Well, I'm sorry. I've been busy. I'll see you tomorrow. Bye."

He started to argue, but the phone was already dead.

She didn't come in the next day. At three o'clock he went to the Anthropology Department and asked the secretary if Helen had been in that morning.

"No," she answered, shaking her head. "And they've got her down as AWOL. She hasn't been in all week." She hesitated before whispering. "Leo, she hasn't looked very good lately. You think maybe . . . ." Her voice died and she shrugged, "Who knows," and turned to answer the phone.

He left work early, walking his bicycle up the garage ramp and wheeling it to the right, toward Helen's neighborhood. He was fuming, but a sliver of fear had worked its way through his anger. He had almost gone to her supervisor; almost phoned Helen first. Instead, he pedaled quickly down Pennsylvania Avenue, skirting the first lanes of rush hour traffic. Union Station loomed a few blocks ahead. He recalled an article in yesterday's *Post:* vandals had destroyed the rose garden in front of the station. He detoured through the bus lane that circled the building and skimmed around the desecrated garden, shaking his head and staring back in dismay. All the roses: gone. Someone had lopped each bloom from its stem. In spots the cobblestones were littered with mounds of blossoms, brown with decay. Here and there dead flowers still dangled from hacked stems. Swearing in disgust Leo made a final loop, nearly skidding into a bus as he looked back at the plundered garden. Then he headed toward Helen's apartment building a few blocks north.

Her windows were dark. Even from the street the curtains looked filthy, as though dirt and exhaust had matted them to the glass. Leo stood on the curb and stared at the blank eyes of each apartment window gaping in the stark concrete façade.

Who would want to live here? he thought ashamed. He should have come sooner. Shame froze into apprehension and the faintest icy sheath of fear. Hurriedly he locked his bike to a parking meter and approached her window, standing on tiptoe to peer inside. Nothing. The discolored curtains hid the rooms from him like clouds of ivory smoke. He tapped once, tentatively; then, emboldened by silence, rapped for several minutes, squinting to see any movement inside.

Still nothing. Leo swore out loud and slung his hands into his pockets, wondering lamely what to do. Call the police? Next of kin? He winced at the thought: as if she couldn't do that herself. Helen had always made it clear that she enjoyed being on her own. But the broken glass beneath his sneakers, windblown newspapers tugging at the bottom steps; the whole unkempt neighborhood denied that. Why here?

he thought angrily; and then he was taking the steps two at a time, kicking bottles and burger wrappers out of his path.

He waited by the door for five minutes before a teenage boy ran out. Leo barely caught the door before it slammed behind him. Inside, a fluorescent light hung askew from the ceiling, buzzing like a wasp. Helen's was the first door to the right. Circulars from convenience stores drifted on the floor, and on the far wall was a bank of mailboxes. One was ajar, stuffed with unclaimed bills and magazines. More envelopes piled on the steps. Each bore Helen's name.

His knocking went unanswered; but he thought he heard someone moving inside.

"Helen," he called softly. "It's Leo. You okay?"

He knocked harder, called her name, finally pounded with both fists. Still nothing. He should leave; he should call the police. Better still, forget ever coming here. But he was here, now; the police would question him no matter what; the curator for Indo-Asian Studies would look at him askance. Leo bit his lip and tested the doorknob. Locked; but the wood gave way slightly as he leaned against it. He rattled the knob and braced himself to kick the door in.

He didn't have to. In his hand the knob twisted and the door swung inwards, so abruptly that he fell inside. The door banged shut behind him. He glanced across the room, looking for her; but all he saw was gray light, the gauzy shadows cast by gritty curtains. Then he breathed in, gagging, and pulled his sleeve to his mouth until he gasped through the cotton. He backed toward the door, slipping on something dank, like piles of wet clothing. He glanced at his feet and grunted in disgust.

Roses. They were everywhere: heaps of rotting flowers, broken branches, leaves stripped from bushes, an entire small ficus tree tossed into the corner. He forgot Helen, turned to grab the doorknob and tripped on an uprooted azalea. He fell, clawing at the wall to balance himself. His palms splayed against the plaster and slid as though the surface was till wet. Then, staring upward he saw that it *was* wet. Water streamed from the ceiling, flowing down the wall to soak his shirt cuffs. Leo moaned. His knees buckled as he sank, arms flailing, into the mass of decaying blossoms. Their stench suffocated him; his eyes watered as he retched and tried to stagger back to his feet.

Then he heard something, like a bell, or a telephone; then another faint sound, like an animal scratching overhead, Carefully he twisted to stare upwards, trying not to betray himself by moving too fast. Something skittered across the ceiling, and Leo's stomach turned dizzily. What could be up there? A second blur dashed to join the first; golden eyes stared down at him, unblinking.

Geckos, he thought frantically. She had pet geckos. She *has* pet geckos. Jesus.

She couldn't be here. It was too hot, the stench horrible: putrid water, decaying plants, water everywhere. His trousers were soaked from where he had fallen, his knees ached from kneeling in a trough of water pooling against the wall. The floor had warped and more flowers protruded from cracks between the linoleum, brown fronds of iris and rooting honeysuckle. From another room trickled the sound of water dripping steadily, as though a tap was running.

He had to get out. He'd leave the door open—police, a landlord. Someone would call for help. But he couldn't reach the door. He couldn't stand. His feet skated across the slick tiles as his hands tore uselessly through wads of petals. It grew darker. Golden bands rippled across the floor as sunlight filtered through the gray curtains. Leo dragged himself through rotting leaves, his clothes sopping, tugging aside mats of greenery and broken branches. His leg ached where he'd fallen on it and his hands stung, prickcd by unseen thorns.

Something brushed against his fingers and he forced himself to look down, shuddering. A shattered nautilus left a thin red line across his hand, the sharp fragments gilded by the dying light. As he looked around he noticed other things, myriad small objects caught in the morass of rotting flowers like a nightmarish ebb tide on the linoleum floor. Agates and feathered masks; bird of paradise plumes encrusted with mud; cracked skulls and bones and cloth of gold. He recognized the carved puppet Helen had been playing with that afternoon in the Indonesian corridor, its headdress glittering in the twilight. About its neck was strung a plait of flowers, amber and cerulean blossoms glowing like phosphorescence among the ruins.

Through the room echoed a dull clang. Leo jerked to his knees, relieved. Surely someone had knocked?

But the sound came from somewhere behind him, and was echoed in another harsher, note. As this second bell died he heard the geckos' feet pattering as they fled across the ceiling. A louder note rang out, the windowpanes vibrating to the sound as though wind-battered. In the corner the leaves of the ficus turned as if to welcome rain, and the rosebushes stirred.

Leo heard something else, then: a small sound like a cat stretching to wakefulness. Now both of his legs ached, and he had to pull himself forward on his hands and elbows, striving to reach the front door. The clanging grew louder, more resonant. A higher tone echoed it monotonously, like the echo of rain in a well. Leo glanced over his shoulder to the empty doorway that led to the kitchen, the dark mouth of the hallway to Helen's bedroom. Something moved there.

At his elbow moved something else and he struck at it feebly, knocking the puppet across the floor. Uncomprehending, he stared after it, then cowered as he watched the ceiling, wondering if one of the geckos had crept down beside him.

There was no gecko. When Leo glanced back at the puppet it was moving across the floor toward him, pulling itself forward on its long slender arms.

The gongs thundered now. A shape humped across the room, something large enough to blot out the empty doorway behind it. Before he was blinded by petals, Leo saw that it was a shrunken figure, a woman whose elongated arms clutched broken branches to propel herself, legs dragging uselessly through the tangled leaves. About her swayed a host of brilliant figures no bigger than dolls. They had roped her neck and hands with wreaths of flowers and scattered blossoms onto the floor about them. Like a flock of chattering butterflies they surged toward him, tiny hands outstretched, their long tongues unfurling like crimson pistils, and the gongs rang like golden bells as they gathered about him to feed.

FROM A DISTANCE

by Kathe Koja

Thirteen: lucky number, jinx number. Unseen on clocks, no part of time; the unmarked floor in a high-rise; it even carries the distinction of its own specific phobia (triskaidekaphobia, if you're interested). Thirteen years ago, *Asimov's SF Magazine* published my short story "Distances" in its Mid-December issue, a story later reprinted in Gardner Dozois' prestigious *Year's Best Science Fiction* anthology, a story that got me noticed and effectively launched my writing career.

Where were you thirteen years ago? What were you doing, where were you living, how did you feel about your life? Can you remember, will you never forget? Does it seem like a long time ago? I remember being a nervous novice writer four years out of the Clarion workshop, with a three-year-old son who is, as I write this, a sophomore in high school. If you asked him, he might tell you that thirteen years is a very long time indeed.

For the characters in this story time moves elliptically: in bursts, in wide circles; it drags and lags and leaps too fast for counting. For them, as for anyone whose inner and outer landscapes are at large variance or outright war—those in physical pain, or enduring great want, or separated by iron circumstance from the ones they love—this is always so. Desire is a chasm steeper than time, unbridgeable as deep space; you may travel it obsessively but grow no nearer to what you seek. Like the Red Queen and Alice, it will take all the running you can do simply to stay where you are.

I see this story through a lens of time, of other stories (and novels) conceived and completed, of discoveries made in the landscape of my own life, most of them good, all of them necessary. If I were to write "Distances" over again today, would the same things happen to those characters, the same resolution be reached? I'm not sure. "Write what you know," is the old good advice, but what we know, or think we know, changes as we do, becomes deeper or dearer or paradoxically disappears; growth is unpredictable, pain is sure, and vision is the tool a writer uses to cope with both, on the page and (we hope) in the life that makes the page possible. All of it, of course, marinated in the brine of time, which has a way of altering perception, of diluting—or concentrating—desire, making of one thing another quite different, without perceptible effort on our part. It is

243

a kind of magic trick, but a very serious and permanent one. Just like life itself.

Thirteen years ago; thirteen years to come; and this second, *now,* sandwiched in their middle, this slice of time where the once-made world of "Distances" is read again and made, by you, its reader, into a living place: where technology flowers, and ambition rages, and two hands reach out to clasp together, in the airless dome of silent space and the great warm darkness of the mind. . . . Time *is* distance. See you in thirteen years.

DISTANCES

by Kathe Koja

MICHAEL, naked on the table, hospital reek curling down his throat, the base of his skull rich with the ache it has had every day since the first one, will probably never lose. He remembers that day: parts of him stone-numb, other parts prickling and alive; moving to make sure he still could; exhilaration; and the sense of the jacks. They had said he would not, physically could not, feel the implants. Wrong—needle-slim, they seemed like pylons, silver pillars underskin.

He is tall, under the straps; his feet are cold. Three

months' postsurgery growth of yellow hair, already curling. Gray eyes' glance roams the ceiling, bare peripherals.

He shifts, a little; the attendant gives him a faraway scowl. The old familiar strap-in: immobilize the head, check CNS response, check for fluid leak, check check check. "I am *fine*," he growls, chin strap digging into his jawline, "just fucking fine," but the attendant, rhino-sized, silent, ignores him entirely.

The ceiling monitor lights, bright and unexpected. Now what?

A woman, dark hair, wide mouth, cheekbones like a cat's, white baggy labcoat shoulders. "Hi," she says. "Doing all right?"

"Just ducky," tightmouthed, tin man with rusted jaw. Don't tell me, he thinks, more tests. "Who're you? A doctor?"

She appears to find this pretty funny. "Not hardly. I'm your handler. My name's Halloran." Something offscreen causes that wide mouth to turn down, impatient curvature. "I'll be in in a couple of minutes, we've got a meeting— Yeah I *heard* you!" and the screen blanks.

Check-up over, Michael rubs the spots where the straps were. "Excuse me," he says to the attendant. "That woman who was just onscreen—you know her?"

"Yeah, I know her." The attendant seems affronted. "She's a real bitch."

That charcoal drawl, bass whisper from babyface: "Oh good. I hate synthetics."

      *   *   *

"So who's he? General Custer?"

Halloran beside him, scent of contraband chocolate mints, slipping him handfuls. They are part of a ten-pair group in an egg-shaped conference room, white jacket and bald head droning away in accentless med-speak at the chopped-down podium. The air is ripe with dedication.

"That's Bruce, Dr. Bruce, the director. You're supposed to be listening to this."

"I am. Just not continuously."

Dreamy genius meets genius-dreamer. Bad kids in the back of the class, jokes and deadpan, catching on faster than anyone anyway. NASA'd done its profile work magnificently this time: the minute of physical meeting told them that, told them also that, if it was engineered (and it was), so what: it's great. Maybe all the other pairs feel the same. That's the goal, anyway. NASA believes there must be something better than a working relationship between handler and glasshead, more than a merely professional bond.

"He always snort like that when he talks?"

"You should hear him when he's not talking."

Dr. Bruce: ". . . bidirectional. The sealed fiber interface, or SFI, affords us—"

"Glass fibers for glassheads."

"Beats an extension cord."

Her hair is a year longer than his, but looking in the mirror would show Michael the back of her skull: it's his. Handlers are first-generation glassheads, just technically imperfect enough to warrant a new improved version—but hey, don't feel bad, you're still useful. We can put you to work training your successors, the ones who'll fly where you can never go; train them to do what you want to; brutally practical demonstration of the Those Who Can't principle. But who better to handle a glasshead but a glasshead?

". . . which by now I'm sure you're all used to." Dr. Bruce again. "But these are extremely important tests. We'll be using the results to determine your final project placement. I know Project Arrowhead is the plum assignment, but the others are valuable, very much so, if not as strictly 'glamorous.' " He says it that way, quotes and all, into a room that suddenly stinks of raw tension. "Handlers, you'll be final-prepping the tandem quarters. Also there's a meeting at 1700. Subjects—"

"That's you," sucking on a mint. Hint of chocolate on those wide lips.

"Actually I'm more of an object."

"—under supervisory care for the balance of the day. Everyone, please remember and observe the security regulations."

"No shootouts in the hallways, huh?"

"No. But don't worry." Halloran gives him a sideways look. "We'll figure out a way to have fun."

Arrowhead: inhouse they call it "Voyager's big brother." Far, far away: Proxima Centauri. The big news came from the van de Kamp lunar telescope, where the results of new proper motion studies confirmed what everyone had, happily, suspected: bedrock

247

evidence of at least three plants. At *least*. The possibility of others, and the complexity of their facefirst exploration, precluded the use of even the most sophisticated AI probe. Build new ones, right? No. Something better.

Thus Arrowhead. And glasshead tech gives it eyes and ears, with almost zero lagtime. This last is accomplished by beaucoup-FTL comlink: two big tin cans on a tachyon string. The tech itself was diplomatically extorted from the Japanese, who nearly twelve years before had helped to construct and launch the machine half of Arrowhead, engineered to interface with a human component that did not yet exist, and proved far more difficult to develop.

At last: the glassheads. Manned exploration without live-body risk and inherent baggage. Data absorbed by the lucky subject through thinnest fibers, jacked from receiving port into said subject's brain. The void as seen by human eyes.

Who wanted a humdrum assignment like sneaking spysat, or making tanks squaredance, when you could ride Arrowhead and be Cortez?

"Hey. State of the art barracks." Michael takes a slow self-conscious seat on the aggressively new, orthopedically sound bed. "Kinda makes you glad this isn't the bad old days, when NASA got the shitty end of every stick."

"Oh yeah, they thought of everything but good taste." Halloran's voice is exquisitely tired. She settles on the other side of the bed, one foot up, one dangling, and talks— inevitably—of Arrowhead. As she speaks her face shifts and changes play across the mobile muscles, taut stalks of bone. She could be a woman talking of her lover, explaining to a stranger. One hand rubs the back of her neck, erratic rhythm.

"It was so *nuts,*" that first group. "Everybody just out for blood. Especially me and Ferrante." Paranoia, envy, round-the-clock jockeying, rumors of sabotage and doctored scores. "Everybody in high-gear bastard twenty-four hours a day. It was all I could think of. I'd wake up in the middle of the night, my heart's going a mile a minute, thinking. Did Bruce see my scores today, really *see* them? I mean does he know I'm the only one who can *do* this?" Her hands stray from neck to hair, weave and twist among the dark locks. Her want shines like a lamp.

"You got it, didn't you." It's no question, and she knows it.

"Yeah, I got it. That's how they found out the tech wasn't up to spec." Her voice is absolutely level. "Fucked up, you know, in a simulator. When they told me I'd never be able to go, in any capacity—and I thought of them all, believe me—when they told me, I wanted to just cut out the jacks and die." She says this without self-pity, without the faintest taint of melodrama, as if it is the only natural thing to want under the circumstances. "Then they told me about Plan B. Which is you."

"And so you stayed."

"And so I stayed."

Quiet. The sonorous hum of air, recirculating. Low

nimbus of greenish light around Michael's head, his glance down, almost shy, trying to see those days, knowing her pain too well to imagine it. Halloran's hand grabs at her neck; he knows it aches.

"You better not fuck me up, Michael."

"I won't."

"I know."

Silence. Where another would retreat, he pushes forward. "Know what I was doing, when they called me? When they told me I made the cut?"

"What?" her hands leave her neck, clasp, unclasp, settle like skittish birds. "What were you doing?"

"Singing," promptly, grinning, delighted with the memory. "It was late, they were trying to find me all day and I didn't know it. I was sure I hadn't made it and I was sad, and pissed, so I went down to the bar and started drinking, and by midnight I was up on-stage. And at twenty after one—I'll never forget it— this guy comes up to me and says, Hey Michael, some guy from NASA's on the phone, he wants to talk to you. And I knew it! And you know what else?" He leans forward, not noticing then that she loves this story almost as much as he does, not surprised that a comparative stranger can share this glee so fully. "I'd been drinkin' all night, right, and I should've been drunk, but I wasn't. Not till he called." He laughs, still floored, having the joy of it all over again. "I was so drunk when I talked to him, I thought, Boy you must sound like a real *ripe* asshole, boy, but I was so happy I didn't give a shit." He laughs again. "I hung up and went back onstage and sang like a son of a bitch till four thirty in the morning, and then I got some eggs and grits and got on the plane for Atlanta."

She puts up an eyebrow. "What's the name of the band?"

"Chronic Six. Chronics one through five busted up." It is the perfect question, and nobody's surprised, or surprised that they're not.

Early days: the pairs, teams as Bruce calls them, solidify. Very little talk between them, and all of it polite. Scrupulous. The glassheads-turned-handlers are avid to better last time's run: they sniff the way old packmates will, hunt weaknesses and soft spots, watch around the clock. The ones they want most are Halloran and her smartass protegé; the Two-Headed Monster; the self-proclaimed Team Chronic.

Too-loud music from their quarters, morning ritual of killer coffee drunk only from twin black handleless mugs, labcoats sleeve-slashed and mutilated, "Team Chronic" in black laundry marker across the back, chocolate mints and slogans and mystic aggression, attitude with a capital A. Her snap and his drawl, her detail-stare and his big-picture sprawl, their way of finishing each other's sentences, of knowing as if by eyeless instinct what the other will do. Above all, their way of winning. And winning.

"Everybody hates us," Halloran at meal break, murmuring behind a crust of lunch. "They hated me, too, before."

Michael shrugs with vast satisfaction. "All the world hates a winner."

251

"And," smiling now, coffee steam fragrant around bright eyes, "they can't even scream teacher's pet, because Bruce hates us too."

"Bruce doesn't hate us. He loathes us."

They're laughing this over when: "Halloran." White hand on her shoulder, faint smell of mustard: Ferrante. Old foe, pudgy in immaculate whites, handsome heavy face bare with anger. Behind him, standing like a duelist's second, Ruthann Duvall, his glasshead, her expression aping his. The whole cafeteria is watching.

"I want to talk to you, Halloran."

"Feel free. I've had all my shots."

"Shots is right," Ferrante says. He is obviously on the verge of some kind of fury-fit. "You're *enhanced,*" meaning chemically enhanced, meaning illegally doctored; no Inquisitor could have denounced her with more élan. Everyone leans forward, spectators around the cockfight pit. "I'd think that even you would recognize that you're disrupting the integrity of the whole project, but that's never mattered to you, has it? *Or,*" sparing, then, a look for Michael, who sits finger-linked and mild, looking up at Ferrante with what appears to be innocent interest, "your foul-mouthed shadow."

Halloran, cocked head, voice sweet with insult: "Oh, I know the species of bug that's up *your* ass—you're stuck in second best and you can't figure out why. Well, let me make it crystal for you, slim: you suck."

"What if I go to Dr. Bruce and ask for a chem scan?"

"What if I jack you into the sanitation system, you big piece of shit?"

His fat white hand clops on her shoulder, shoving her so she slews into Michael and both nearly topple. Immediately she is on her feet, on the attack, pursuing, slapping, driving him towards the cafeteria door. Michael, beside her, grabs the avenging arms: "Let him go, the son of a bitch," and indeed Ferrante takes almost indecent advantage of the moment, leaves, with Ruthann Duvall—contemptuously shaking her still-nearly bald head—following, muttering, in her mentor's wake.

"Fuck you too, tennis ball head!" Halloran yells, then notices a strange sound coming from Michael: the grunt of suppressed laughter. It's too much, it blows out of him, hands on thighs and bent over with hilarity, and somebody else joins and somebody else too and finally the whole room is laughing. Even Halloran, who is first to stop.

"Let's go," she says.

Michael rubs helplessly at his eyes. "Tennis ball head!" He can't stop laughing.

Third week. Long, long day. In their quarters, blast music on, Michael bare-chested on the floor, Halloran rubbing her neck, the muscles thick and painful. Michael watches her, the sore motions.

"Do your jacks ever hurt?"

"No!"

"Mine do. All the time."

"No they *don't*! They're not supposed to!"

253

He raises his brows at her vehemence, waits.

"All right," she says at last, "you're right. They hurt. But I thought it was because I'm— you know. Defective." Fiercely: "*You're* not defective. It must just be phantom pain."

"A phantom pain in the ass." He sits up, pushes her hands away, begins to massage her hunched shoulders. "Listen, Halloran." His hands are very strong. "There isn't anything wrong with me. Got that? Nothing. So relax." He squeezes, harder and harder, forcing the muscles to give.

"So," squeezing, "when do we jack?"

"We've been jacking all damn day."

"I mean together."

"I don't know." Pleasure in her voice, the pain lessening. "That's up to Bruce, he does all the scheduling."

"The hell with Bruce. Let's do it now."

"What?" Even she, rebel, has not considered this. "We can't," already wondering why not, really—if they can jack into the computer—"It's never been done, that I know of, not so early."

"Now we *really* have to." He's already on his feet, making for his labcoat, taking from the inner breast pocket a two-meter length of fiber, cased in protective cord, swings it gently jackend like a pendulum at Halloran, a magic tool, you are getting verrrry sleeeepy. "Come on," he says. "Just for fun."

There is no resisting. "All right," she says. "Just wait a minute." There's a little timer on her wall desk; she sets it for ten minutes. "When this times out, so do we. Agreed?"

"Sure thing." He's already plugged in, conjurer's hands, quicker than her eye. He reaches up to guide her down. "Ready?"

"Yeah."

They've jacked in simulation, to prepare; it is, now, the difference between seeing the ocean and swimming, seeing food and eating. They are swamped with it, carried, tumbled, at the moment of mutual entry eyes flash wide, twinned, seeing, knowing, hot with it, incredible

Michael it's *strong* stronger than I thought it would know I know great *look* at this

and faster than belief thoughts and images burst between them, claiming them, devouring them as they devour, all of each shown to the other without edit or exception, all of it running the link, the living line, a knowing vaster than any other, unthinkably complex, here, now, us, look look see *this,* without any words; they dance the long corridors of memory, and pain, and sorrow, see old fears, old joys, dead dreams, new happiness bright as silver streamers, nuance of being direct and pure, sledgehammer in the blood, going on forever, profound communion and

finally it is Halloran who pulls back, draws them out, whose caution wakes enough to warn that time is over. They unplug simultaneously, mutual shudder of disunity, a chill of spirit strong enough to pain. They sit back, stunned; the real world is too flat after such a dimensionless feast.

Words are less than useless. In silence is comfort, the knowing—*knowing*—that one lives who knows you beyond intimacy; two souls, strung hard, adrift on the peculiar fear of the proud, the fear of being forced to go naked in terrible weakness and distress, and finding here the fear is toothless, that knowing and being utterly known could be, is, not exposure but safety, the doctrine of ultimate trust made perfect by glasshead tech.

They move into each other's arms, still not speaking.

Tears are running down Michael's face; his eyes are closed.

Halloran's hands are ice-cold on his wrists.

"We've been jacked all night," she says, "it's almost morning."

She can feel his body shaking, gently, the slow regular hitching of his chest. She has never loved anyone so much in all her life.

Is it chance, rogue coincidence, that the next day Bruce schedules a dual jack, a climatizer as he calls it? Between them, there is much secret hilarity, expressed in a smile here, a less-than-gesture there, and when they do dual, for real and on the record, they swoop and march in flawless tandem, working as one; the simulated tasks are almost ridiculously simple to complete, and perfectly.

Bruce still loathes them, but is undeniably impressed. "There's something about them," he tells a subordinate, who tells someone else, who mentions it sotto voce at dinner break, mostly to piss off Ferrante, who is nobody's favorite either. Michael and Halloran hear, too, but go on eating, serene, prefab biscuits and freeze-dried stew.

The tests seem, now, redundant, and Michael is impatient, growing more so. He lusts for the void, can almost taste its unforgiving null. "What is this shit?" he complains one night, face sideways-pressed into pillow, Halloran's small hands strong on back and buttocks. "The damn thing'll be there and back before we ever get a chance to ride it."

More tests. NASA is stultifyingly thorough.

More tests. Intense. Ruthann Duvall vomits her morning sausage in simulation; the sausage, of course, is very real. "Don't you know," Michael tells her, "that's not the way to send back your breakfast?"

More tests.

"Fuck!" Halloran feels like wrecking something. She contents herself with smokebomb curses. "This is getting to me, you know that, this is really fucking *getting* to me."

Maybe even Bruce, the king of caution, has had enough. The waiting is driving everyone mad, madder than before, the daily speculation, the aura of tension thick as gasoline smoke. Surely they must know, those testers, those considerers of results, surely they must know who is meant to fly, who is the best.

They don't need a victory party. They are a victory party.

No one is really, truly, happy for them. Michael is no darling, and this is Halloran's second sweep; besides, Team Chronic has rubbed too many raw spots

to be favorites now. All the others can hope for, in
their darkest moments, is project failure, but then of
course they feel like shits: nobody really wants Arrowhead to fail, no matter who's riding it.

The winners are wild in their joy; the strain has
broken, the goal achieved, the certainty blue-ribbon
and bright confirmed. They order up beer, the closest
they can get to champagne, and one by one, team by
team, the others drift by to join in. Ferrante and Duvall do not, of course, attend, instead spending the
evening reviewing data, searching for the flaw that
cannot be found.

Everyone gets drunk, yells, laughs loud. Even in
losing out there is a certain comfort—at least the waiting is over. And their assignments, while (as Bruce
noted) not "glamorous," are still interesting, worthy
of excitement. Everyone talks about what they're
going to do, while silently, unanimously, envying the
radiant Michael.

Somebody takes a picture: Michael, beer in hand,
mutilated labcoat and denim cap askew, sneakered
feet crossed at the ankles, hair a halo and eyes—
they are—like stars; one arm around Halloran, dark,
intent, a flush on her cheekbones, hair pushed messily back, wearing a button on her lapel—if you look
very closely at the picture you can read the words:
"Has The World Gone Mad, Or Am I At Work?"

His work area is almost ludicrously bare. The physical
jacking in, 2mm cord running to a superconducting
supercomputer—that's all. The comlink system is

housed elsewhere. In contrast to the manual backup equipment, resembling the cockpit of a suborbital fighter in its daunting complexity, he could be in a broom closet.

He has taken almost obsessive care to furnish his domain. Totems of various meanings and symbolisms are placed with fastidious precision. His bicycle bottle of mineral water, here; the remnants of his original labcoat, draped over his chairback here; his handleless black mug, sticky, most times, with aging grounds, here; pertinent memos and directives that no one must disturb, in this messy heap here; a bumpersticker that reads "Even if I gave a shit, I still wouldn't care," pasted at a strict diagonal across the wall before him; and, in the place of honor, the party-picture.

He loves his work.

It goes without saying, but he does. He cannot imagine, now, another way to live, as if, meeting by chance the lover he has always dreamed of, he thinks of life without her scent and kiss, her morning joke. Riding Arrowhead is all he ever expected, dreamed it to be, only better, better. He does his work—now, guiding Arrowhead through systems check in deceleration mode, realtime course correction to prepare for the big show—and has his play, the sheer flying, ecstasy of blackness, emptiness at his fingertips, in his mouth, flowing over his pores so hungry for mystery that they soak like new sponges. He eats it, all of it, drunk with delight, absorbing every morsel.

In their quarters is a remote terminal. It goes unused.

Other handlers work their subjects still, guiding them through maintenance routines, or geosynchronous dances, or linkups close and far; they are needed, to some degree; their tech has uses. Not that the subjects will not leave them behind, to NASA's prosaic mercies, to other work for handlers whose glassheads have outstripped them. They are on their way out. It was the pre-est of preordained. But not just yet.

Halloran is useless.

Her tech cannot fly Arrowhead—*that* was graphically proved. She cannot interface directly with the audacious bundle streaking across heaven; cannot in fact guide Michael; he is already far beyond her abilities. Despite any projections to the contrary, she has no function. She is required, now, only to keep Michael happy, on an even keel; when he stabilizes, breaks completely to harness, she will no longer be even marginally necessary.

She has busywork, of course. She "charts." She "observes." She "documents." She is strictly prohibited to use the room emote. It will hurt her. She knows this.

She is in the room one twilight, finishing the last of her daily "reports." She is wearing a castoff flightsuit, the irony of which only she can honestly appreciate. Her hair is clubbed back in a greasy bow. She refuses to think about the future. Sometimes, at night, her stomach aches so sourly she wants to scream, knows she will, doesn't.

"Hi." Michael, tray in hand, smile he tries to make natural. Her pain makes him miserable. He goes, every day, where she is technologically forbidden to enter: she stands at the gate while he soars inside. There is never any hint that she begrudges: she would scream like a banshee if ever came the slightest whisper of withdrawal from the project. He is as close as she can get; even the light of the fire is warmth, of a kind.

"Brought you some slop. Here," and sets it before her, gentle, seats himself at her side. "Mind if I graze?"

"Help yourself."

He eats, or tries to. She messes the food, rubs it across the plate, pretends. "Music?" she asks, trying to do her part.

"Sure. How 'bout some Transplant?"

"Okay." She turns it on, the loudest of the blast purveyors, nihilism in 4/4 time. "Good run today?"

"Great. You see the sheets?"

"Yeah. Outstanding."

He cannot answer that. They play at eating for a little while longer, Transplant thrashing in the background; then Michael shoves the tray aside.

"Jack with me," he says, pleads, commands.

This is what she lives for. "Okay," she says.

Inner workings, corridors, a vastness she can know, share. O, she tells him. Without words, trying to hide what cannot be hidden, trying to bear the brunt. He sees, knows, breaks into her courage, as he does each time; his way of sharing it, of taking what he can onto his shoulders. Don't, he says. No, she says.

Wordless, they undress, fit bodies together, make physical love. He is crying. He often cries, now. She is dry-eyed, wet below. The pleasure suffuses, brings its own panacea, is enough for the moment. They ride those waves, peak after peak, trailing down, whispering sighs into each other's open mouths. Her sweat smells sweet to him, like nothing else. He licks her shoulders. He has stopped crying, but only just.

To stay jacked this way too long, after a day of Arrowhead, will exhaust him, perhaps mar his efficiency. She is the one who broaches a stop.

No

Don't get an asshole yes

No

I am

and she does. He grapples, wide-eyed, for a moment, tears free his own jack. "Don't *do* that!" he cries, then sinks back, rubbing rough at his neck.

"I don't want to hurt you," she says, and the cry she has withheld so sternly for so long breaks out; she weeps, explosion, and he holds her, helpless. What to do, what to do; nothing. Nothing to do.

The symptoms are subtle.

Besides the nighttime bellyache, which Halloran has learned to ignore if not subdue, come other things, less palatable. Her jacks pain her, sometimes outrageously. Her joints hurt. She has no appetite. It is so difficult to sleep that she has requested, and received, barbiturates. The fact that they gave her no argument about the drugs makes her wonder. Do they A) just not care if she dopes herself stupid or B) have another reason, i.e., more requests? Is everybody breaking down?

Incredibly, yes. The handlers are beginning—in the startlingly crude NASAspeak—to corrode. The glassheads are still okay, doing swimmingly, making hay with their billion-dollar tech. The handlers are slowly going to shit, each in his or her own destructive orbit but with some symptoms universal. Entropy, Halloran thinks, laughing in a cold hysteric way. Built-in bye-bye.

But it is not built in. She accesses Bruce's files, breaking their so-called security with contemptuous angry ease, finds that this situation is as shocking to the brass as it is to the handlers. The ex-glassheads. Broken glassheads.

No one is discussing it, not that she knows of. In the cafeteria, at the now-infrequent meetings, she searches them, looks minute and increasingly desperate, hunting their dissolution: does Ryerson look thinner? Wickerman's face seems blotchy. Ferrante has big bags under his eyes. She knows they are watching her, too, seeing her corrosion, drawing conclusions that must inevitably coincide. While in the meantime hell freezes over, waiting for Bruce to bring it up.

She says nothing to Michael about any of it. When they jack, the relief of not having to think about it sweeps her mind clean; she is there, in that moment, in a way she is never anywhere else, at any time, anymore.

Bruce comes to see her one morning. She logs off,

faces him, feels the numb patches around lips and wrist begin to throb.

"We don't understand it," he begins.

"Yeah, I know."

"There are various treatments being contemplated." He looks genuinely distressed. For the first time it begins to dawn: this is more than breakdown. This is death. Or maybe. Probably. Otherwise why the careful face, the eyes that won't, will *not,* meet hers. Her voice rises, high vowels, hating the fear of it but unable to quell.

"We're thinking of relocating you," Bruce says. "All the handlers."

"Where?"

"South Carolina," he says. "The treatments—" Pause. "We don't want the subjects . . . we don't want to dismay them."

Dismay? "What am I supposed to tell him?" She is shouting. No, she is screaming. "What am I supposed to *tell* him? That I'm going on VACATION?!" Really screaming now. Get hold of yourself, girl, part of her says, while the other keeps making noise.

"For God's sake, Halloran!" Bruce is shaking her. That in itself quiets her down; it's so damned theatrical. For God's Sake Halloran! oh ha ha ha, HA HA HA stop it!

"We have no concrete plans, yet," he says, when she is calm enough to listen. "In fact if you have any ideas—about how to inform the subjects—" He looks at her, hopeful.

Get out, Bruce. I can't think about dying with that face of yours in the room. "I'll be sure and send you a memo." It is dismissal; the tone comes easy. In the face of death, getting reprimanded seems, somehow, unimportant. Ha HA: you better stop it or you're going to flip right out.

No more bogus "reports." She sits, stares at her hands, thinking of Michael flying in the dark, thinking of that other dark, the real dark, the biggest dark of all. Oh God, not me. Please not me.

"Something's wrong."

Michael, holding her close, his breath in her damp hair.

"Something's *bad* wrong, Halloran, and you better tell me what it is."

Silence.

"Halloran—"

"I don't . . . I don't want to—" dismay "—worry you. It's a metabolic disturbance," and how easily, how gracefully, the lies roll off her tongue. She could give lessons. Teach a course. A short course. "Don't get your balls in a uproar," and she laughs.

"You," he says, measured, considering, "are a fucking liar." He is plugged in, oh yes, he's going to get to the bottom of this and none of her bullshit about metabolic disturbances, and he pins her down, jacks her in. One way or another he's going to find out what the hell's going on around here.

He finds out.

* * *

"South Carolina, what the hell do you mean South Carolina!"

"That's where they want to send us. Some kind of treatment center, a clinic." Voice rough and exhausted from hours of crying, of fighting to comfort. "Bruce seems to think— well, you know, you saw." She is so immensely tired, and somehow, selfishly, relieved: they share this, too. "Don't ask me, I—"

"Why can't they do whatever they have to do right here?" There is that in him that refuses to think of it in any way other than a temporary malfunction. She will be treated, she will be cured. "Why do they have to send you away?"

"You know why."

"How the fuck can I work anyway!" He is the one screaming, now. "How do they expect me to do anything!"

The bond, the tie that binds, cuts deeper than NASA intended, or wants. For all the teams it is the same: the glassheads, even those whose handlers have, like Halloran, become token presences, *want their handlers*. They *need* them. Bruce and his people are in the unhappy position of trying to separate high-strung children from their very favorite stuffed animals now that the stuffing is coming out. *And* trying to disguise the disintegration at the same time. It is the quintessential no-win situation. Uncountable dollars down the drain with one batch, the other batch sniffing stress and getting antsy and maybe not able to work at all.

266

And for the closest of them, Team Chronic, it is even worse. How do Siamese twins, *happy* Siamese twins, feel when the scalpel bites?

"Just a little more."

"Stop it." She is surly in her pain. "You're not my mother. Stop trying to make me eat."

"You have to eat, asshole!" He is all at once furious, weeks' worth of worry geysering now. "How do you ever expect to get better if you don't eat?"

"I'm not going to get better!"

"Yes you are. Don't even say that. You are going to get better." He says each word with the unshakable conviction of terror. "And you'd be getting better faster if you'd just cooperate a little."

"Stop it! Stop making it my fault!" She stands up, shaking; an observer, seeing her last a year ago, would be shocked silent at her deterioration. She is translucent with her illness; not ugly or wasted, but simply less and less *there*. "*They* did this to me!" She scratches at her neck, wild, as if trying to dig out the jacks. "*They* made me sick! It's not my fault, Michael, none of it is my fault!"

He starts to cry. "I know I know," hands over his face, "I know I know I know," monotonously, and she sweeps the tray from the table, slapping food on floor, spattering walls, kicking the plastic plate into flight. Then, on her knees beside him, exhausted from the strain of anger, her arms around him, rocking him gently back and forth as he grips her forearms, and sobs as if his heart will break, as if his body will splin-

267

ter with the force. "I know," she says, softly, into his ear. "I know just how you feel. Don't cry. Please, don't cry."

"There goes the bastard," says a subordinate to Bruce, as Michael slips past them down the corridor. "One minute he's tearing your head off because you touched his coffee cup, the next minute he won't even answer you or acknowledge you're alive."

"He's under enormous stress, Lou."

"Yeah, I know." Lou bites a knuckle, considering. "You don't think he'll—*do* anything, do you? To himself?"

"No." Bruce looks unsure.

"How about Arrowhead?"

"No." Very sure. "He's totally committed to the project, that I know. His performance is still perfect," which is simple truth. Michael's work is excellent, his findings impeccable; essential. It is his refuge; he clings to it as fiercely and stubbornly as he clings to Halloran.

Bruce, and Lou, and all the Lous, are meeting today, to decide the next step in he separation process. The tandem quarters will be vacated; each handler— how empty the title sounds now!—will be put on a ward; the glassheads will be housed in new quarters, with no memories in their walls or under their beds. This move will just be done, no discussion, no chance of input or hysterics or tantrums. Better for everyone, they tell each other solemnly. For them, too, but they don't say it. This daily tragedy is wearing everybody down.

The move is a success, with one exception.

"No," Michael says, with the simplicity of imminent violence. "Nope," hand on the door, very calm. "No, she's not moving anywhere, I don't care who decided, I don't care about anything. She's staying right here and you can go tell Bruce to fuck himself." And the door closes. Bruce is consulted. He says, Let them be for today and we'll think of something else tomorrow.

What they think of is ways to mollify the other teams. Halloran is not moved. Arrowhead is, at bedrock, *the* project, essential. Everything else is a tangent. If consistent, outstanding results are obtained—as they are—then ways can be found, any ways, to keep them coming; the glasshead project in toto is not such a crushing success, what with the first batch proving unsuitable and then unusable, that they can afford to tamper with that which produces its only reason for existing, its reason, to be crude, for any budget at all. Without Arrowhead they can all fold up their tents tomorrow. And the data in itself is so compelling that it is unthinkable that the project not continue.

So Halloran stays.

A conversation tires her; her feet swell and deflate, swell and deflate, with grim comic regularity; her lips bleed, her gums. She plays Transplant, very loud, tells Michael she wishes she could jack right into the music so as to feel it, literally, in her bones. She lets him do almost everything for her, when he is there; it calms and pleases him, as much as he can be pleased, any-more. When they make love he holds her like china, like thinnest crystal that a thought could shatter. They spend a lot of time in tears.

"Oh this is old," she whispers, stroking his back as he lies atop her. "This is just getting so old."

The is no answer to that, so he gives none. He is too tired even to cry, or pound fists, or scream that their treatments are shit, shit! He feels her heart beat. It seems so strong. How can anyone who looks so sick have such a robust heartbeat? Thank God for it. Let it beat forever, till he and all the world is dust.

"Know what?"

"What?"

"Know what I'd like to do, more than anything?"

He raises himself from her, moves to his side, cra-dles her that way. "What would you like to do?"

"Arrowhead."

The word makes a silence. Vacuum. Each knows what the other is thinking.

Finally, Michael: "It's a neurological strain. A *big* strain. You might—it could hurt you."

She laughs, not sarcastically, with genuine humor. "What a tragedy *that* would be."

More silence.

"There isn't a lot left," she says, very gently, "that I can do. This," running her hand down his body, her touch ethereal. "And that. Just one. Just one ride."

He doesn't answer. He can't answer. Anything he says would be cruel. She puts her hand on his cheek, strokes his skin, the blond stubble. There is a lot she could say, many things: If you love me—one last chance—last favor. She would rather die, and for her it is not an academic pronouncement, than say those things, any of those things.

"All I care about," he says finally, his voice deeper than she has ever heard it, "is that I don't want to be a part of something that hurts you. But I guess it's already too late, isn't it?"

For her, there is no answer to that.

Much later: "You really want to do it?"

He can feel her nod in the dark.

"Shit."

"Okay," Michael says, for the tenth time. "It'll take me a couple minutes to get there, get plugged in. I'll get going, and then this—" indicating a red LED "—will pulse. You jack in then. Okay?"

"Please, Mister," in a little girl's voice, undertone of pure delight, "how do you work this thing?"

"Okay, okay. I'm sorry." He is smiling too, finally. "Fasten your seatbelt, then." She is pale with excitement, back almost painfully rigid, his denim cap jaunty on her head. When he kisses her, he tastes the coppery flavor of blood. He leaves, to march down the hall like Ghenghis Khan.

Halloran's heart is thrashing as she jacks in, to the accompaniment of the LED. She feels Michael at once, a strong presence, then—go.

The slow dazzle of the slipstream night, rushing over

her like black water, rich phosphorescence, things, passing, the alien perfection of Arrowhead, the flow and flower of things whose names she knows but now cannot fathom or try, the sense of flying, literal arrowhead splicing near to far, here to there, cutting, riding, past the farthest edge— it is wonder beyond dreams, more than she could have wished, for either of them. Worth everything, every second of every pain, every impatience and disappointment, of the last two years. She does not think these things in words, or terms; the concept of rightness unfolds, origami, as she flies, and if she could spare the second she would nod Yes, that's so.

Michael, beside her, feels this rightness too; on his own or as a gift from her, he cannot tell, would not bother making the distinction. She is in ecstasy, she is inside him, they are both inside Arrowhead. He could ride this way forever, world without end.

They find out, of course, Bruce and the others; almost at once. There is a warning monitor that is made to detect just this thing. They are in the tandem quarters, they forcibly unplug her. Michael feels her leaving, the abrupt disunity, and eyes-open screams, hands splayed across the air, as Arrowhead gives a lurch. As soon as she is out of the system she collapses. Grinning.

Bruce teeters on the edge of speechlessness. One assistant says, voice loud with disbelief, "Do you have any idea what you've just done to yourself? Do you know what's—"

"No," she corrects, from the bottom of the tunnel,

faces ringing her like people looking down a manhole. "No, *you* have no idea."

South Carolina is a lot farther away than Proxima Centauri.

INTRODUCTION TO

"THE WIND BREATHES COLD"

by P.N. Elrod

In 1990, when I got my first invitation to contribute a story to a theme anthology (*Dracula: Prince of Darkness,* DAW, edited by Martin H. Greenberg), I already had the idea of writing a Dracula novel bumping around in my head. It was inspired by Clive Leatherdale's commentary on Bram Stoker's work. Clive pointed out that Quincey P. Morris was one of the more enigmatic characters in *Dracula.* He was the only one of the band of vampire hunters who did not keep a journal. Except for a few telegrams, nothing in the book is written by him. His actions throughout are occasionally odd, though he was a capable fighter and when he felt things, his emotions ran deep. In the end he was the one to slam his bowie knife into Dracula's heart (of course we all know it should have been a wooden stake) and he is the only one of the hunting party who dies. He goes gladly, after seeing that he has indeed saved Miss Mina from a Terrible Fate. What a hero!

It struck my twisted brain that perhaps Mr. Morris was in some way on Dracula's side of things, whether by his travels throughout the world or by some supernatural connection. Maybe he knew more than even Van Helsing, and chose to play his cards close to the chest. If Dracula was so all-powerful why didn't he just kill his enemies and get on with his business? Did he have a reason for holding back? And just *what* was Quincey's agenda?

Possibilities were jumping about for me that day when I imagined myself inside Quincey's head, waking up from his sleep of death to discover he's become that which he most despises. Being a man of action he's not one to wallow in the angst of it all and sets out to do something about his changed condition, and that turned out to be my plot.

I'd always intended this story—whose title is from something Dracula said to Jonathan Harker in the early chapters—to become a full-blown novel, and a decade later realized the intent. Though I'd meant to write the book soon after finishing the short story, circumstances dictated otherwise, but it worked out for the best. The book that might have been written then and the one presently on the racks are two different critters. All that life in between made me grow as a writer. The final product, *Quincey Morris, Vampire,* is much better for the wait. I've heard other writers declare the same thing about themselves and their works, and so I gratefully join their ranks.

The idea of turning a short story into a novel was something I swiped from Raymond Chandler, Dashiell Hammett, and others from the golden age of pulps. They would frequently take a story and develop it further, which struck me as being remarkably thrifty. This one was ever meant to be the first chapter of something larger. It was fun for me to go back for another look at it, to compare it to the novel's version and see where I expanded and polished things. It's still one of my favorites!

THE WIND BREATHES COLD

by P.N. Elrod

NO one sense returned first; my inability to move or see, the cold, the soft whine of dogs, and the rough jostling all jumbled together in my awakening brain like different kinds of beans in a pot. I slipped to and fro between awareness and nothing until a particularly sharp lurch and bump caught my attention for longer than a few seconds. It was enough for me to realize that something was wrong and needed investigating. The next moment of consciousness I managed to keep hold of; the moments to follow had me wishing I'd done otherwise.

They were tugging at my feet, which seemed to be bound up, but then so was the rest of my body. I was wrapped snugly in a blanket from head to toe. The thing was right over my face, which I never could abide. I twisted my head to free myself but could not.

The tugging abruptly stopped and several dogs snuffled my immobile form. I felt an icy, tingling jump all along my nerves as I realized they were not dogs, but wolves. They whimpered and growled over me, then strong jaws clamped down on my wrappings and they resumed their work. Emboldened by hunger, they had actually entered our camp and were dragging me off to a safe distance.

I wanted to shout and bring my friends, but that might also set off the wolves. Outright panic would only kill me and I was that close to giving in to it. Holding my breath tight, I waited and listened for my life.

There must have been dozens of them. I could hear their eager panting and claws clicking against stone. Wolves usually shy away from men—such had been my experience when Art and I had been trailed by that pack in Siberia—but this was a far different place and I'd already seen proof that a tall tale in one part of the world was God's own awful truth in another.

They pulled me along another few feet. My weight, and I was aware of every solid pound of it going over those rocks, was nothing to them. Once they felt secure, they'd rip through my blanket and clothes like taking the hide off a deer. I'd seen that happen once. The deer had still been alive when they'd started in and though quick enough, it hadn't been an easy death.

Panic surged up like bile in my throat. It choked off any scream for help I might have had. I fought against the restraining blanket. Startled, the wolves at my feet let go. One of them snarled, stirring up the others. They moved all around me, excited, nipping at the blanket as though in play. Fresh air knifed my face as the damned thing finally came loose.

Bright-eyed, with lolling tongues, and rows of tearing teeth, they scampered about like puppies. Some darted close to snap at me, wagging their tails at the sport of it. I wrenched my hands free, but they were of little use without a weapon and some dim memory told me I had no gun or knife. I scrabbled in the inches deep snow and found a chunk of rock. Better than nothing.

Then a big black one, one that I would have chosen to be the leader, raised his head to the wild gray sky and howled. The others instantly broke off their game and crowded around him, their tails tucked down like fawning supplicants seeking a favor. One after another joined him, blending and weaving their many voices into a triumphant song only they could fully understand.

The leader broke off and focused his huge green eyes upon me. It's a mistake to ascribe human attributes to an animal, but I couldn't help myself. The thing looked not just interested, but curious, in the way that a human is curious.

The wolf snarled and snapped at those nearest him. The pack stopped howling and obediently scattered. After a sharp, low bark they formed themselves into a wide circle like trained circus dogs. I was at its exact center. Some stood, others sat, but all were watching me attentively. Though I'd had more contact with wolves than most other men, I'd never seen or heard of anything like this before. Had the hair on my neck not already been raised to its limit, it would have gone that much higher.

Some of them growled questioningly, no doubt scenting my fear.

Clutching the nearly useless rock with one hand, I tore at the bindings around my ankles with the other. It was desperate work, made slow by my reluctance to take my eyes from the pack. Despite the distraction caused by their presence, I saw that for some reason I'd been wrapped like a bundle for the mail, first in the blanket, then by ropes. Why? Who had tied me up so? A burst of anger helped me get through the next few moments as I cursed the bastard who had done me such an ill turn.

Free. I kicked the blanket away and staggered upright, half expecting the wolves to close in. They remained in their great circle, watching. There were no trees within it to climb to safety and if I tried to break through their line at any point they'd be on me, so I kept still and stared back. One of the wolves sneezed; another shook himself. They knew they had me.

Winter wind sent the ground snow flying. Dry flakes skittered and drifted over the discarded blanket. With my free hand, I slowly picked it up and looped it around my arm. The big leader stepped forward. I turned to face him, thinking I was as ready as I'd ever be, only to find an instant later that I'd been utterly wrong. No man could possibly prepare himself for what came next.

The wolf lowered his head, but rocked back on his haunches, like a dog about to do a begging trick. A darkness that seemed to come from within the thing's body blurred the details as bones and joints soundlessly shifted, muzzle and fur retreated, skin swelled. It rose on its hind legs and kept rising, until it was as tall as myself. The crook of its legs straightened, thickened, and became the legs of a man, a tall, thin man, clothed all in black. Only the bright green eyes remained the same and when he smiled at me, I clearly saw the wolf lurking beneath the surface.

I was as scared as I'd ever been and could have expressed it, loudly, but there didn't seem much point. In a few minutes, I'd either be dead or worse than dead and making a lot of noise about it wouldn't help one way or another.

"I can respect a brave man, Mr. Morris," he said, pitching his deep voice to rise above the wind. In it was some of the harsh tone I'd heard when he had taunted us from the stable yard of his Piccadilly house just over a month ago. He clasped his hands behind his back and continued to regard me with the same mixture of interest and curiosity manifested in his wolf

form. The wind bounced against him with little effect
other than to whip at his dark clothes and pale hair.
Black on white was the mark Harker had left on his
forehead, a deep cut in the pallid flesh. That was how
I knew for certain who he was. I'd had only glimpses
before, and the last time I'd seen that face I'd . . .
I'd. . . .

Something very like the wind, but existing solely
within my mind, whirled inside my skull. The man
before me, the circle of wolves, the snow, the cold,
all faded for an instant of nothing before asserting
themselves again. It was like the focus of a poorly
made telescope sifting in and out.

"I killed you," I said faintly. I recalled the impact
going right up my arm when my bowie knife slammed
firmly into his chest.

"So you did," he admitted. "With some help from
Jonathan Harker, do not forget."

"Yes. . . ." Harker had buried his own knife in the
monster's throat. We'd fought our way through those
Gypsies to get to the wagon and the box on top of it.
The Gypsies had drawn their own knives and one of
them had . . .

I dropped the stone, my hand going to my side.
The clothes there were thick and stiff with dried and
frozen blood.

My blood. It had fairly poured out of me. Jack Seward and Van Helsing had tried their best to stop the
flow, but the cut was too deep, the damage beyond
any skill to heal. Thank God it hadn't been very painful. The last memory I had was of poor Mina Harker,

her face twisted by bitter grief as I slipped away into what seemed like sleep.

Not sleep. Nothing so human as that had taken me, changed me, turned me into . . .

"No need for such alarm, Mr. Morris," Dracula said, reading my face. "It's not as bad as you've been led to think."

Not knowing my own voice, a cry escaped me and, heedless of the wolves, I turned and ran. Some of them started to follow, but were headed off by a sharp word from their master. I crashed through the snow-drifts, blundered against trees, and tripped on invisible snares at my feet but kept going. Not far ahead was the warm yellow light of our campfire. If I could just get there, if Van Helsing still had some of his Holy Wafer left, there might yet be protection for us.

For *them*. At least for them.

I was close enough to see their huddled forms: the Harkers lying together, Van Helsing and Seward, Art a little off from the others, presumably taking his turn at watch. All of them were fast asleep, worn out by the hard travel and the chase, but just one shout from me would bring Art instantly awake. . . .

A hand, colder than ice, slapped over my mouth just as I drew breath. As though I were a child and not a grown man, he lifted me right off my feet and back into the cover of the forest. I struggled with in-different success, but got in a few good kicks that made him grunt. Then he spun me suddenly and my head cracked against one of the trees.

Lights brighter than the sun blinded me, or maybe it was the ungodly pain that went with them. I dropped, paralyzed and sick from the shock. My vision slowly cleared. Dracula stood over me, his sharp teeth bared and hellfire fury blazing from his eyes.

"Fool," he hissed. "Do you think they'll show you any mercy once they know?"

"I'm counting on it," I snapped back. "I know what to expect and shall welcome it."

"Well, I do not. Give yourself away to them if you must, but not me. I've been to enough trouble over this matter and want no more."

"Go to hell."

I didn't think his eyes could hold more rage. I was wrong. He raised a hand as though to smash me like a fly, then forbore at the last second. His anger beat against me like heat from a forge, but after a long and terrible moment it dissipated into nothing.

"You're but an infant," he sighed. "You don't understand yet."

"I know enough."

"I think not. Come with me and I might be of some help to that end."

"No—"

"Stay behind and your friends will be food for my children." He gestured meaningfully at the forest around us. There was no need for him to explain who his "children" were; I could hear and occasionally see them well enough. "Come with me and all will be safe."

"For how long?"

"As long as you remain sensible. And that is entirely up to you."

He stepped back and waited, watching as his wolves had watched. He did not offer to help as I found my feet, leaning hard on the tree. Though dizzy, I was able to think, but no idea running through my mind could be remotely mistaken for a way out of this spot.

"Where?" I asked unhappily.

He pointed behind me. We were to go deeper into the trees, away from the camp. I didn't like that, but followed as he led the way along what looked like a deer trail. The wolves kept pace with us, whining and wagging their tails like dogs out for a walk. Glancing back, I saw more than a dozen of them padding almost at my heels. I realized that they were completely obliterating my tracks in the snow. Was it accidental or intentional? I made a step off to one side as a test and went on. The wolves, tongues hanging as if with laughter, sniffed the spot and easily blotted the boot print out as they swarmed over it.

Rocks rose up next to us, forming a natural wall that cut the wind. The snow underfoot thinned and vanished. The wolves followed, ears raised attentively. Dracula waited until I was well upon this trackless surface, then stretched his arms out before him, spreading them wide. As though the pack were one animal and not many, his children instantly retreated into the trees and were lost to sight.

"Where are they going?" I demanded.

The question surprised him. "To hunt, to play, to

run with the moon, whatever they desire. Your friends are still safe from them, as are you."

"What do you want of me?"

"Nothing more than the answers to a few questions."

"What questions?"

He pointed to a knee-high boulder. "Please seat yourself, Mr. Morris."

He had a presence about him that could not be ignored. I sat. There was a similar rock not four feet away and he took it, facing me, and spent several minutes studying me intently.

"With your permission," he said and held his hand out, palm upward, looking for all the world like some Gypsy ready to read my fortune if I but mirrored him. I hesitated only a little, for my own curiosity was awake and on the move by now. He inspected my hands, finally comparing them to his own, which were broad and blunt. "Your fingers are of different lengths," he pronounced.

"What of it?"

"They are also quite bare, not at all like mine, as you see."

From Harker's journal I already knew about the hair on his palms and the sharp nails, so there was little need to gape in wonder.

"I see when you speak that your teeth appear to be perfectly normal. The same may not be said for my own," he added, letting them show in an almost wry smile.

"Have you a purpose to this?"

"To confirm to myself and prove to you that we are similar, but not very alike."

"We are most certainly not alike!" My voice was rising.

"I am so glad that we are in agreement," he said with a calm sarcasm that took all the wind out of me. "Such differences should reassure, rather than alarm you."

"What do you mean?"

"You know that well enough for yourself."

I did, but the agonizing terror inside made me consciously obtuse. To face the truth, to actually *speak* about it. . . .

"As I told you," he said with a glimmer of sympathy I would have never otherwise ascribed to that hard, unpleasant face, "it is not as bad as you have been led to think."

A short explosion of a laugh burst from me, a laugh that might have turned to a sob had I not forcibly swallowed it back.

"You are *nosferatu,* Mr. Morris, nothing more. I am *nosferatu,* but much more, hence the visible differences." He opened his palms again, as though that explained everything. "I know how I became as I am, but I want to know your story. Who took your blood and gave it back again? Who initiated the change in you? And when?"

I was speechless for many long moments as he expectantly waited for an answer. "Why do you want to know?"

"Those of your kind are rare. I would know more about you. You are also the first I have ever met both before and after dying. Our encounters in London and in Seward's house were brief, but I sensed the change in you. For that alone I would have spared your friends had I not made other plans."

"Plans?"

"To rid myself of the hunters without killing them. Look not so surprised, Mr. Morris. At any time of my choosing I could have destroyed the lot of you and left no trace to rouse the suspicion of the law. Knowing what you do about me, could you doubt my ability to accomplish that?"

"You're saying you spared us?"

"Your deaths were unnecessary. Better to lead you to believe in my own demise than to— "

"I saw you die, we all did."

"You saw me vanish," he corrected. "Things might not have gone so well for me had you used wood instead of metal. I am content with the results. Now you see why I had to stop you from rousing your friends; to do so would have meant their deaths and yours as well. Large parties have disappeared before in these mountains. Accidents are easily managed—I chose to avoid such an extreme action. Believe me or not, as you will."

And I did believe him, though I couldn't have explained why.

"Now as for your own change . . ." he prompted.

"It was a few years back, in South America," I said.

"Art—Lord Godalming now—and I were at an embassy ball. I met her there. She was the most beautiful woman I'd ever seen. She and I—"

"Her name?"

"Nora. She was European, I think, though she had dark hair and eyes and that wonderful olive skin. . . ." Which I'd been on fire to touch the moment I saw her. I hadn't been the only man trying to claim her attention at that gathering, but I was the one she picked as escort for a walk in the embassy garden. I reveled in my good fortune and hoped to give her a favorable impression of myself in the time we had, but it was she who took the lead in things, which surprised me mightily. That night, holding true to a promise and plan made in the garden, she found her way to my room and we fulfilled one another's expectations—exceeded them, I should say.

I'd been exhausted the next morning, of course, not from blood loss so much as from excess champagne and sheer physical activity. Her biting into my neck had startled me only a little. Young as I was, I'd known more than one woman in my travels and learned that each had her own path to pleasure and it was my privilege to assist her there. It was always to my own advantage to be ready to learn something new and Nora was a delightful teacher. My body's explosive reaction to this lesson was like nothing I'd ever felt before or since.

I rested throughout the day and the next night we expanded and explored our range of talent. It was then, caught up in the lust of the moment, that she frantically opened a vein in her own throat and invited me to drink from her in turn. Brain clouded and body aching for release I gladly did so, taking us to a climax that left us both unconscious for many hours afterward. I woke up a little before dawn in time to see her throw on a dressing gown and leave, then dropped away into sweet oblivion.

The word vampire was not unfamiliar, but its context for me had to do with a species of bat that plagued the area. In our drowsy love talk, the subject came up, but Nora told me not to worry about it and, lost in the warmth of her dark eyes, I dismissed any and all misgivings . . . until that day in the Westenra dining room when I volunteered my blood to save Lucy.

I had no mind for Nora then—she was years behind me, an exquisite and happy memory—and put myself forward without another thought. It was afterward, when I began to hear more from Jack and Van Helsing about Lucy's condition that the doubts crept in. I feared that Lucy had fallen victim to someone like Nora, but a rapist rather than a lover. From that point everything Van Helsing told us confirmed my many fears. It was only after Lucy's death and the hideous proof of her return that I realized what horror was in store for me when I died.

Dracula took that moment to interject. "If by that you mean being staked through the heart by your well-meaning friends, then you have every right to be horrified."

"If it will free me to go to God, then so be it."

"I doubt if He would welcome such an enthusiastic suicide," he said dryly. "Do not look so amazed, you are still one of His children—yet another difference you may rejoice in."

"How is that possible? I am—am *nosferatu,* one of the Un-Dead."

"Exactly. Un-Dead and nothing more. Do you not see?" I did not and he threw his hands up in exasperation. "Your so-sweet Nora has much to answer for. She should have told you all this and saved me the trouble and you your anguish. You *do* understand that she was, and probably still is, *nosferatu?*"

"Yes."

"And you must know by now that she was not as I am. Her offspring, which now includes you, will be like her. I have already had ample proof that my offspring, no matter how lovingly taken, will never be so tame. Mine to hers are as the wolf to the hunting hound. *Now* do you see?"

My reply was whispered, but he heard me.

"Good. You know that your soul is your own . . . and His," he said with quirk of his heavy brows toward the sky. "With some small changes you are free to live as before, but as *you* choose, for good or ill as all things will be judged in their time. For me, it is not so simple."

"What do you mean?"

"I can do that which you cannot. The wolf, the bat, the curling mist, are natural forms to me but not for you. I prefer the shadows, but may walk in the sun if necessary, you would die from it. You can no more command the weather or my wild children now than you could as a human, but that is of no matter to you. I read in your heart and by your manner that you would refuse to pay the price for such powers. Long ago I paid and still do. My body bears the signs of that payment, marking me as different from other men, and as for my soul . . . I think you would be more comfortable to remain ignorant of such things."

From the look that crossed his face I silently agreed with him. "And what of Lucy? Am I to let you go free after what you did to her?"

"I did nothing that was not a part of my nature, a part of any man's nature. She was beautiful and willing—no, do not gainsay me for you were not there and never knew her true heart. I loved her in the only way left to me."

"Until she died."

"We all die, but if you wish to fix a blame for her death, then you need look no farther than her attending physicians. Had they left her alone she would still be walking in the sun. Doctors, bah!" His ruddy lips curled with contempt.

"And my blood . . ."

"Made no difference to her health. The seeds of becoming Un-Dead were within you, but you were not Un-Dead then. To create your own offspring now you must first take blood from your lover, then return it."

"As you've done to Mina Harker? What is to happen to her?"

"Nothing. The miracle she prayed for—" he touched the red mark on his forehead, for it nearly mirrored the one she had carried—"came to pass. Seward and Van Helsing will not bother her. That alone should suffice to guarantee her a long and fruitful life."

"But what you did to her—"

"That which passed between Mrs. Harker and myself is really none of your business, Mr. Morris," he rumbled, his brows lowering.

"But that poor woman—"

"Is quite capable of making her own decisions." By his tone, I knew that to pursue the matter would result in unhappy consequences to myself. And he was right. It was none of my business. Besides, to be honestly selfish about it, I had problems of my own.

Now that my eyes had been opened a little wider than before, I looked out into the night. Though all would have been pitch blackness to my friends, it was as daylight to me. The snow put a silver gleam upon everything it touched. Beautiful, but marred by the questions troubling me.

"Must I do as you—as Nora—to . . . to . . ." The words refused to emerge.

"Sustain yourself? Hardly. To drink from a lover is one matter, but you'll find that the blood of animals is your real food. One may live upon love alone for a while, but sooner or later one must come down from the clouds and take more practical nourishment. This is as true for vampires as it is for humans. Are you hungry?"

I said nothing.

He shrugged. "When you're ready, then."

"What about my friends? When they wake—"

"They will find that you have been dragged off by a pack of ravenous wolves. So very tidy, is it not?"

"It's monstrous!"

"Far better that than to see your footprints in the snow walking away from the blanket that shrouded your dead body. I suspected you might revive and rise tonight, so I made sure my children and I could cover your escape."

"But they are my friends. Must they be put through such grief?"

"Yes." He was not to be moved on this point. There would be no return to them, not for now, anyway, not while his wolves were within call.

"Very well," I murmured. Perhaps later I might be able to talk to Art or Jack and persuade them to reason as I had been persuaded, but in the meantime I was feeling very lost and miserable. The icy November air, something I'd been able to ignore because of my changed condition, was sinking heavily into my body. It would take more than the coat I wore to dispel it. I shook out the blanket I still carried and threw it over my shoulders.

Dracula nodded. "Yes. It is time to go inside. My castle is not too terribly far from here. Van Helsing thinks he has sealed me from it, but there are entrances he knows not."

"Harker wrote of your . . . companions." I nearly said "mistresses" and diplomatically changed the word at the last moment.

"They are no more. In their deaths Van Helsing

was more careful and they too careless. I felt them go and could do nothing." His face darkened then cleared, like the shadow of a cloud running over a mountain. "But to avenge them would bring no gain, and only reveal my deception." He gave another shrug, this time with his hands, and stood tall. "Come then, Quincey Morris, I will show you any number of dark places for you to shelter from the day, places much safer than the ones they had."

"Won't I need my home earth as you do?"

"This has become your home, Mr. Morris. When a brave man's blood strikes the ground he has purchased it for his own. You will find rest here and may carry away as much earth as you want when you leave. But perhaps you will stop a while and visit with me? The wind breathes cold through the broken battlements and casements of my castle, but you will find more comfort there than in these wastes. We two have many griefs to settle in our hearts and though I would be alone with my thoughts, in such a time of mourning it is better to have company."

My answer was to follow him. As we picked our way over the rocks and up a narrow path, his children began to sing again.

INTRODUCTION TO

"DEEP SLEEP"

by Matthew J. Costello

First a disclaimer about the story to follow, "Deep
Sleep" . . . it really isn't—

Um, on second thought, how about a teaser first,
some nugget designed to urge you to read this nifty
little introduction all the way to the end? And the
teaser is that . . . at the end of this intro you will
learn how I passed on an absolutely once-in-a-lifetime
experience—and why.

Back to the disclaimer.

"Deep Sleep" is my first professional *horror* story.
Unlike most authors, I jumped into novel writing without the yeoman years crafting shorter gems. Not that
I just woke up one day, put my pinky finger to lips,
and said, "I think today I'll write a novel."

Though I kind of did that, writing an early novel
that garnered some nice feedback but no sale. Some
important lessons there—but that's for another
introduction.

But I had years of journalism, writing for everything

ranging from *Sports Illustrated* to the *Los Angeles Times* to *Playboy*. I had found that hidden authorial grail, one's "voice," well before my first novel was sold.

And once I sold that novel, I never looked back—and short stories were a step skipped. But then people started asking for stories, for this magazine, for that anthology, and that has been the only way I've done them, on request. And I viewed them as a welcome respite from my novels and scripting.

Hence, there is an antic quality to most of them. I've done everything from an erotic adventure of young Robin Hood, in faux Olde English, to a mystery story starring everyone's favorite fat man, the Santa dude.

They have been a lark, enjoyable, a chance to play, and I hope to keep doing them.

"Deep Sleep" was written in 1991 for the anthology *Dracula, Prince of Darkness* (edited by Martin Greenberg and published by DAW Books). All the stories in the anthology starred . . . guess who.

And the premise of the story was born of my fascination with a major disaster. Ever since I was kid, I'd been mesmerized by the sinking of the *Titanic*. From the old films about the event, like *A Night to Remember,* to the artist recreations of the crash and what the ship might look like miles below the Atlantic, I remained completely absorbed in the horror of the tale.

The themes were so powerful—hubris versus nature, speed against ice, stupidity and lack of planning meets the briny deep, awash with furs, jewels, briefcases and, for audio, imagine the terrible screams.

The setup of the story was simple. What if Dracula was making his trans-Atlantic crossing on this doomed ship?

For the implications of that fateful decision, I recommend the story that follows. I can say no more. As for my teaser . . . ?

This story appeared years before my own fateful near-encounter with RMS *Titanic*.

In 1996, F. Paul Wilson and I met with James Cameron about the game possibilities for a film he was making . . . *Titanic*. It was an incredible visit, seeing the footage he had shot using a small ROV sub matched to the vintage photos. Cameron was electrifying, obsessed, and knee-deep into a production that no one at the time expected could recoup its mammoth budget.

He was going down there again in a few weeks time, in the Russian sub *Mir,* to shoot more footage.

And then, after Cameron and I bonded over scuba diving, he turned to me and said, "Would you like to go down with me?"

Imagine. . . .

Invited down to the *Titanic,* with James Cameron. (All right, it takes eight hours to get down and you have to pee into a bottle, but still. . . .)

To see the wreck close up, and the debris field littered with everything from dinner plates to porcelain dolls. The strange fish hiding in the ship's bowels. The experience of a lifetime.

But I was committed to a major Disney project and a week of brainstorming in the Adirondacks for that same week. Oh the horror! I asked the Disney producer. Could I go? And he said no. Without me, there was no point in the week's work. I would blow the project out of the water.

I could have said to hell with you. I'm going to see the *Titanic*!

I could have. And people say—all the time—I should have.

But I didn't.

And now, unlike Vlad the Impaler in the upcoming tale, a trip to the *Titanic* will always be my personal tale about the one voyage that got away. . . .

DEEP SLEEP

by Matt Costello

HE looked across the expanse of the first-class dining room, through the maze of bustling waiters sleekly presenting the passengers with their chosen dessert. A chocolate mousse perhaps, or fraise à la crème? Great dark wedges of Black Forest cake sailed through the room while the chamber quartet played too much Strauss.

Andre Farrand—such was the name on his passport—was traveling alone. But he felt them looking at him. One, two—yes—three pairs of eyes, ignoring their meal, their dessert course, their husbands. The room was filled with wealthy robber barons and overstuffed captains of industry.

The women looked at him. He felt their eyes devouring him, hungry.

"Monsieur, some cafe for monsieur?" The waiter was at his elbow. This was the first meal that Farrand had made an appearance at, nibbling some of the greens, tasting the escalope de veau before declaring the lemon sauce much too tart.

It was not uncommon for travelers to have distressed stomachs at sea.

Though—to be sure—that was not the reason Farrand didn't eat.

He caught the eye of one woman looking at him. Her eyes attempted to speak, urging him to confirm that they would dance again that evening, that they'd again take a walk on the first class promenade. That—in the chill of the North Atlantic—he'd pull her close, muttering words to make her forget her husband, then closer. . . .

"Still not feeling better, Monsieur Farrand?"

He looked up. A woman in a white dress heavy with brocade gave him a motherly purse of the lips. Perhaps the bejeweled dowager was so solicitous of his appetite since hers was never in disrepair.

He smiled. Monsieur Andre Farrand, a world famous dealer in antiquarian furniture, favored the woman with a charming grin. "No, Madame Welch. I'm feeling much better. Much . . . but I'd best not test myself. A nibble here, a nibble there—it will more than satisfy me."

The dowager smiled, so pleased that he was well.

He felt the eyes around the room, perhaps not quite in control, perhaps in danger of embarrassing him, of creating a scene. That would not do, not on this ship, not here. There was no place to hide . . . no place to go.

Monsieur Farrand pushed his chair back. He looked around at the table, smiling at the noisy Americans and a pair of British bankers with their wives—repulsive, cowlike creatures with no appeal, despite the rolls of skin that jiggled on their arms.

"But I think I'd like to take some air. And see if it's gotten any colder outside."

He nodded to the table. One of the American men stuck out his lip. "Perhaps I'll—"

The man was offering to join him, but Farrand pretended not to hear. He turned away and walked to the front of the grand dining hall, the hungry eyes still watching him, looking for a signal, something to give them hope. He forced his face to remain impassive.

Farrand pushed open one of the doors, pressing against the center section of cut beveled glass. It led to the main hall and the giant staircase of first class. He walked out.

Just outside, he saw the purser talking to the captain. Captain Smith had excused himself early from dinner and now was engaged in what looked like a most serious conversation.

The Captain saw him pass by. He turned, and nodded—a diplomat. "Good evening, monsieur."

"Captain," he said, nodding to the man.

Farrand turned to go up the staircase. He looked up. At the landing where the staircase split in two there was a carved wooden panel and a clock . . . a frieze representing "Honor and Glory crowning Time."

He smiled at that, enjoying the irony, the private joke. Time is the ruler. Yes, it's the despot in people's lives. Unless . . . unless it can be defeated—and made the servant.

He walked up the stairs and stopped on the landing. He looked at the clock. It was 8 P.M. Then he touched the clock, and the two wooden figures holding the crown. And then he continued up the grand stairway.

Farrand went to his stateroom. It looked untouched, except for one open bag containing some clothes. He had given instructions, fortified with a ten pound note, that his room was to be left undisturbed. He didn't wish his bed to be made or his washroom to be cleaned. Nothing was to be done.

There was little need. He barely used it.

He stood in the darkness, feeling the rolling of the ship, the swells of the icy North Atlantic. He felt his hunger, and he stood there, savoring the warmth, the meaning it gave to him.

And when he was sure that supper had ended, he opened the cabin door and left his suite.

He made his way to another corridor, and the staterooms farther toward the bow.

She'd be waiting. They'd all be waiting, he knew, while their husbands played cards and smoked cigars and drank brandy.

He came to the door and knocked. If, perchance, the husband was there, Farrand would claim it was a mistake. It was so easy to get confused on this giant ship.

But the woman opened the door. She had the top of her dress open, wantonly, invitingly, so eager. She grabbed his hand.

"No," he whispered, gently shutting the door behind him. She was beautiful, with dark eyes and jet black hair. Her body pressed against him, lean, hungry. She was young, and so very unhappy with her life.

He grabbed her hard with his hands and pulled her away, fixing her with his eyes.

He heard sounds from the corridor. Some people were moving this way.

The woman looked hurt. Her lower lip—full, beet red—quivered in shock, in pain. He let go of her and brought his hand to her cheek. She brushed against it.

"Not here," he said. "You must wait. Meet me on the promenade deck. In an hour. Meet me there. . . ."

She licked her lips, the fever was on her. It was always this way, and he enjoyed her pain, her turmoil. To want something so badly, to crave it above all

other things, something that would take everything
away from you . . . your whole world.

It was wonderful.

He released her. He listened at the door. The corridor sounded empty.

He picked her because of her great need, the way
she would kick and moan when he kissed her, when
he touched her—I must not get carried away, he
thought. Not on the ship. There was no way to explain
such things. He turned and grabbed the door handle.

"You'll be there?" she said. Her voice had a wheedling quality, a small child, unsure, afraid.

He opened the door an inch. He looked at her
again, his face not smiling.

"Don't ever doubt my word. Ever."

He left the stateroom. He smelled the cigar smoke,
lingering here, the hint of perfume. I can't wait too
long, he thought.

My senses become aroused, inflamed.

Even I can't wait too long. . . .

He pulled his coat close. The churning water, white,
frothing, spitting at the hull of the ship, was alive with
phosphorescent specks. He wrapped his coat tight.

A couple walked by, their shoes clicking noisily on
the wood of the deck. He turned to look at them,
close together, perhaps newlyweds. They moved on,
oblivious to him.

And then he was alone. He wondered if anyone
doubted his name . . . Monsieur Farrand, from Paris.
His accent is nearly parfait . . . still, he wondered if

he made any slips. There was a Frenchmen, a writer, sitting two tables over, and a Marseilles businessman and his family sat all the way on the other side of the room.

But—so far—he had avoided meeting them, having them probe his background, asking questions, difficult questions.

It was cold, frigid. It felt as if the wet cold seeped right through his overcoat, through his suit, his shirt, and held his skin tight. It reminded him of what he faced every morning.

There is a price for conquering time. . . .

He turned his gaze away from the wake of the great ship up to the stars. The sky was white with stars, the Milky Way was a gossamer belt around the night sky. Even in the mountains, in his homeland, there were never nights like this, so clear, so bright. He turned to search for Perseus, the Pleiades, other familiar constellations, his companions friends in the night. . . .

But the giant smokestacks of the ship blocked out the southeast sky, four great black columns outlined by the twinkling stars.

He heard a door creak open, yards away, leading from the first-class lounge to the open deck. He took a deep breath. The icy air stung his nostrils. He saw her outline, and he heard her steps on the wood.

He waited, arms open, ready to pull her close, to hold her tight, surrounding her warmth, possessing it.

"He—he came back, my husband," she said. Her words made small eddies of fog in front of her face. "I had to say I needed to walk. He wanted to come—"

He took her, grabbing her shoulders.

"But you told him no? You said that you needed to be alone?"

There was just the glow of a few lights, the pale light of the stars, the billowing clouds of her breathing. He dug his hands into her shoulders, hard, locking her to him. He watched her face delirious with joy. Her hands fiddled with the neck of her dress, unhooking it, exposing the creamy flesh to the icy air.

She was cold, shivering.

Slowly savoring the moment, he pulled her close, pulling her tight against him. He saw the twin black dots on her neck.

"My sweet," he whispered. "My precious. . . ."

"Andre . . ." she said, using a name that meant nothing to him. A convenience. It was best to be careful.

He opened his mouth. Her eyes were locked on his mouth. He pulled back, ready to hurry now, to quicken the moment when he'd open her skin again, and taste the warmth, let it drip onto his lips, sucking at it, not wasting a drop.

While she moaned and mewled.

He brought a hand behind her neck and pulled her to him. He bit down.

She gasped and kicked against him, quivering from pleasure.

And when she was done, she fell to the deck.

He waited, giving her a few minutes. And then he helped her up. She was dazed, shivering, weak, even confused.

305

He helped her button up her dress.

"You must go," he said. "Hurry back to your room. I'll see you tomorrow—"

There was a voice. It didn't come from the deck.

The woman started backing away. The voice yelled out something, and Farrand looked up. It was coming from the giant mast, a lookout, saying words.

The woman staggered backwards, maybe too dazed, too confused to find her way back to her stateroom, her husband.

But again the words, and a bell ringing, so loud, raucous, disturbing the quiet. The bell ringing over and over. He understood the words this time.

"Iceberg! Straight ahead!"

He looked up, and he saw the slab of white so close, as if it suddenly appeared in the water. The ship was moving right toward it, as if it was landfall.

We're going to hit it, Farrand knew. He had that thought, and there was an alarm attached. We're going to hit that iceberg.

And then—slowly—the blood still fresh on his lips—he started to think what that meant. . . .

He moved to the bow. People were coming on deck, a few summoned by the bell, others by the frantic shouting.

The iceberg was ahead, but already the ship was turning, cutting sharply to the left. But this ship, this *Titanic,* was moving too fast, and the berg looked so large, a great rectangular block with jagged white peaks jutting into the sky.

A crewman appeared beside him.

"We're goin' to hit 'er," he said.

Farrand recognized the accent. Cheapside, he thought. A thick, guttural accent used by sailors and fishmongers and whores.

"But 'twill be aright." The crewman looked over at him. "We'll just graze the berg." The crewman laughed. "A bit of a bashing around, sir, I say. That's all that will—"

Together, they watched the berg approach as if it were a white island, and RMS *Titanic* was set to dock.

The accent. It brought memories. . . .

Farrand had to leave Carfax Abbey. They would have found him after one of his servants began to kill, crazily. When the man began to slaughter whores, he had to do something.

The white island was close. . . .

"There we are, sir—" the crewman said. The bow was gliding past the berg.

And that's when Farrand heard the groan. The boat staggered as if it was beached, and then moved on, sluggishly, filling the night with the sound of metal tearing.

The man knew the ship was taking a gash on its side. He could feel it. But we missed it, he thought. Didn't we? This isn't so bad.

It was over in a matter of seconds, the ship slowed, still veering away from the berg, the ghost island now left behind.

The deck was suddenly filed with people. From the other side of the promenade someone tossed an icy snowball. It landed at Farrand's feet. He reached down and touched the ice, musing about where it came from, how long since it had fallen and how many miles had it traveled to reach his fingertips.

It felt so cold. . . .

People were talking excitedly.

The ship moved.

But—and here he hoped that he wasn't letting his senses, his finely-tuned senses run away from him— he thought he detected a difference, a subtle change in the motion of the ship.

He moved past the elegantly dressed first class passengers, some pointing back at the berg, pulling their white silk scarfs tight around their neck, talking animatedly about the disaster narrowly averted.

He moved back into the ship.

The ship was—he had no doubt now—moving differently.

No . . . doubt.

He went down the stairs. The captain's office was located in a wing off the grand staircase. He hurried down an abandoned corridor, moving quietly on the red carpet. Everyone was outside, gathered together, chattering about this great event.

But he expected that the captain would be down here.

He saw the door. It was shut.

Farrand moved against it, breathing deeply. He pressed an ear close to the wood and listened.

He heard the fluttering rustle of paper, of big sheets

being flipped, and then a voice. The captain, he wondered. Yes, it was Captain Smith.

"But how much could be damaged, Mr. Andrews?"

More rustling of paper.

Another voice, one he didn't know. . . .

"There are tears, gashes here, and here, and here. Perhaps at least three more. There are three more bulkheads gone, all flooding."

"But the others? Surely, they are fine. And that leaves—"

"Ten. Yes, those compartments were spared any damage."

"Then—"

The papers rustled again, and Farrand could picture the blueprints, the giant schematic drawings of the ship. He imagined them with the water flooding in—

"*Titanic* can float with one, two, even three compartments completely flooded. But the berg tore a gash right along this line— With those six watertight compartments gone, she will sink."

There was silence. Farrand held his breath. His mind was racing now, calculating—what does this mean? What does this mean to me?

"How long?" Captain Smith asked.

"Two hours . . . maybe a bit longer. But only a bit. . . ."

He backed away. He turned, numb, his mind a jumble of ideas, of dangers met and surpassed, of moments when his victory was nearly snatched from him. This was all too incredible, too improbable.

He turned back to the staircase . . . back to the wooden frieze, the clock now ticking so noisily.

Two hours, maybe less. He stared at the wood carving . . . at honor and glory bowing before time.

Farrand pulled his lips back, and he snarled at the carving. He snarled, exposing his fangs, not caring who saw, not giving a goddamn who watched him rage at the stupid joke.

And then he drifted outside again. . . .

There were not enough lifeboats. Women and children first, those were the instructions. But some men were jumping right in. They'd be damned if they'd go down with the ship. Even some crewmen jumped in, leaving women and children crying, begging to get into the lifeboat.

Out in the dark sea, he could spot a few lifeboats already bobbing around the great ship, a funeral watch.

He saw John Jacob Astor back away from one boat. The American raised his hand to his wife as the lifeboat was lowered. Then the millionaire turned and looked over at Farrand. They had briefly spoken that day. . . .

Other men looked around at the boats being loaded, looking for a chance to jump on.

But Astor looked over resignedly. He smiled.

Perhaps he respects me because I'm not getting into the boats, Farrand thought.

Farrand looked down at the water.

I would—if it was a possibility, if that was something that I could do—oh, yes, I wouldn't hesitate. . . .

He shook his head. The ship was tilted now, the angle growing more severe by the minute. Signal rockets were being launched from the stern. There were muttered stories of a ship on the other side, a mystery ship sitting in the distance that wasn't answering the distress signal.

Some people had jumped into the water, the panic claiming them. And they screamed, crying out as the incredibly cold water squeezed their chest and made it impossible to breathe.

The boat's angle increased.

There was only one thing to do. He knew that. He had considered every other possibility, including getting into a lifeboat and chancing that it would be found before the sun came up, that he could somehow hide and—

Another lurch, more fireworks. The band was playing. a hymn, treacle, the bleating sounding so pompous, so stupid while the hungry sea ate the ship and all who clung to it.

He turned away. He walked off the deck, and hurried inside, past gamblers playing a final hand of poker, and passengers drinking until the room wobbled, trying to blot out the last terrible moments.

He hurried. The ship groaned continuously now as if it very rivets, every metal plate was under stress.

He reached a door that was marked FOR CREWMEN ONLY.

It was a door he had used before. It was supposed to be locked, but Farrand had arranged it so that with a jiggle of the handle, the bolt slipped open. Then he hurried down the metal staircase. He heard people yelling, perhaps second class passengers searching for life vests or a way to the boats reserved for first class.

And on down deeper, to the nightmare corridors of steerage, past crying children, the angry sounds of crewmen trying to keep order, to make the poor passengers line up while they fought their way up the stairs, past Farrand.

Farrand stepped aside to let the first wave go, and then he pressed tight against the green wall of the stairwell and inched his way down.

One man punched him, screaming, "Where ya goin', you fool? Go up, go—"

But Farrand kept sliding past them until he was finally able to move below the damp and smelly corridors of the lowliest passengers on the ship.

Just below was the cargo area. His heart beat madly.

What if it's already underwater? What if I can't get to it—

But the boat's tilt was making this part of the ship rise out of the water.

He lost his footing, and slid forward at one point, banging his head against a metal stair. But then he quickly scurried up.

The lights were still on, but surely the power, the electricity that fed them would be gone soon.

The boat moved, sliding down quickly now, the weight in the front pulling it down. He heard crashes and—even here, so far below the decks—he heard the screaming, the band playing, the noise of things collapsing, and—

He reached one cargo room. Great crates blocked his way and he had to clamber over them, digging his long manicured nails into the wood, climbing over the jumbled hill to the next cargo compartment.

To the metal vault.

It looked like a silvery metal crate. An oddity to be sure, but no one questioned what valuable items Monsieur Farrand might be transporting.

It stood alone. No other heavy cargo had fallen to block the opening.

Again the ship moved, and the bow had to be fully in the ocean's grasp.

Time . . . I have just moments, he knew.

He went to the metal vault. He felt the front, feeling for the small moving pieces, imperceptible, unnoticeable, the panels of metal that were a secret lock, a combination.

He pushed at the shiny metal, but nothing happened.

I made a mistake, he thought. I'm rushing.

He took a breath. Another movement, and a stack of boxes fell into his arm; he felt his skin tear. It would heal—quickly—but still there was pain, and now his arm did not move so quickly, or so well. He shoved the boxes away and returned to the metal vault.

Again, he pushed at the moving pieces, the puzzle he devised from a Chinese box he purchased in his travels.

There was click. And the vault opened.

And he saw—strapped to the other side, fastened with great metal clamps—the coffin.

He stepped into the vault. The lights sputtered out-side, the naked bulbs protesting the loss of power.

Darkness is coming, he thought. For how long . . .

He pulled the metal vault shut. He felt his way to the coffin lid, feeling the letters, the name.

His hand ran across the metal plaque. Vlad Tepes. And underneath . . . Count Dracula.

He opened the coffin. It smelled of his body, of centu-ries of sleep, and perfume, and blood drying on his lips, and now—of something new—a salty smell, oil, and soon—

He lay down.

The cracking sound, like an explosion, traveled even inside here, inside the watertight vault. . . .

He shut his eyes.

Darkness, he thought. Darkness . . . for how long?

He felt movement, banging, even as he forced his consciousness to that near-death state. Movement, sliding down, *Titanic* breaking in two . . . groaning, the twisted metal crying out.

Until there was nothingness.

And nothing except waiting.

He slept for decades.

And then there was a sound.

He was sure of it. A sound here, and it wasn't just a natural movement, some shifting of the sea floor. It was a man-made sound. Dracula was sure of it.

Twice before he had made himself come to a state of

awareness. There had been some earthquake, a tremendous movement of the sea floor. As he came to awareness he listened to the rumbling, wondering whether something might make his vault pop open, exposing his coffin, his body, to the hungry creatures in the sea.

It had been years, maybe a decade or two after the accident.

Of course, that was his great fear. He was trapped here. What if he emerged? To do what? To crawl on the ocean floor, to make his way to a shore maybe a thousand miles away while sharks and hungry fish chewed at his withered flesh? They'd tear at him until he was nothing, his immortality squandered like grains of sand thrown into the sea.

He knew that, as dark as the ocean floor was, it offered him no escape from his tomb.

And of the lifeboats? What if he had still been in one when the sun rose? He would have been trapped in the open boat, seared on the small wooden ship like an animal cooked alive in a skillet.

The sound again, a whirring noise, came closer. He opened his eyes in the darkness, looking at the total blackness inside his coffin.

Another time, there had been a noise overhead—certainly decades ago, as much as he could figure time. There had been the sound of a motor overhead.

But it went away, and he waited.

Thinking all the time thinking, that there was no way out. To be immortal and trapped at the bottom of the sea. . . .

It was a terrible irony.

The sound grew in volume. A whirring noise, an engine of some kind. And he thought, what could it be? It's not on the surface. It's not a ship. It's something down here, something outside the *Titanic*, looking at the ship.

That makes sense. He had no idea how many years had passed. But surely the day would come when people would be able to come down here, to see and—

The whirring seemed almost loud. It paused, just outside.

Perhaps—perhaps looking at his steel vault.

Then—a terrible moment—it moved on, growing fainter, moving to other parts of the ship, the *Titanic*'s carcass probably broken into pieces, its innards exposed for this thing outside.

Then it went away completely.

But Dracula didn't close his eyes. He stayed awake, for just a bit. To savor the thought, the realization.

They'll be back. And someday when they return, they'll be able to bring things to the surface. They will see the silvery metal vault, and think it such an odd thing. They will wonder about it and, as people do, they will become even more curious until they must have it, must bring it to the surface.

It may not be for a very long time.

But I can wait. I'm used to waiting. I have all time to wait.

And only then did he shut his eyes and give himself over to the void, the blankness, the emptiness of his deep sleep.

C.S. Friedman

The Coldfire Trilogy

"A feast for those who like their fantasies dark, and as emotionally heady as a rich red wine." —*Locus*

Centuries after being stranded on the planet Erna, humans have achieved an uneasy stalemate with the fae, a terrifying natural force with the power to prey upon people's minds. Damien Vryce, the warrior priest, and Gerald Tarrant, the undead sorcerer must join together in an uneasy alliance confront a power that threatens the very essence of the human spirit, in a battle which could cost them not only their lives, but the soul of all mankind.

BLACK SUN RISING   0-88677-527-2
WHEN TRUE NIGHT FALLS   0-88677-615-5
CROWN OF SHADOWS   0-88677-717-8

To Order Call: 1-800-788-6262